TOLL THE BELL FOR MURDER

ALSO BY GEORGE BELLAIRS

Littlejohn on Leave
The Four Unfaithful Servants
Death of a Busybody
The Dead Shall be Raised
Death Stops the Frolic
The Murder of a Quack
✓ He'd Rather be Dead
Calamity at Harwood
Death in the Night Watches
The Crime at Halfpenny Bridge
The Case of the Scared Rabbits
✓ Death on the Last Train
The Case of the Seven Whistlers
The Case of the Famished Parson
Outrage on Gallows Hill
The Case of the Demented Spiv
Death Brings in the New Year
Dead March for Penelope Blow
✓ Death in Dark Glasses
✓ Crime in Lepers' Hollow
A Knife for Harry Dodd
✓ Half-Mast for the Deemster
The Cursing Stones Murder
Death in Room Five
Death Treads Softly
Death Drops the Pilot
Death in High Provence
✓ Death Sends for the Doctor
✓ Corpse at the Carnival

Murder Makes Mistakes
Bones in the Wilderness
✓ Toll the Bell for Murder
Corpses in Enderby
Death in the Fearful Night
Death in Despair
Death of a Tin God
The Body in the Dumb River
Death Before Breakfast
The Tormentors
Death in the Wasteland
Surfeit of Suspects
Death of a Shadow
Death Spins the Wheel
Intruder in the Dark
Strangers Among the Dead
Death in Desolation
Single Ticket to Death
Fatal Alibi
Murder Gone Mad
Tycoon's Deathbed
The Night They Killed Joss Varran
Pomeroy, Deceased
Murder Adrift
Devious Murder
Fear Round About
Close All Roads to Sospel
The Downhill Ride of Leeman
Popple An Old Man Dies

TOLL THE BELL FOR MURDER
AN INSPECTOR LITTLEJOHN MYSTERY

GEORGE BELLAIRS

INTEGRATED MEDIA

NEW YORK

All rights reserved, including without limitation the right to reproduce this book or any portion thereof in any form or by any means, whether electronic or mechanical, now known or hereinafter invented, without the express written permission of the publisher.

This is a work of fiction. Names, characters, places, events, and incidents either are the product of the author's imagination or are used fictitiously. Any resemblance to actual persons, living or dead, businesses, companies, events, or locales is entirely coincidental.

Copyright © 1959 by George Bellairs

ISBN: 978-1-5040-9258-6

This edition published in 2024 by Open Road Integrated Media, Inc.
180 Maiden Lane
New York, NY 10038
www.openroadmedia.com

To
PROFESSOR VICTOR LAMBERT, F.R.C.S.
With Affection and High Esteem

TOLL THE BELL FOR MURDER

1
SOMETHING WRONG IN THE CURRAGH

In the schoolroom of the village of Mylecharaine, in the north of the Isle of Man, the local women were holding a 'Tay'—Manx for Tea-in preparation for a jumble sale next day. The proceeds were to go to a fund for decorating the church. There were around thirty there; about a third of them occupied in laying food on long tables, and the rest sorting out the loot which had been collected from their own and neighbouring parishes for the morrow's big event.

It was well past tea-time. The sun had just set across the sea behind Jurby Head, which meant it was seven o'clock, the end of a lovely April day. All around the squat little whitewashed school stretched the flat curragh lands, marshy still from the recent rains but green with the onset of Spring, with wisps of mist rising from them with the coming of night. In the background to the south, the great bastion of the Manx hills, ending suddenly and spectacularly where the fenlands began.

But the assembled women had no time for admiring the evening or the view. They were busy with the spoils, assessing their values with experienced eyes and hands, ticketing them with prices, and maintaining a running commentary on the donors of the jumble.

A pile of soiled raincoats, some brass fire-irons, a washtub, a heap of bound religious magazines, old boots and shoes, a decrepit carpet-sweeper, a tumbledown chair with a worn horse-hair seat, a musical-box, and a hand-driven sewing machine were all swiftly dealt with. Then Mrs. Lace, of Ballagot, wearing a hat which ought to have been with the jumble, opened a parcel and gingerly held aloft a pair of shabby riding-breeches, two soiled old dress-shirts, a grey morning coat and a topper to match, and a velvet smoking jacket with a red lining and the pile suffering from moths or some obscure, mangy disease.

"I can hardly persuade myself to touch them for fear they contaminate me," said Mrs. Lace, seeing nothing funny at all in the variety of the bundle or how its contents might be used.

"Who sent it?"

"You might know. Who else but a transgressor, a wicked transgressor, would wear such stuff."

"Not Sir Martin?"

"His very self."

All work ceased as the women scuffled to inspect the apparel of sin and shame, for Sir Martin Skollick, unofficial squire of Mylecharaine and tenant of Myrescogh House, had a dirty reputation. Two good-looking farm girls had already, it was said, had to go to England to bear his illicit offspring, and no woman was safe from him.

Here, in the very schoolroom itself, he seemed to have dumped the cast-offs of his sin, and some of the younger and livelier members of the party were already reconstructing Sir Martin in the sporting breeches, the flame-lined jacket, the elegant topper and the shabby Ascot coat, which once he wore in wicked haunts across the water.

All this rush of dangerous emotion was violently interrupted by a scream from one corner, occupied by Miss Caley, a maiden lady from Ballaugh, who was unwrapping parcels and surrounding herself with their contents. Barricaded by a pile of cracked plates, a black-steel kitchen fender, a pair of old Wellington boots, an ancient object like an accordion marked 'vacuum-cleaner', and two flatirons, she was now holding aloft an object which might have been, judging from her handling, red-hot. It was an old fashioned sporting-gun. In the other hand, Miss Caley balanced a cardboard box half full of cartridges.

"Whatever 'ave you got there?" said a large fat woman with a dead-pan face, called Armistead, who had arrived from England only two years ago, but who nevertheless tried to boss the show. "Give 'ere. Squealin' like that. One would think you was bein' murdered."

She took the gun savagely. "Where'd this come from?"

"Mrs. Quayle, from Balladoole."

There arose a sympathetic noise, like a dismal cheer, from the onlookers. Mrs. Quayle, following the death of her husband around Christmas, had broken-up her home, sold out, and gone to live with her son at Ballakilpheric.

"She said she'd no use for it, so we might as well have it."

"It's an old-fashioned one."

It was. An ancient breech-loading pin-fire about a hundred years old. All the same, it was in good condition.

"*Two* pounds?" said one of the assessors, and the rest nodded.

"And the cartridges?"

"I'd throw that lot in. Like as not they don't make that sort anymore and they'll be needed if somebody buys the gun."

The weapon was labelled £2 and left, with its ammunition, leaning against an old chair in one corner.

"Tay's ready."

A woman arrived with a huge urn and set it at the head of the table, which was covered to capacity with plates of food. Bread and butter, jam, Manx soda cakes, scones, buns, shortbread, potato cakes and large currant slabs like solid blocks of concrete.

And on top of that lot, a strapping girl entered, struggling with a huge steaming cauldron which she had to put on the floor, for there was no room on the table. It was the hot-pot.

"Where's pazon? We want him to say grace before the hot-pot gets cold."

"He's in church. Prayin', leek as not. He's in one of his bad moods to-day, poor man."

Another melancholy and sympathetic cheer from the company.

The Rev. Sullivan Lee, vicar of Mylecharaine, had arrived from London during the war, after the death of his wife in an air raid. He had been a nervous wreck and it had been thought that this scattered parish, entailing a lot of walking in good air, would do him a world of good. Now and then, Mr. Lee had relapses and behaved a bit wildly. Otherwise, he was a good priest and was well-liked.

"Somebody go get him."

Miss Caley scuttered off, chattering to herself, and the rest took their places round the table. It was almost dark outside. Lights twinkled from the scattered cottages sprinkled over the curraghs, where the menfolk were entertaining themselves whilst the women were away.

The Rev. Sullivan Lee entered. He blinked as the light of the room caught him and he looked around him as though he'd never seen the place before. A tall, well-built man, with a great dome of a head, almost bald, hollow cheeks and a Roman nose. He wore a sad, tortured look and his dark eyes might have been those of a blind man. There was no recognition or light in them. Then, suddenly, it was as if a shutter had clicked open, and he smiled at the company. It lit-up his whole face and completely changed him.

"I'm so sorry. Mustn't let the hash get cold."

"It's 'at-pot," corrected Mrs. Armistead.

Lee took his place at the top of the table. He said grace and they all fell-to. He presided like the head of some strange order.

He wore a cassock with a leather belt and this, combining with the natural tonsure of his hair, gave him a monastic appearance. He enjoyed his food. They all did, and continued eating until far into the early night. Then they set to work again and he helped them. Nothing exciting happened until long after the party had dispersed.

Then, as the clock at Ballaugh was striking two musical notes which floated across the flat curraghs in the stillness, there was a terrific explosion. It seemed to hang on the air for a good half minute and then it died away.

Lights went on one after another in the upper rooms of the scattered cottages, until the curragh around Mylecharaine seemed infested by swarms of fireflies.

Mr. and Mrs. Armistead, retired from an eating-house in Oldham, awoke. He was as big as his wife and their joint bed looked like a great tent pitched in a desert of oilcloth in the low-roofed room.

"It's an atom bomb," said Armistead, pulling his trousers over the vest and long pants in which it was his habit to sleep.

He was the first abroad and the road was deserted as, shod in his carpet slippers, he gingerly made his way to the garden gate. Around stretched the dark countryside, fragrant with the scents of bog-plants, dotted with the lighted bedroom windows of the startled homesteads. Overhead swept a magnificence of stars. In the northern distance, the lighthouse at the Point of Ayre swung its great beam, like a huge besom pushing rubbish from the land into the sea. To the west, the far-off lights of the Irish coast.

Mrs. Armistead appeared at the door, her heavy features embellished by a nimbus of curl-papers. Armistead turned his head to address her.

"There's a light on in th' church. I'd better go and see what's the matter. Stay where you are, mother. Leave this to me."

By this time, others were afield. They assembled round the telephone kiosk, which shone like a beacon at the crossroads in the middle of the village, and formed themselves in a silent group without even greeting one another. They looked in each other's faces questioningly and then someone spoke.

"What was that explosion? Think it was a mine at sea?"
"Too loud for that. Sounded like someborry blastin'.
Like as if there was quarryin' goin' on."
"There's a light on in the church."

They went off like one man. It gave them a lead, something to do. They marched to the door of the church, a motley little army, braces dangling, some of them with their raincoats over their night clothes and without collars and ties, wearing carpet slippers or unlaced boots. Two of them had hurried out without putting in their dentures. Only Mr. Jeremiah Kermode, an eccentric, was impeccably turned out. He wore his best suit and billycock, his shoes were bright with polish, and he even seemed to have had a wash and a shave. Nobody ever knew or asked how he'd done it.

The church was a little stone building, a solid-looking oblong, with a simple bell-tower rising at the west end and carrying a small bell rung by a rope which dangled outside the door. A dim light shone through the east window, illuminating the old gravestones of the churchyard and the great square vaults of the families of Mylecharaine and Myrescogh, now long departed from the neighbourhood and from human memory.

The little squad of men halted at the iron gates of the churchyard, whence a paved path, now framed in daffodils shaking in the night breeze, led to the church door. They were like visitors hesitating on the threshold of a sick-room, wondering what they would find inside. All around them' stretched the graves of the silent dead, their memorials silhouetted against the background of the night, some new and upright, others askew or fallen and forgotten altogether. Their hesitancy lasted just long enough to give dramatic pause for the final stroke of terror which was a prelude to what was yet to come.

A dark shadow emerged from the open door of the church.

It seemed, for a moment, to flutter like a great bat, and then shaped itself into the form of the vicar, his tall body leaning forward, groping for something in the darkness like a blind man. He quickly found what he sought, grasped the dangling rope, and began to ring the bell. He did it in a frenzy of despair, panting as he pulled and leaping in the air as the bell swung back and shortened the rope. Across the silent marshes, fields, roads and homesteads the silvery note floated. It wakened everybody for miles around. Those aroused from peaceful sleep to practical everyday things thought of a fire or a shipwreck. Others, less clear in their minds, fumbled about for reasons, imagined invasion tocsins or practical jokes. The superstitious-and they were thick on the ground in the curraghs-surmised the work of fairies or Things far worse. And two very old people, patiently waiting for the ebb-tide to carry them home, died, thinking they heard the bells of heaven.

The solitary ghostly note was heard for miles before the waiting men sprang to life and clawed down the frenzied parson, who seemed to be floating and flapping in mid-air in the vigour of his efforts. Silence fell, however, before the intruders gathered the Rev. Sullivan Lee in their arms and tried to calm his still jerking body, for the bell, in the fury of the attack, had finally made a complete circle over the beam, entangled the rope in its wild flight, and come to a dead stop.

The whole countryside was now sparkling with lights.

Jurby, Ballaugh, Sulby, Ballamanagh in the dark hills; some in distant Kirk Michael, and even six miles away in Ramsey heard it, too. There was a lot of quarrelling and arguing in the light of succeeding days as to who did hear it, but in the nearer places, the illuminations were proof enough that it reached them.

"Somethin's wrong in the curragh," said those who knew the unique note of the Mylecharaine bell, the like of which there was not in any other part of the isle. It was said to have been cast from the metal of an earlier one, that of the monastery of Rozelean long lost in the bogs.

Meanwhile, the men in the churchyard were trying to make head or tail of the strange behaviour of their priest. His own flock dealt more sympathetically with him than some of their nonconformist companions who, on account of his style of dress and his fondness for ritual, (mee-maw, Mr. Armistead called it) accused him of being an idolater and capable of any folly.

"What are you doin' here at this time of night, reverend?" asked Armistead, who seemed to have elected himself leader of the posse. He was wearing a cloth cap pulled down to his ears and a long woollen muffler. He sneezed, and wound the muffler tighter round his fat neck.

The vicar did not answer. Instead, he regarded his questioners with glazed eyes, holding his long hands before him as though to fend them off.

"'ow dare you make all that row in the middle of the night, scaring the women and the little children? And what was all that bang about, too?"

Still the Rev. Sullivan Lee said nothing. He rolled his head from side to side like someone being tortured, until one of the men made for the church porch through which the light was still streaming. Then the vicar moved. He ran to get to the door before the other, turned the key, and put it in his pocket.

"You've left the lights on."

Armistead looked from one to the other of the surrounding faces under the glow from the windows. He seemed to be seeking help or inspiration as to what they should do next. "Hadn't we better put out the lights?"

But Mr. Lee was on his way home to the vicarage, standing surrounded by a circle of dark trees behind the church. The little group of men remained under the window, their bewildered faces illuminated in dim blues, yellows, purples and reds from the stained glass given in memory of a dead and gone Myrescogh and depicting Abraham about to sacrifice Isaac. He held a long knife and in the eerie glow looked alive and resentful and about to set

TOLL THE BELL FOR MURDER

upon the gang of interlopers who were disturbing him at his sacred task. Mr. Jeremiah Kermode sadly tried to restore his bowler to its original shape. It had been trampled on in the commotion.

Then, suddenly, one of the twinkling lamps on the curragh began to move, drew nearer and nearer, (and so did the scared men), burst into noise as well as light, and a motor-bike took shape, ridden by a shadow in a helmet.

"What's goin' on there?"

Some of the men almost cried with relief. It was as if, in a realm of hopeless shades, one living, useful, human form had intruded with help and news of another world they loved.

P.C. Killip silenced his bike, dismounted, and approached the party. They all began to talk at once, like a crowd in a theatre scene, unintelligible gibberish, with here and there an odd dear word. All except Mr. Jeremiah Kermode, who was still mournfully remodelling the hat he had bought for his wedding forty years last Easter.

"Parson's gone balmy and been firin' guns and ringin' the bell," said Armistead above all the rest.

"Where is he now?"

"Gone 'orne," said a man without his dentures and therefore unintelligible.

"Eh?"

"Gone 'ome," translated Armistead.

"And left the church lights all on?"

"He wouldn't let us go in. He locked the door."

"He did, did he? We'll soon see about that."

P.C. Killip tried the door just to be sure and then he tipped his helmet from behind and scratched the back of his head. This was like a nightmare. Cycling on patrol from Jurby to Ballaugh, he had suddenly heard a loud report which reminded him of attack fire during the war. Then a lot of lights had gone on across the curragh. And to cap the lot, bells had started to ring. He'd wondered at first if it was some sort of celebration, perhaps a royal birth. Or even God forbid! -Russian space-men invading the Island. He'd got there as quickly as he could, no easy matter among the maze of ditches, hedges, swamps and narrow roads of the curraghs. And here he was. The vicar had gone off his rocker. He hadn't thought of that one!

"I'd better go and see if things are all right and get the key at the same time. Light is too dear to waste. Some of you had better stick around. If he's gone mad, he might get a bit rough and I'll need help."

They were only too glad to find a leader. They agreed with acclamation to remain.

"Blow yer whistle if you want us," shouted Armistead, in a voice intended to convey that he wasn't afraid of anything or anybody.

P.C. Killip gingerly made his way across the parson's path between the graves to the vicarage. He was a reliable officer, solid in mind and body, red-faced, beefy, a good husband and father of four, and a good churchman, as well. He kept his mind on his job, too, otherwise he would have halted transfixed by the horror of parading among the rows of the dead he had once known, at such an unearthly hour. He protected himself from evil in the Manx fashion by holding his thumbs between his index and second fingers in the form of a cross.

The vicar lived alone and a woman from the village came daily to attend to his needs. The vicarage itself was cold and damp, a little square-built stone place in a wild garden, set in a ring of old trees, with a lot of windows, un-curtained because the rooms were empty. There was a dark pool overhung by a twisted tree with limbs like long clawing fingers in one neglected corner. Rats scuttered about the dead leaves of past summers and there was a sudden splash in the black water of the pond.

A dim glow shone through the fanlight of the house. P.C. Killip beat on the stiff rusty knocker. Nobody replied, so he tried the door, found it loose, and entered. The hall smelled of mildew and neglect and was covered in the old linoleum left by the previous tenant, a miser who had been found dead behind the door. There was a bamboo hat stand against the soiled whitewashed wall with a few coats hanging from pegs, with some walking-sticks and old umbrellas in the lower part. A staircase rose into the dark upper regions. The whole was lighted by a small smoking paraffin lamp set on a chair beside the hat stand.

P.C. Killip stood and listened. The hair rose on the back of his neck. From a dark room to the right of the hall emerged a noise like something whispering signals in Morse code. Now and then the sound changed to a wail or a great sob. The bobby's heart began to race and his feet were glued to the floorboards. Funny things happened in the curraghs. He remembered old Standish, the miser, dead behind the very door now open at his back. And ghosts and wild cries of monks brutally tortured and strangled there long ago, as their pursuers ran them to earth in their fenland hideouts. The phosphorescent wraiths of travellers, too, murdered by the Carashdhoo men. He pulled himself together, turned the beam of his lamp in the room, and met the agonized eyes of a man on his knees, praying.

"You've left the lights on in the church, sir."

It was an anti-climax and sounded out of place somehow.

The vicar seemed to think so, too, for he made no reply, but knelt there, transfixed, staring blankly at the torch without even blinking. The policeman raised him gently to his feet.

"You're not very well, Mr. Lee, are you? Better come along with me, then. We'll get somebody to make you a nice cup of tea, or maybe take you in for the night."

Mr. Lee allowed himself to be led like a child. P.C. Killip helped him on with his threadbare coat and even had to put his hat on his head for him. It was back to front and gave the priest an even wilder look.

"Give me the keys of the church and we'll switch off the lights."

No reply.

"The keys, please, sir."

"The keys? No! No!"

The parson recoiled into the blackness beyond the rays of the lamp.

"Come now, sir. Nobody's going to hurt you. You're with friends."

"No!"

This was ridiculous. Arguing with a dotty priest in the small hours. To make matters worse, Killip's lumbago was beginning to twitch. His wife had only just rubbed it away with a secret embrocation supplied by a wise woman in Smeale, and here he was.

"Give me the keys, reverend, in the name of the Law!"

"The Law! God forgive me. I'd forgotten the Law."

P.C. Killip didn't understand what the man was getting at but he took the keys obediently handed over by the parson.

"Now come along with me, sir."

Killip closed the door behind them and they set off back between the graves and joined the working-party in the churchyard. Killip left the vicar with the rest and was making for the church again.

"No! No!" shouted the parson, tore himself from the group, and leapt after Killip with large bounding jumps. "Like a bloomin' kangaroo", was how Mr. Armistead later described it to his loving wife. Killip turned and faced him.

"Take him away and keep him quiet."

Ten or a dozen hands seized the now demented man, who was babbling and praying incoherently in turn. Killip unlocked the door, sought the switches in the porch, and turned them off with hardly a glance inside. Then he paused. There was a small vestibule to keep out the draught and then a padded swing door into the main building. Killip turned again, opened the inner door, and shone his lamp round the dark church. A gust of warm air, smelling of stone and old books emerged. A few rows of plain wooden pews, with prayer and hymn-books on the racks in front of them. A large coke-stove in the middle of the aisle. Memorial tablets on the walls. *Peter Killip, who died in Burma.* His cousin Pete. And then the simple chancel, carpeted, with the altar in the background, its brass candlesticks and pewter chalice and paten reflecting the beams of the constable's lamp. A pause, a gasp, and then Killip rushed back and put on all the lights.

A body lay sprawled, face upwards, across the steps of the chancel. Killip hurried to it, gently touched it, recoiled, and then hurried out.

"Hey! Come here, two of you. I said two, not the lot." Armistead was first, hurried in, and then quickly hurried out to be sick.

He had seen quite enough of the body of Sir Martin Skollick. Half the head had been blown away by a shot-gun. The gun was there beside the body. The one which had been given to the ladies of Mylecharaine for the jumble sale.

2
THE NIGHT THE BELL TOLLED

When Littlejohn got out of the 'plane at Ronaldsway airport the first person he saw was the Rev. Caesar Kinrade, Archdeacon of Man and his very dear friend.

He was standing beside the operator who, by brandishing a couple of objects like ping-pong paddles, indicates exactly where the 'plane must come to rest. There was no mistaking the parson, with his froth of white whiskers, his fine way of holding high his head, his easy gracious manner, and his shovel hat and workmanlike gaiters.

The Archdeacon met him as he descended from the 'plane, both hands outstretched.

It was always the same. As soon as Littlejohn set foot on Manx soil it was as though he had never been away; as though, somehow, the time between one visit and the next had vanished and didn't count.

"I felt sure you'd come, Littlejohn."

The letter from the Archdeacon had only arrived that morning, just as Littlejohn was ruefully contemplating a few days' holiday in the Fens, where his wife's youngest sister was just about to produce her eighth child. Mrs. Littlejohn had gone on ahead, as usual, to keep up the morale of her brother-in-law, a Canon of Ely. It only needed a telephone-call to her to switch Littlejohn's arrangements.

In his letter the Archdeacon had asked Littlejohn to come over and help him with the problems of the Rev. Sullivan Lee.

> He is a highly-strung man, who at times manifests a perverted sense of duty. He seemed completely off his head when the constable arrived on the scene. He had been ringing the church bell at long past midnight and local people now speak of the night when the bell tolled. He was known to detest the dead man, whom he had often accused of perverting the district. He refused to defend himself or speak of his whereabouts at the time of the crime. He has been arrested and committed for trial at the next Court of General Gaol Delivery-our Assize and is now lodged, calm and collected, in prison in Douglas. But I cannot believe he would, in any circumstances, take the law in his own hands and kill a sinner to prevent his continuing in his evil ways.

So here Littlejohn was and the usual routine of his arrival on the Isle of Man was unrolling. He was already well known there and a number of people came to shake hands with him and welcome him. Two small boys approached with autograph-albums and the sergeant-in-charge of the police-post at Ronaldsway quietly entered his office and picked up the telephone.

"Give me Douglas police. Inspector Knell." Teddy Looney's old taxi was waiting for them at the entrance.

"Good to be puttin' a sight on ye again, Inspector," said Teddy, a conservative Manxman who hadn't got used yet to Littlejohn's official promotion.

The sun was setting over the gentle Manx hills and casting shadows across the little fields which seemed to climb almost to their summits, as the car turned into the quiet interior, past the signpost to Grenaby, through the domains of Ballamaddrell, Quayle's Orchard and Moaney Mooar, and then over the bridge and through the trees to Grenaby vicarage.

Maggie Keggin, the Archdeacon's housekeeper, was waiting for them at the door. She was overjoyed to see Littlejohn again, but wore a slightly exasperated look, as though something in the events of the day had annoyed her.

"Let me take your things, Inspector."

Here was another who called him Inspector, deliberately, too, because she associated Superintendents with Sunday Schools, and Inspectors to her mind were better sounding and more dignified.

The table was laid. White linen, silver, an old tea-service of the finest china. Someone had that day brought the Archdeacon a choice salmon-no questions asked-and it reposed on a silver trencher surrounded by a most appetizing salad.

"You must be hungry, sir."

No reference had been made to the case of the tolling bell or to anything else to do with crime and nothing was said until the meal was over. The only hint of why Littlejohn was there at all was dropped by Maggie Keggin who casually mentioned in an acid voice to the Archdeacon that *he* had been on the telephone.

"I gather you mean Knell, Maggie?"

"Who else? As soon as Inspector Littlejohn shows his nose in Grenaby, that Knell's buzzin' around like a wasp over a ripe pear. I told him you wasn't here yet, and he could wait till he was told to come. I said we'd telephone."

She halted, her lips tightened, and she clasped her old hands across her stomach in a gesture of disgust. A police car was drawing-up at the gate.

There emerged a tall, powerful man, with large teeth and a perpetual, pleasant smile. He wore a raincoat and a soft black hat with the brim turned down all round, like Littlejohn's. It was Inspector Knell of the Manx C.I.D. He always reminded Littlejohn of Fernandel.

Knell, unaware that he was watched, trotted up the garden path, joyfully seized the knocker of the front door, and beat upon it a cheery rat-a- tat.

"You can wait," replied Maggie Keggin to herself, and she proceeded to clear the table and serve coffee.

Knell looked puzzled at his reception, then listened for sounds from within. Then he trotted to the dining-room window, looked in, and came face to face with Maggie Keggin, her nose pressed angrily to the pane. Quite unperturbed, he indicated that he would like her presence at the front door. Then he saw Littlejohn in the shadows, and pantomimed a joyful greeting. He made as if to raise the sash and enter that way, whereat Maggie Keggin surrendered and let him in by the proper entrance.

"And now, that will do," said the Archdeacon to his house-keeper, for he saw signs of the eternal Keggin-Knell feud breaking out again. "You can kindly give Knell some coffee, Maggie, and then leave him in peace."

Knell was not as reticent as the Archdeacon about the murder. He made it clear right away that although Scotland Yard had not been called-in on the case, Littlejohn was *persona grata* as far as the Manx police were concerned and that Knell and the rest of them would be very much obliged for anything he could do in the way of proving that the obstinate Sullivan Lee was either innocent or guilty.

A pause. It seemed as if Littlejohn were expected to ask questions right away.

"When did it happen, Knell?"

"In the early morning of Wednesday, the 14th of April."

"And now it's the 21st."

"Yes. We never dreamed of accusing the Rev. Lee at first.

We simply thought he'd come across the dead body and taken it in the church to pray over until somebody arrived. Then, when he thought nobody was going to turn up and he'd finished his prayers, he'd raised the alarm by ringing the church bell."

"And then?"

"Well, sir. There was the gun. There weren't any other prints than those of the parson on it. It had been locked up in the schoolroom overnight. It had been given along with a lot of other stuff for a jumble sale to be held by the Mylecharaine women next day."

"Who had the key?"

"The vicar had one, Miss Caley, secretary of the Women's Union, another, and Mrs. Dalgleish, from the village, who cleans the place, had the third."

"And you suspected the vicar had entered the school after they'd all gone, and taken away the gun?"

Knell shrugged his shoulders apologetically.

"That and other things made it we could do no other.

Mr. Lee was said to have hated Sir Martin... that's the murdered man, sir. Sir Martin Skollick, of Myrescogh Manor."

"A comeover?"

"Yes. He bought the manor and farm about four years ago. Said to have come from the south of England. A wealthy man, over here to save himself on income-tax."

"Was he popular?"

"You couldn't call him that. He had a way with the ladies, though. Or, at least, some of them. He was in his late fifties, but the young ones still seemed to find him fascinating. There've been two scandals already in the locality. Two good-looking farm girls were mixed-up with Sir Martin and it became the talk of the whole neighbourhood. They left the island in the end; one rather hurriedly, it's said. It was whispered she was in the family way."

"A typical melodrama squire."

"Beg pardon, sir?"

Knell raised bewildered eyebrows. He'd evidently never heard of rascally squires or of *droit de seigneur*.

"It doesn't matter, old chap."

Knell flushed. Old chap! Things were looking up. "He was married?"

"Yes. Lady Skollick is a real lady. One of the best. It's a shame he treated her so badly."

"Badly?"

"Well. Going off after other women."

"Did she know?"

"We asked her was she alarmed when he hadn't arrived home in the early hours. She said she wasn't, as he sometimes stayed opt all hours of the night."

"Where?"

"In Ramsey. The police there knew all about it. A woman called Mrs. Vacey, widow of an army officer who retired there. She's in her forties, but you wouldn't think so."

"Sir Martin apparently didn't think so, either."

"No."

"Had he been there the night he was killed?"

"Yes, sir."

"In his car?"

"Yes. He'd left Mrs. Vacey's place just after midnight, she said. His car was found, locked, on the main road just through Lezayre. He'd run out of petrol."

"So he had set out to walk home. How many miles?"

"Four or five."

"An energetic man."

"He'd plenty of energy of one kind or another. Besides, it was well past midnight."

"He'd forgotten to fill-up his car?"

"Or else somebody had emptied it for him."

"Thus making the crime premeditated."

"Yes."

"And now to return to the Reverend Lee. He disliked Skollick naturally."

"Disliked is putting it mild, sir. He hated the man with a fanatical sort of frenzy. He said he'd demoralized the whole neighbourhood."

The Archdeacon, who had been smoking his pipe quietly and listening to it all, intervened.

"As I told you, Littlejohn, Lee was not the kind who would take the law into his own hands. He would wait for divine retribution."

Knell shook his head.

"But we couldn't depend on that, your reverence. In the first place, Mr. Lee wouldn't explain how he came by the body. We gave him every chance, He's just remained mute ever since the crime. He wouldn't say where he was at the time when the big explosion was heard. Neither would he say whether or not he fired the shot. Nor would he explain the presence of the gun in the church with two discharged cartridges in the breech. He hated Sir Martin and had been heard to say he wished he were dead..."

"Not quite, Knell. His reported words were, he wished the Lord would smite him down."

Knell said nothing, but his look implied that there wasn't much difference between the two.

"So, he was arrested."

"What else could we do, sir? He'd packed his bag and was off. One of our men spotted him making for the morning boat and detained him. Even then, he wouldn't say what it was all about or where he was going."

"Did he seem normal?"

"Yes. Cool as a cucumber. We had to put him in gaol and he had to appear before the magistrates so that we could keep him under lock and key. Otherwise, he'd have bolted again. Whether or not he'll put up some defence when he appears before the Deemster, I can't say. It's all very awkward."

"Do you believe he's guilty?"

"Well, no, I don't."

"Why?"

Knell hemmed and hawed.

"Well. he's not that kind. I doubt if he knows the right end of a gun. He's the sort who'd fire both barrels at once in his ignorance, but he's a mild, kindly man. In spite of his adventures and loss in the bombing of London, he's a pacifist."

The Archdeacon might have claimed a tactical victory over Knell, but he didn't.

"That's why I asked you to come, Littlejohn. If Lee won't talk, then we want someone who will *deduce* what happened. You are the man, my friend. We're relying on you. Aren't we, Knell?"

Knell nodded vigorously.

Night had fallen and outside all was silent. The curtains were drawn and the lamp had been lit. When there was a lull in the talk, there was no sound at all, except the steady tick of the old clock in the hall and the breathing and crackling of the log fire.

"I suppose you'll want to start right at the beginning, sir?"

Knell knew Littlejohn's methods, if such they could be called, and was prepared.

"If you don't mind. I suppose you've worked very painstakingly, old chap, and accumulated a lot of evidence and interviews for the files, but I'd like to go and work on the spot and absorb the atmosphere. It all happened in the curraghs, I believe."

"Yes. It was actually in the Lezayre curragh. Mylecharaine was once a chapel-of-ease to Kirk Christ, Lezayre, but the Rev. Lee took it over under the vicar of Lezayre, more or less as a full-time job. It's a scattered little area and as Mr. Lee inherited quite a bit of money from his wife, he wasn't dependent on his stipend. Or at least, that's what I'm told. The Archdeacon will know."

"That is quite right. Lezayre is the largest parish on the Island and the vicar of Kirk Christ is always glad of a little help. Mr. Lee is officially chaplain-in-charge, although known as vicar by the villagers."

"It's a locality I haven't visited much. I gather curragh means fen, is that it?"

"Yes. That's right. Much of the area has been drained, of course. The curraghs are attached to their separate parishes according to their situation. They're tacked on to Ballaugh, Lezayre and Jurby. I'll show you."

The old man hauled down old and new books from the shelves and produced ancient and modern maps. Maps with strange and musical place names which made Littlejohn feel he was in a foreign land. Alkest, Regaby, Breryk, Rozelean, Aust and Mullen Lowne. The Archdeacon placed his finger on a spot labelled *Ellanbane-White* Island-and travelled north with it through lands quaintly studded with symbols of rushes.

"The Curraghs. Here is Myrescogh, once owned by the monks of Rushen Abbey. It was then a huge lake, studded with islands. Myrescogh means Wood of the Swamp. It has now been drained and Myrescogh manor, which is on the border of Ballaugh, is a comparatively modern place, built around 1780. It adjoins the village of Mylecharaine, composed of isolated cottages and farms, with a knot of small thatched houses in the centre near a little store and post-office. We'll go to-morrow, if you like."

"That will suit me."

Maggie Keggin entered with cups of cocoa and a large cake, which although it looked to have been quarried at Billown, ate delectably. She remarked in passing that it was past ten and that she was going to bed, and she nodded her head convulsively at Knell to indicate that it was time he went home. She smiled at him faintly, to show her anger had passed. After all, they were cousins twice removed, and thus their family quarrels were their own business. She said goodnight and turned to Littlejohn as she reached the door and uttered a thrifty reminder.

"The cheap rate goes off at half-past ten."

"Thank you, Maggie," replied Littlejohn and hurried out to telephone his wife.

When he returned, the Archdeacon and Knell were discussing the curraghs and exchanging yarns and reminiscences about the people there.

"We were just talking of the curraghs, Littlejohn.

There's no place quite like them anywhere else. The houses and farms stand on little islands of land amid the drained acres and are built stoutly for human protection. In winter they are flayed by the gales from all directions and in the heat of summer they're scorched by the sun. So the massive walls retain the heat and cold and neutralize the seasons and withstand their fury. At this time of the year, the whole place is ablaze with wild flowers and breathes cool air full of their fragrance and verdure."

"I shall enjoy it all."

"And the people, too, are a little world of their own. The same families have lived there for generation after generation. Crowes, Curpheys, Casements, Ratcliffes, Corletts, Garretts. Many of their old homesteads are now deserted and in ruins and their gardens bramble-strewn and still guarded by the fuchsia hedges they planted long ago, and the elder-trees-the Manx trammans-which protected all within from evil. Strange, quiet people, living a life of their own, marrying within each other's families. I have traced as many as fifteen marriages between two families over three generations."

"Awful superstitious, too."

Knell fell into the vernacular as they spoke of old days. "Yes. The living mingled easily with the dead there until very recently. They missed their departed ones and spoke often of them. The shades were always present."

"Aren't the Kilbegs an old family there?"

"Yes, Knell. It's a wonder you didn't meet some of them crossing on your 'plane, Littlejohn. Old Juan Kilbeg, of Ballaugh Curragh, will be ninety years old next week. He had two sons who emigrated to America and, in their turn, produced seven pure Americans. All told, I believe he has living descendants totalling forty in the U.S.A. Many of them are coming over to celebrate the birthday. Ballaugh, where they are staying, is like a little America for a while."

"The old man is hale and hearty, Archdeacon?"

"Sure enough, Littlejohn. I, at eighty, feel quite a boy before him. His wife's alive. his second. He married again at sixty, a girl of thirty-five. He's one of the few native Manx speakers left and has taught his wife. I hear their American descendants have been annoyed now and then by the old man and his wife conversing in a strange tongue about things they wished to keep to themselves!"

Knell, torn between going home and talking until the small hours, returned to the crime at Mylecharaine.

"I gather that Sir Martin Skollick didn't get on too well with the local farmers. He was a comeover and wasn't at all pleasant to them. He thought money would buy anything."

"Yes. He tried to create around his own property a belt of prohibited land behind which he could be alone when he wanted. He wished to build a large estate and tried to buy up holdings from local owners. He didn't succeed, because the men there hold the land very dear. It is in trust for those who have gone and those who will come. Some fierce conflicts arose between Sir Martin and the other landowners. There was a lawsuit or two about the boundaries of certain treens, as we call them, in which Skollick came off badly."

"Yes. And a rick or two caught fire and although the police couldn't pin down the blame, it was said that Skollick had something to do with it. One nasty habit he indulged in. He used to encourage a half-mad handyman of his to light grass fires when the wind was blowing in the direction of his enemies and cover them with a pall of stinking smoke. One or two peaceable men talked of taking a gun to him."

Knell paused and looked startled.

"He might have been murdered by any of his neighbours, mightn't he?"

Littlejohn laughed.

"The sooner I get in the curraghs and find out what's been going on there, the better it will be, judging from the looks of things."

As he lay in bed later, waiting for sleep and listening to the rush of the river under Grenaby bridge, the sighing of the great trees, and the barking of a dog in the desolate direction of Moaney Mooar, he thought of the lonely curraghs, their strange secret people, their deep still waters, their swamps of terrifying depths, and the mysteries of their deserted homesteads. When sleep at length came, he dreamed he was lost there and that a solitary awful bell was tolling in the dark, and he awoke full of indescribable fear as the clock in the hall was striking four.

3

THE SILENT MAN

A radiant spring morning. Slow white frothy clouds gently drifting across the clean blue sky and a slight breeze teasing the sea and making it sparkle in the sunshine. The air was like wine and easy going pleasure shone on the faces of the few passers-by on Douglas promenade. A horse hitched to a milk-cart neighed out of sheer joy and a dog, taking a morning stroll, looked here and there admiringly and seemed to smile to himself.

There are many days like that on the Isle of Man. Days when the atmosphere seems charged with a new vitality and everything possesses a heightened significance and stands out clear and fresh, with all that is commonplace washed away.

It was the day after Littlejohn's arrival. Knell had turned up early with a police car and picked up Littlejohn and the Archdeacon for a visit to the Manx prison in Douglas. If they could persuade the Rev. Sullivan Lee to break his silence, the trouble in the curragh might be quickly explained.

Knell turned off the promenade, changed gear, and drove up a hill to the left, *dawn* a few pleasant side-streets, and drew-up in front of a smallish building which might have been a comfortable dwelling-house.

"This is it."

Not a bad place for a gaol, especially with the sun shining through the windows and the clean sea air filling all the cells. They found the warder reading the morning paper and sipping tea from a large mug. The twin headlines of the news hit them in the eye as they entered. *Superintendent Littlejohn on the Curragh Case. Calf with Six Legs born at Ronague.*

The warder leapt to his feet, greeted them with a pleasant smile, and put his hat on to show that he was on duty again. He was the only one there for the time being. They weren't busy. There were only three prisoners at present. A teddyboy, who'd thrown a pal through a shop window, a drunk who'd been sick and was now cleaning out his cell before they'd release him, and the Rev. Sullivan Lee.

Knell got to business right away. "You've told him we're calling on him?"

"Yes, as soon as you telephoned."

"What did he say?"

"He said it was nice of you."

A long passage with linoleum on the floor. The man might have been showing some new arrivals on holidays to their rooms.

"Here we are."

The warder turned the key in the lock and opened the door. A plain, clean cell, with a barred window overlooking a courtyard in which large trees were just bursting into leaf. Birds were singing and someone was whistling happily in the street behind. It all looked nice and comfortable. There was even a rubber mattress on the bed, which had been neatly made. The warder removed an empty teacup and saucer from the table.

The occupant rose to his feet from the solitary chair. He was well-groomed and recently shaved and wore his cassock which was neat and tidy. He slipped an old envelope to mark the place in the book he'd been reading, and closed it.

A strange situation. Here was a man who very soon might be

convicted of murder and yet it seemed impossible to take it seriously. He looked innocent from the beginning and that altered the whole attitude of his visitors. Even the warder treated Mr. Lee deferentially.

The Archdeacon offered Lee his hand as soon as he entered, and Lee shook it warmly without hesitation. They might have been visiting a monk in his cell instead of a man accused of murder in a gaol.

"This is Superintendent Littlejohn, a very dear friend of mine, who's come over to help us."

Littlejohn shook hands as well and he and Lee smiled at each other. Friendly smiles, too. It was fantastic.

The warder brought in three more chairs and then left them, for the drunk had finished his cleaning-up, and was shouting for freedom.

They all sat down and the Archdeacon was the first to speak.

"Well, Lee? How are you?"

"Very well, thank you, Archdeacon. It's kind of you all to call."

Just as though nothing at all were the matter.

Lee was tall and heavily built, with his dark hair combed back from a broad brow. He had troubled dark eyes and well cut features. He was calm and self-possessed. He could even have asked, in the circumstances, why Littlejohn was there at all, but he merely smiled and might have been getting ready to invite them to stay for lunch.

"I said Littlejohn had come over to help us, Lee. I must tell you quite frankly that you're causing us a lot of trouble by taking the whole of this business on your own shoulders. If you'd only speak and tell us what happened. You're not the stuff murderers are made of."

Sullivan Lee lowered his head under the scrutiny of the Archdeacon's keen blue eyes. For the first time since the affair had started he seemed uneasy.

"I'm sorry. Truly sorry. But I don't wish to say anything."

He said it almost in a whisper.

There was no pose about him, no show of martyrdom.

"I know, Lee, you're a high churchman and you believe in confession. Has somebody confessed this crime to you? Are you shielding someone? I've asked you this before, but I must persist for your own sake."

"I cannot."

Lee's hands lay placidly on his lap and he shook his head sadly as though regretting to refuse the help he was offered. "Very well, Lee. Then we must act without you."

Lee looked up sharply.

"I mean if you will not talk about the matter, Littlejohn will have to start and find out all about it by deduction without your co-operation. He will arrive at the truth and you will have caused him all the trouble out of what I cannot do other than describe as a misplaced sense of duty, even stupidity."

"I'm really very sorry. I beg you do no such thing. This is my affair and I will pay the price."

Nothing was said by Lee about his being guilty of the crime. He just knew the facts, wholly or in part, and would not disclose them.

Littlejohn spoke to him.

"You were in London, sir, before you came over here?"

"Yes. They have been so good to me. I'm sorry to."

"Have you always been in the ministry?"

"Since I left school and college, yes."

"Country livings?"

"No. Always town parishes. I was curate in two industrial towns in Yorkshire. I was born in Bradford. Then, I got my first living in Bristol, and since then have had two east-end parishes in London. St. Thomas's-by-the-Wall and St. Andrew's, Barking. You know them?"

"Very well indeed, sir. St. Andrew's was wrecked in the bombing."

Lee winced.

"Yes. So was the vicarage, and my dear wife was in it."

"I'm very sorry, sir. Did you like work in the city?"

"I did, indeed. I'm not a countryman, Superintendent, by any stretch of imagination. I admit, my present work is among country people and in the heart of lovely scenery, but it is the work and the parishioners I love, not the rural pursuits."

"The fishing and shooting then, wouldn't make good hobbies for your off-hours?"

"They certainly wouldn't. I have never handled a fishing line in my life, nor will I."

He paused.

"I beg of you, Superintendent, do not try to trick me into giving you information about the tragedy of my parish. I have already said, it is my sole responsibility."

"Until whoever committed the crime decides to confess?"

"I cannot answer that question."

"You are prepared to allow whoever did it, sir, to remain free until you yourself might be found guilty? In which case, he will come forward with a confession? If you are acquitted, he will escape scot-free."

"Please do not think badly of me. I know my duty."

"I'm afraid you don't, sir. You must be very sure of your man if you can be willing to leave him at liberty all the time you are bearing the present strain. He might even commit another crime, or maybe flee, and leave you to suffer for your quixotic behaviour. Instead, you are content to give the police all the trouble of a most difficult investigation, one rendered all the more difficult by your refusing to co-operate."

Lee was now wringing his hands gently. The strain of keeping quiet and allowing nothing in the few words he said to betray him was beginning to tell on him. Littlejohn was not one who favoured a third-degree. He rose and offered Lee his hand.

"I can see, Mr. Lee that you are either prepared to sacrifice yourself, to go the whole way for someone else, or you trust such a person so much, that you believe he will not let you down. I'm afraid I can't wait to test your theory or beliefs. I shall try to find out without you."

"Don't think I don't appreciate what you are doing, Superintendent. I'm very grateful. But I can't do other than what my conscience bids me."

"Neither can I sir. Whoever has allowed you to put yourself in this position deserves the fullest punishment the law can give him."

"I tell you, Superintendent, I am a guilty man and I must pay for my sins."

"Whatever else you're guilty of, it's not the murder of Skollick. I'm sure of that. Am I right?"

"I have nothing to say."

"Good-bye for the present, then, sir."

The Archdeacon shook hands as well.

"Do you need any books, Lee? I see you're passing the time reading."

He indicated the volume with which Lee had been occupied when they entered, and a Bible and a prayer-book on the table, as well.

"If you would be so good as to lend me some more books about the Isle of Man. The one I'm reading now is *Manx Worthies* and I find it most enjoyable."

"I'll send some along right away."

"No religious books, please, Archdeacon."

The old man turned and faced him.

"Do you find your Bible and prayer-book enough, then?"

"My kind warder brought those in. I didn't bring my own. They are not for me any longer. I am irretrievably damned. I am an outcast."

The Archdeacon replied in his quiet serious way.

"That is foolish talk. No matter whom you are protecting, you know you are doing wrong. You are an outcast, because you are making yourself one, Lee, and the sooner you decide to tell the truth, the sooner you'll find your faith again. I'll bring the books myself this afternoon."

The door closed behind them and Littlejohn knew the good old man was returning to the fray alone with Lee when next he called. They left the Archdeacon in Douglas where he proposed to visit friends and collect books for the prisoner. They promised to pick him up later in the day.

Knell now suggested taking Littlejohn to the curraghs and the scene of the crime. As usual, when Littlejohn arrived unofficially to give his friends as much help as he could, he was finding himself once more in charge of the case, with Knell as his official sponsor and apprentice.

The car took the road through the lovely Baldwin valley, now green with Spring and alight with primroses. A steady climb all the way to the massive graceful hills which form the interior of the island. After passing the beautiful artificial lake at Ingebreck, the local waterworks, the road mounted steeply along a ridge of hills, with wide lonely valleys beneath, to a cottage at the main crossroads. It was a spot with which Littlejohn was familiar, for, in Druidale, for which they were now making, he had once investigated a murder. They drove past the very farmstead, ruined and grim, where the body had been found. It was just the same as it was long ago. Time seemed to stand still in the silences of the Isle of Man.

The Druidale road ended in Ballaugh, capital of the curraghs. Thence, a perfect maze of lanes led through the drained marshland to Mylecharaine.

It was hardly a village at all. Two or three houses in a cluster by the roadside, one of them acting as a local stores and post-office. The church and vicarage stood completely isolated at the end of a by-road. The rest of the place was scattered piecemeal. Cottages on their own, built on little islands of dry ground standing above the general level of the land. Farms just visible through the rings of willows and sycamores which protected them from the winds and were twisted and tortured in the process.

Knell pulled-up near the telephone kiosk which, since its recent erection, had become the official centre of the parish. There was nobody about. If there had been, what was the use? Knell realized that he had brought Littlejohn there simply to show him the scene of the crime. Or rather, the scene of the grim nocturnal drama staged by the Rev. Sullivan Lee.

They sat in the car, side by side, not moving for a minute or two. Littlejohn was quietly smoking his pipe and Knell took a cigarette from a packet and lit it. There was hardly enough breeze to blow the smoke away: The land shimmered under the hot Spring sunshine, birds were singing and chattering, and in the distance they could hear the calling of plovers and bitterns. The turns in the road and the heavy tall hedges of shrubs and trees prevented their seeing far around them.

Knell began to speak in a low apologetic voice, like a penitent making his confession.

"It's the strangest case I've ever been on, sir. We know Sir Martin Skollick was a rascal, cynical, a woman chaser, a twister. He was disliked everywhere and had enemies among the farmers, villagers, and Lord knows who else, that he'd offended or robbed or meddled with their women. Half a dozen people hated him enough to wish him dead. That we know."

He drew hard on his cigarette and then threw the end of it through the car window with a gesture of disgust.

"That's all. We haven't even found out where the murder happened. Or who was up at the unearthly hour when people heard the shot. We just know that Skollick and somebody else were abroad in the dark together, and that unknown somebody and Skollick met, and one killed the other."

"You've searched the roads for traces of blood and questioned everybody in the vicinity?"

"Yes. Our men have been to every farm and cottage in the neighbourhood where the shot was fired. Not a thing. We've searched every road and by-path, too. Unluckily, there was a short shower the day after the murder. It might have been sent to bailie us. After it had washed away all traces, it cleared up and it's been fine ever since."

"And yet, none of us think Lee did it."

"No, sir. He either saw the crime and knows who did it, and is for some goddam reason shielding him. Or else he came across the body and the shock drove him round the bend. He carried it to the church, prayed over it, rang the bell, wakened everybody, and then froze into a sort of silence ever since."

Littlejohn climbed out of the car, knocked out his pipe against the heel of his shoe, and leaned over a gate in the hedge, looking across at the stark lonely buildings which constituted the church and vicarage of Mylecharaine.

"You searched the house, the vicarage, I mean?"

"Yes, sir. There was nothing there to help us. Would you care to see the church and the parsonage?"

Then a diversion occurred before Littlejohn could reply.

Down the road ahead of their car trotted a little flock of sheep. About four ewes and half a dozen lambs. They were unattended, but were obviously being pressed from behind. The reason for their hurry appeared almost on their heels. A smart, dark-blue saloon car rounded the curve, came to a halt, and a handsome middle-aged man stepped out and shouted to Knell.

"Hi, Knell! Open the gate you're leaning over and let in these blasted sheep. Wandering unattended on the road and me unable to get past 'em. Who the hell owns 'em, I don't know, but he'll soon know where to find them. I see Mrs. Cashen peeping round the curtains there."

The newcomer indicated the nearest cottage, the curtains of which were in a state of agitation.

"She'll convey the information to the proper quarter in no time. It's like the jungle drums here in the curraghs for passing on news."

Between them Knell and the stranger shepherded the little flock into the field beyond the gate, the sheep showing their approval by immediately starting to gnaw the grass and the lambs by plunging at their mothers' udders and enjoying a convulsed meal.

The stranger was still complaining.

"What a ruddy place for a doctor! If it isn't floods blocking the roads, it's cattle. And if it isn't cattle, it's sheep. Half my time's spent in removing obstacles."

Knell introduced Littlejohn to the doctor.

"This is Dr. Pakeman, sir. Superintendent Littlejohn, of Scotland Yard, doctor."

"Ah. So you're the man! I'm glad to meet you, Superintendent."

He gave Littlejohn a remarkably fine and well-kept hand for a countryman. For Dr. Pakeman had all the appearances of one. He looked nearer sixty than fifty; a tall, forthright man, with a small grey moustache, rugged features full of character, and shrewd grey eyes. He wore a tweed suit, and a cap which he now removed to mop his forehead, which was broad and intelligent. The moustache, the bushy eyebrows, and plentiful grey hair cut short and bristling over his fine head all gave him a look of strength and dependability.

"They brought in Dr. Pakeman when the body of Sir Martin was found."

Pakeman put on his cap again and took out and lighted a pipe.

"Not much I could do. Hardly anything left of his head. All the brain had been shot away."

Knell winced.

"You live near here, doctor?"

"In Ramsey actually. On the Lezayre Road, the nearest doctor to the curraghs. That's why I have to navigate this maze every day. Not that I don't know it like the back of my hand after nearly thirty years of it."

"What do you think of all this, doctor? The murder, I mean."

"Your guess is as good as mine, Littlejohn. In fact, it's better. You're a trained man. I'm not. All the same, I'm not surprised. What I'm surprised at is that nobody's done it before."

"He could hardly be described as a popular favourite, doctor?"

"Not by a long way. In fact, nobody liked him. He was a strong man, determined, he had money, he could be described as successful. Even when it came to seducing a virtuous girl, he seemed to succeed. Some people are that way, aren't they? Can't put a foot wrong. And yet, Skollick was a Wilshout, a failure and a freak. You ask why? Because for all his success, he could never be content with what he'd got. He couldn't rest. He'd his own estate; he wanted that of the man next door. He'd his own wife-and she's a damned nice one, too--but he wanted somebody else's as well. He'd enough money of his own, but whilst the chap across the way had some, too, Skollick couldn't sleep for hatching schemes to twist him out of it. He was a real bad lat."

It wasn't said in heat or passion. The doctor might have been calmly describing some disease or other to a colleague.

"Which reminds me, I'm on my way to Myrescogh Manor now. I've got to see Lady Skollick. This business had put her out. You'd think she'd jump for joy to be rid of such a scoundrel. Not a bit of it. She's heartbroken and a nervous wreck. Going my way?"

"We may as well. I'd like to see the manor. It doesn't seem much use staying here, doctor. There's nothing to see and nobody to talk to."

"You don't know how to go about it, Littlejohn. These are cautious people, sly, and with a shy sense of humour. You'd like them immensely if you got to know them. But it takes a long time, *Traa di Liooar*, as they say in Marne Plenty of time. You should come round with me for a spell. We must see what we can do about it. Well, Knell, get back in that car of yours and let's get going. Better follow me and hoot at every turn in the road. One car's enough for the natives to cope with in these parts. Two coming round a corner together would just paralyse them."

He jumped in his car, patted an old springer spaniel which had been sitting beside him, started off, and they followed his route. The road wound and twisted, crossing little bridges over the drainage ditches. Here and there an old by-road, metalled in sharp flints, branched off, but now led nowhere, for the homestead at the end of it had fallen into decay and its land had become waste or been joined to that of others.

They reached Myrescogh Manor at last. An avenue of wind-twisted firs broke away from the main road and they followed it between hedges of daffodils and unkempt gorse to the house itself, which faced the hills to the south. A square-built place, simply constructed in rectangular fashion, with a great front door, a row of five windows above it and four on the ground floor. It seemed to huddle for shelter among its giant weather-tortured trees. In front, a wild garden sprawled about, with forlorn unkempt rose beds, profuse thorny bushes and tall scraggy palms and eucalyptus trees, which shook in the breeze, struggling for life in unhospitable soil. All the blinds were drawn, no chimneys smoked, and there was no sign of human habitation. Behind stretched acres of neglected curragh land, much of it bearing the rotten appearance of peat-bog with masses of gorse growing like a black and yellow fleece in the midst of it. An ominous, foreboding house, whose windows looked like blind eyes, and the door of which seemed firmly closed against intruders.

4

THE HOUSE AT TANTALOO

Dr. Pakeman Beat upon the thick oak panels of the front door of the manor. He was too impatient even to use the knocker. A pause, footsteps which seemed to approach from afar off and sounded like a crescendo of drum-beats. Then the door was flung wide open and an elderly woman in cap and apron stood gravely there looking them all over.

"Good day to ye, docthor," she said at length in the lilting Manx brogue.

"Well, Jinnie. And how's your mistress to-day?"

"Middlin', middlin', docthor. She's still in her bed."

"Did she sleep well last night?"

"Afther the tablets you gave her, yes."

"I'd better go up and take a look at her."

"She's awake."

"These two gentlemen are from the police."

The woman's face had been set woodenly until now. This was the expression she thought meet for a servant in a house of tragedy and death. Now her look changed to one of surly, defiant hostility.

"What will they be wantin' here?"

"I met them in the curragh and I'm taking them home with me. Better let them wait in the morning-room until I come down."

The maid turned and indicated by a motion of the head that they could follow her.

Littlejohn was not superstitious, but as soon as he crossed the threshold, a queer feeling took hold of him as though round the next corner something or someone might have been lurking to do him harm. It wasn't physical harm, either. It went deeper than that. It might have been due to the thick walls, or the dead hush which pervaded the place, or again, the chill might have risen from deep foundations stretching far into the damp underground waters of the ancient bog.

The hall was wide and a broad staircase rose at the end of it and disappeared upwards in a right-angled turn. Persian rugs on the polished oak floor, mounted heads of foxes and deer on the walls, a carved ebony hat stand, a huge gong, and a print of Frith's *Derby Day* filling half of one side.

The maid opened a door to the right and bade Littlejohn and Knell enter. From here came the smell which pervaded the whole house, that of aromatic wood. There was a small fire of apple wood and gorse roots burning in the large fireplace.

"Better draw the curtains, Jinnie. No sense in keeping out the light of day."

The old woman obeyed and swished back the heavy chenille curtains on brass rings. She did it with a gesture of protest, but it was obvious she was an admirer of the doctor and would go far to please him.

"You'll excuse me if I go up to see my patient. I won't be long."

They were left alone. Knell hadn't said a word since they arrived at the manor. He was obviously out of his element and uncomfortable.

"I can't say I like this place much. I'll bet it's haunted."

He looked around as though expecting a ghost or something even more monstrous to materialize.

"You feel it, too?"

"Yes, sir. It gives me the creeps."

All the same, the little morning-room was a pleasant place and obviously much used. It overlooked the front garden, facing the hills between Sulby and Kirk Michael on which the sun of high noon was shining and revealing a wide graceful sweep of coloured bracken and gorse. A blackbird was busy on the lawn listening for worms and digging them up and another was singing in a tree. Daffodils running riot everywhere. Wild roses and honeysuckle in the hedges. A pleasant sight. They might have been looking out on a world full of good things, like unattainable pleasures set-out in a shop window.

The room itself was furnished in well-used Victorian chairs, a small table, a sideboard and an oak chest. Books on either side of the fireplace, a television set, and in one corner, a large radiogram with a record cabinet. There was just space in which to move round among the various odds and ends. There were two large pictures on the walls, indifferently painted aspects of the manor itself, one from the front, and the other from the side, which showed the avenue of tortured trees in the winter, leafless, twisted, with a stretch of bare curragh in the background. It made you feel cold and depressed to look at it.

Over the fireplace were photographs and miniatures on ivory. A number of the photographs were of the same beautiful woman. Leaving a 'plane all smiles; in the process of what looked like accepting gifts from children at a bazaar or fete; then in evening dress as though ready to mount the platform and sing a song; and finally, dressed up like Mimi in *La Boheme.*

Littlejohn took it all in casually, whilst Knell looked through the window whistling *Don't Knock the Rock* through his teeth absent-mindedly. He had learned it by heart one night as he supervised the arrest of half a dozen berserk teddy-boys at a Douglas dance-hall, where the band kept on playing to keep everybody busy.

There was not a sound in the house and the doctor was back before they realized he was there.

"Sit down. Lady Skollick says you're to have a drink.

Jinnie's bringing in the whisky."

No sooner said than done. The maid entered with a tray on which were a bottle and glasses. She held it far from her as though it were something vile and dangerous. She put it on a table and left the room and the doctor poured out helpings.

"Say when. Soda?"

"Your health, gentlemen."

"Good health, doctor."

Knell drank gingerly. He'd been brought-up teetotal and had signed the pledge at the Band of Hope in his youth. He eased his conscience by telling it that this was in the course of duty and that the whisky was distasteful to him. Then he took a good swig and smacked his lips.

The doctor seemed at home there. He even bent and took a couple of handfuls of gorse roots and flung them on the fire. The flame licked them up and the scent of the burning wood filled the room again.

"I was just looking at all the photographs round the fireplace, doctor. Are the ones of the same woman those of Lady Skollick?"

"Yes. She was a fine singer in her time. Opera and concert platform. She still has a splendid voice although she's middle-aged now. I've heard her a time or two."

"Soprano?"

The doctor raised his eyebrows. Littlejohn nodded at the picture of Mimi. "Yes. You musical?"

"My wife more than me. We often go to the opera."

"I wonder if I've ever heard Lady Skollick."

"She was Jean Calloway in those days."

Littlejohn shook his head. No. He didn't remember the name.

"How long was she married to Sir Martin?"

"Twelve years or so, I think. I did hear her mention it once."

"How old was he?"

"Fifty-eight. She was ten years younger."

"She ought to be in her prime."

"*Ought* is the right word. But you didn't know Skollick."

"How did he get his knighthood?"

"His father was a baronet. A stockbroker with philanthropic leanings. A very respectable and decent chap, I believe."

"How did Skollick make his money?"

"Followed in father's footsteps, only instead of keeping on the straight and narrow path of respectable stockbroking, after his father's death he converted the firm into a bucket-shop and landed himself in gaol for a spell. He must have salted a lot away. He never seemed to go short of anything after he came from gaol. His wife was waiting when he came out, and they came over here. But don't think Skollick did it to hide himself for very shame. He came to avoid high income-tax and death-duties."

"Did he start being unpleasant as soon as he got here?"

"Right away. But it's time we thought about some lunch. It's turned half-past one. Come to my place for a drink and a sandwich. It's on your way home. There's cold meat, and I'm sorry that's the best I can offer."

"We mustn't impose on you."

"Rubbish. I can see you're both bursting for more information. I'm full of it. In and out the houses on the curragh one doesn't miss much. I've been doctor to the Skollick's since they arrived and there isn't much I don't know about them. Let's go."

They bade Jinnie good-bye and left as they had come, the doctor leading and Knell driving in his wake.

They passed through the domain of Myrescogh again; great sweeps of barren land where rushes and willows flourished and brambles and gorse grew wild and rank. Then, at length, the main road through the curraghs, narrow but well-metalled, which led them quickly on the highway which runs the whole way from Castletown to Ramsey.

Much of the road passed through arches of tall old trees, now almost in full spring leaf. As they travelled along, they could see a panorama of the flat extreme north of the Island with, to the north-east, the first signs of higher ground, rising gently to the tender little hills of Bride. The doctor's car pulled-up in front of a square old house with gothic shaped windows. It was set behind a walled garden and access was through a full-length door like a postern cut in the wall. The doctor ran his car through a gate at the side of the house and down to what appeared to be stables at the back.

"Park yours in the road, Knell. I'll be with you in a minute."

As they made their way along the gravel path down the hidden garden to the front door, there was a heavy scent of wallflowers on the air, bees buzzed among the espaliers which flowered on the walls, and tulips were already blooming to replace the dying daffodils. In this secret sheltered spot, everything seemed weeks ahead of elsewhere.

The doctor led them through a cool dark little hall into a study to the right, which overlooked the garden. Excusing himself, he left them and could be heard talking with a woman in the back quarters, apparently ordering a meal. He was soon back.

The room was small and cosy. A large fireplace in which burned a huge log. Saddleback armchairs, a small sideboard, books in shelves along one wall and in alcoves on each side of the fire. A double-barrelled sporting gun in one corner along with fishing-tackle. Framed photographs of university groups and Rugby teams.

"The river runs just behind," said the doctor, intercepting Littlejohn's glance at the rods. "We get some fine salmon at times, and always trout in season. Look."

He led them to the window and showed them the direction in which the river lay and then indicated a large house to the west.

"That is Ellanbane, which means White Island. Long ago, it stood in a wilderness of bog which stretched from here to

Ballaugh and embraced Myrescogh and Mylecharaine. Ellanbane was for long the home of the Standish family, which included Longfellow's Pilgrim Father, Miles."

"Beer or whisky?"

A small slim woman of sixty or more put in her head and raised her eyebrows in a cheerful question.

"Both, Nessie, please."

They all sat by the fire, for, in spite of the warm sun outside, there was a chill dampness in the room akin to that at Myrescogh, which may have arisen from the hidden waters which probably undermine the whole stretch of flat land bordering the curraghs.

There were no signs whatever of the practice of medicine in the room, which was obviously the den which the doctor usually occupied. Pakeman apparently read Littlejohn's thoughts.

"I've half retired from medicine. I used to live in Ramsey when I was very active, but now I've only kept on the country part of my work. It's a long stretch from the curraghs to Ramsey to see the doctor, and as often as not, I visit my patients at home, except in mild cases where they can walk a mile or two and then get the bus. I love the quiet of the marshlands and I go there most days, even if nobody's sick."

"You must know all that goes on there, then."

"Some of it. As I said, they're secret folk and only tell you what they want you to know. The women will gossip, of course, and once you've won the confidence of the men, they'll confide in you. Great talkers if you get them going. A *li'l cooish,* they call it. A little chat about everything. There's not much in the curraghs but work and talk. At night, they gather round the fires before bedtime and chatter. If they couldn't talk, they'd be eaten up by boredom. Many of them have cars, but they use them merely for church or the mart, or perhaps a visit to nearby neighbours. In winter, the fury of the weather, storms sweeping across the flatlands, isolates them. And in summer, they're busy on the land. It's then that the marshes steam and the earth dries, and in the hot sunshine the villages and farms seem to sleep among the reeds in the heat like exhausted animals."

Nessie had brought in the lunch, a tray bearing two plates piled with sandwiches, glasses and bottles, and a large apple pie in a dish on top of a small pile of plates. She whispered to the doctor.

"Excuse me. A patient for some medicine, they enter by a wicket gate at the side which leads into a sort of conservatory I use as a waiting-room, when there's anybody to wait. Thence a door admits them to the surgery."

He went out leaving the servant to spread the meal on a series of little tables which she set beside the three chairs.

"You live here, Mrs?"

"Mrs. Vondy's the name, sir. Yes, I live in. I've been with the docthor since himself, my husband, died three years since. I like it. Mrs. Joughin, before me, was here about ten years. It's a good place to be at and the docthor that nice, too. Mrs. Joughin would have still been here, leek as not, if her brother in Australia hadn't died an' left 'er twenty thousand pounds."

This was obviously Mrs. Vondy's great news which she passed on to everybody. The awful way in which she said *twenty thousand* was proof of that.

"So she retired?"

"Went to live at Maughold, the other side 0' Ramsey.

The village where she was born and where she says she wants to die and be buried in the old churchyard there."

The doctor was back.

Beer and sandwiches circulated and the doctor talked as they ate.

"What was I saying? Giving you some background about the curraghs, wasn't I? Delightful people, but best at home in their own farms and villages. Like those lovely local wines of France which are ruined by removing them from their native places."

Where was it all leading to? Littlejohn couldn't even guess. Did it concern Skollick and the crime, or was it just a *li'l cooish* which the people so loved in the off hours on the marsh?

At any rate, it was pleasant, sitting there, eating excellent beef sandwiches and drinking good Castletown ale, with the view of the garden and, beyond it, the magnificent chestnut trees of the road and the green rising slopes beyond them.

"What is the name of this place, sir?"

Knell thought he'd better say something between his bites at a large sandwich.

"Tantaloo, Knell. We're in Lezayre parish, and the view at the end of the little valley opposite gives the house its name. Tantaloo. There used to be a little hamlet there and a small tuck-mill, as the Manx call the old fulling-works."

It was very comfortable and the doctor had opened the front window which let in the scent of the flowers. A flock of pigeons swept regularly round and round over the garden.

"That's where Skollick made his mistake." Now it was coming!

"He didn't try to understand people before he started to deal with them. When he arrived at Myrescogh, he was a comeover, a stranger, an interloper. One has to lie low until one gains the confidence and respect of one's neighbours anywhere, most of all in the curraghs. But Skollick was so selfish and avaricious, he wanted to do everything at once."

The doctor rose and poured out more beer for his guests.

He took a good drink himself.

"He seemed to have a mania for acquiring land. He wanted to build up a vast estate at Myrescogh for some reason, probably out of pride and to show-off. Making himself a big landowner. As I told you before, he met with stubborn refusals from the owners to sell even a yard. So he began his peevish tricks. Firing the gorse and old rubbish to annoy his neighbours. And he had a habit of digging out old cattle roads and tracks, long overgrown, and some of them embraced in other people's farms. He'd ride over them on his horse and if the farmer objected, point out the track and challenge him to go to law. One or two tried it out and had their fun but had to pay for it."

Pakeman rose again, cut substantial wedges of apple tart, and poured rich thick cream over them; then he handed them out with a spoon apiece.

"A man will, you know, go to extremes of violence for his land or his women. To suffer injustice is a normal human burden and is often borne with patience. But when it comes to land and women. It creates madness of intoxication which breeds unpredictable passions and evil. Now you see what I'm getting at. Skollick might have been killed by almost anybody in the curraghs."

Knell stopped eating and seemed to be brooding on some point or other. Then, he began to chew his pie again as though he'd reached a decision.

"Do you think that Mr. Lee is protecting someone, then, doctor?"

"What do you mean, Knell?"

"Perhaps he saw the crime committed and won't say who did it."

"I'm sure you're right. Lee wouldn't hurt a fly. Unless."

"Perhaps he knew someone or other would use violence to Skollick one day and decided to avert it by taking the sin of murder on his own shoulders. I remember once when I met him in the curraghs there'd just been a haystack fire and he suggested it might be one of Sir Martin's tricks. He worked himself into quite a frenzy of sympathy for Skollick's victims. You see, like Anatole France's *Putois,* Sir Martin was the scapegoat for every wrong in the district. A girl in the family way… Sir Martin. A cow dies. Sir Martin. A house on fire… Sir Martin. The best silver spoons missing. Sir Martin. It was ridiculous. He had become the modern edition of what the old Manx used to call the Eye, the putting of a curse on one's enemies."

Littlejohn drank the last of his beer. "More beer, Littlejohn?"

"Thanks, doctor. It's a funny thing, I've no idea of what Skollick looked like. Strangely enough, I've made up in my mind a picture of him so vivid that I've not even asked to see a photograph of him."

Littlejohn could have sketched his own mental photograph of Skollick. It was something like his late friend Tad Slaughter taking his famous part of William Corder in *Maria Martin, or the Murder in the Red Barn*. Riding clothes, hunting crop, swagger, lecherous smile.

Pakeman was handing him a photograph apparently taken by a newspaper man. A little group of people obviously at an agricultural show standing with a fine horse, a hunter, on the bridle of which was a rosette indicating a prize winner. On one side of the animal were Pakeman and the woman whose picture was repeated so often in the morning room at Myrescogh Manor. She was still handsome in a dark mature aquiline way, with high cheek-bones, a fine arched nose, pointed chin and large eyes. Her greying hair curled attractively from beneath her little hat. She was smiling at the horse in a fond, melancholy way.

Littlejohn was looking for the villain, Sir Martin, the scoundrel who coveted his neighbour's land and women and who had ruined hundreds through his financial bucket-shop and gone to gaol for doing it.

"Is this him?" said Littlejohn, ungrammatical in his astonishment.

"Yes."

On the other side of the horse, looking away from it possibly at a passing woman-was a small, bareheaded, thin man in tweeds. A caricature of a villain! He was turning bald and had the bandy-legged stance of a cavalryman. He wore a small moustache and had a firm mouth and jaw. The features could have been described as large and strong, the kind which should have gone with six feet or more, instead of with five-feet six. He appeared to be smaller than his wife, but the deep-set eyes and the self-confident smile made you think of a wasp buzzing round a butterfly. However small Skollick might have been, he had a sting hidden somewhere about him.

"Funny. I never thought of Skollick being so small."

"Many people misjudged him, to their regret. Casement, the poacher, for example. Skollick once caught him on his land and struck him with his crop. Casement, an enormous fellow, who loves poaching and would die without it, was flabbergasted. He hit Skollick back; just, as he said later, to teach him not to be so handy with his whip. There was nobody about to prove a case. Skollick told one tale and Casement another. It never went to court, but Skollick took his revenge. He insisted on police assistance against poaching and he and the police so harried and chased poor Casement about, that he became a dangerous savage. The type who might have shot Skollick himself in the end."

"So we have yet another suspect?"

"Yes; but no greater than the rest. Sir Martin was universally disliked."

"You mentioned his wife's continued affection for him.

Was he kind to her in spite of being unfaithful?"

"When he was sober, yes. When he was drunk, he was a devil. He taunted and accused her, made fun of her interest in the village life and especially in the village church. On one or two occasions, he struck her."

"Did she tell you this, doctor?"

"No. Jinnie, who seems to think the world of me, has kept me informed. In fact, she once called here. Sir Martin had had a mild attack of D.T.'s. Jinnie came to ask if it wouldn't be possible for me to do something, certify him as insane or an inebriate fit for a home. People always rush to the doctor with such troubles."

"And yet, Lady Skollick stood by him through it all."

"Yes. She is a good religious woman and said she knew where her duty lay. I noticed her bruised arm once when I called and asked her outright if her husband had done it, in view of what Jinnie had told me."

Littlejohn looked at the rugged, troubled face and sad eyes of the doctor, sad even when he was smiling, and wondered how many more secrets he knew about Myrescogh Manor and the curraghs and people which surrounded it.

The maid was back and whispering to the doctor again.

Another patient.

"We're busy to-day."

Pakeman excused himself and left. They could hear a door open and close along the passage.

"What do you think of it all, Knell?"

"The doctor seems to know plenty. He's a lonely man, isn't he, sir? And he's glad to find a sympathetic friend and get a lot of it off his chest."

"You're right. I wonder what his own history is. What's made him come over here and shut himself up in this place and seek the loneliest community on the island to serve? I'd like to find out."

"What about calling at Maughold and having a word with his old servant. The one Mrs. Vondy mentioned, sir?"

"Not a bad idea. We'll talk about it on the way back."

"We pass the Maughold turning."

Littlejohn stood by the window, smoking his pipe and admiring the garden. In one corner, he noticed a radiogram with a pile of records under it. Casually he raised the lid. There was a disc on the turntable. He slipped on his spectacles and leaned to read the title out of curiosity about the doctor's taste. "*April,* by Tosti, sung by Jean Calloway." The top two of the pile beneath were hers as well. Footsteps were approaching, so he closed the lid quietly and was smoking by the window again when the doctor entered.

"I'll have to leave you, Littlejohn. A child at the Garey choking with croup. Come again any time for another talk. By the way, you seemed surprised at Skollick. Had you imagined him as very different?"

"To tell the truth, doctor, I'd rather stupidly created a picture in my mind of somebody like William Corder in the *Murder in the Red Barn!*"

Pakeman nodded and smiled his sad smile.

"Sorry to disappoint you, Littlejohn, but you may be half right you know. It may *be* the murder in the red barn. If he took the shortest way home to Myrescogh, Skollick would pass the Red Haggart. Haggart's Manx for stackyard. It lies close to Red Island-Rozelean in the old Gaelic and it's a most likely place for an ambush. Well, I must be going."

He saw them out and then went off to the child who was said to be dying from croup, but who survived unhurt after swallowing a safety-pin and six ball-bearings.

5
A WOMAN ON EDGE

They drove straight back to Douglas. No sense in calling at Maughold to speak with Mrs. Joughin, Pakeman's old servant. The arrival of a couple of total strangers asking her to tell them all she knew about the doctor would be enough to make her shut-up for ever. The Archdeacon was the man for such a job.

They picked up the parson in Douglas. He had had another long talk with the Rev. Sullivan Lee. He'd even ordered a special lunch for the pair of them and eaten it with Lee in the gaol. But he had got no nearer; Lee would say nothing about the events on the night of the crime.

"He's as stubborn as a mule. He's quite set for standing trial for murder."

So there they were. Not a bit nearer for all the day's efforts. There were one or two matters to set in motion, though. Knell arranged with the police to go to the Red Haggart in the curraghs and give the whole place a thorough examination for traces of blood or intrusion. Pakeman's guess might prove right.

Then, Littlejohn telephoned to Scotland Yard and asked for as much information as they could quickly gather about Sir Martin Skollick and the Rev. Sullivan Lee.

On the way back to Grenaby, Littlejohn was very thoughtful. He was trying to arrange the pieces of the curragh jigsaw in his mind and his companions maintained a sympathetic silence. Only once did Knell speak. They were passing over the Fairy Bridge at Ballalona.

"Good afternoon, little people." he said and raised his hat, and Littlejohn and the Archdeacon solemnly followed suit. Knell was always ready for a bit of help from the fairies on any case that concerned him.

They ate a meal at the vicarage at Grenaby and then settled down over their pipes to discuss the case.

"Do you think Lee is guilty of the crime, parson, after your further long talk with him?"

"No. But I'm sure that Lee, for some reason, thinks himself guilty. I can't say whether or not he blames himself morally or physically."

"His refusal to speak, his effort to get off the Island, and the fact that he had a key to the school where the gun was lying overnight, are the main props of the prosecution side. There is one big point for the defence, however. The abandoned car."

"You mean leaving it at Lezayre, sir?"

"Yes. What time did the hot-pot supper break-up at Mylecharaine, Knell?"

"The last of them left at just after eleven. Two or three of the women testified to that."

"They were busy to the end?"

"They'd rather a lot of stuff to deal with for the jumble sale. They said they really ought not to have had such a big meal. It made them late starting again. Then, just after half-past ten, when they'd finished pricing and arranging all the stuff, they made themselves another cup of tea, for the road, so to speak."

"Was the Rev. Lee there all the time?"

"Yes. He's a flair for printing labels and wrote them, or rather printed them in block letters, while the women priced and set the goods out. Mr. Lee was there all the time after the hot-pot supper, and left the last. He locked-up, in fact."

"Meanwhile, Sir Martin was with Mrs. Vacey in Ramsey. He left at midnight, his car conked-out short of petrol just through Lezayre, and he started to walk. Did Lee go straight home from the meeting in the school?"

"Mrs. Armistead and another woman, Mrs. Cregeen, walked with him to the cross-roads by the telephone-box. He left them there and was making for the vicarage as they went to their own houses."

"Suppose he got home about eleven-thirty. Unless he went out in the dark long afterwards, prowling the lanes, how could he have met Sir Martin? Furthermore, what was he doing with the gun? And finally, and most important, how could he possibly have got to Ramsey and run-out the petrol from Sir Martin's car? Didn't we say that it might have been a premeditated crime and that whoever committed it, might have arranged beforehand for the car to give out and thus to waylay Skollick and kill him. That would be impossible for Mr. Lee. He couldn't have got to Ramsey in time. He couldn't even have got to Lezayre by the time the car stopped. If Skollick left Ramsey at midnight, he'd be in Lezayre ten minutes later. Lee would have needed powers of precognition as well as a car to do it in time."

"So, he's not guilty after all?"

"I don't know. He's not the type, nor had he the opportunity. And yet."

The telephone interrupted them. Maggie Keggin entered and gave Knell a blistering look. She disliked the instrument as a perpetual disturber of the peace at the best of times. When Knell was around, it never ceased from ringing.

"It's for you."

Knell rose to answer it. He was soon back.

"It's Douglas. They say the Ramsey police have been on. They've been putting a sight on the Red Haggart. There's no sign there of blood or anything. But they went a bit further afield. The schoolroom's not so far away. just over the road. In the grass by the roadside just beyond the schoolroom, they found a petrol-lighter marked M.S. They enquired if it's Sir Martin's. Jinnie Kermeen, the maid, recognized it. She's been in the habit of filling it for him regular. He always carried it."

"So, it might be the Rev. Lee, after all. He might have got up in the night for some reason, perhaps wondering if he'd locked the door, gone to the school, and found Skollick on his way home. He could have gone inside, taken the gun, and shot him there."

"But what about the car, Superintendent?" Littlejohn shook his head.

"The whole thing's a complete puzzle. Why can't Lee talk? What game is he playing?"

"If he were guilty, I'm sure he'd confess. He's that sort.

He's shielding somebody. I'm convinced of it."

"Well, sir, I can't sit here trying to think out a solution.

Do you mind if I leave you for a night or two and go and stay on the spot?"

"If you think that's best, by all means go, my friend."

"Where shall I stay, parson?"

"There's an hotel at Sui by Glen station. It's quite a decent little place. They'd put you in there. Knell could ring them."

It was all arranged.

"It's two or three miles to the middle of the curraghs from there and three miles to Myrescogh and Mylecharaine."

"We could lend you a car, sir."

"No, thanks, Knell. I'll do some walking. It will do me good and I'll get down to earth with the people, too, if I'm on foot. You can drive me there, if you will."

They arrived at Sulby Bridge just in time for dinner and Knell left reluctantly. He even shook hands as though they were parting for ever.

"Don't forget, sir. If you want me at any time of the day or night, let Ramsey police know over the phone and I'll be here right away."

"I'll not forget. Good-bye, old chap."

Knell waved two or three times as he vanished in the distance. Littlejohn liked him better and better the more he knew and worked with him.

A comfortable, quiet hotel, with nobody else staying there.

It was the slack season. In summer they were full-up for months.

Littlejohn's table was set in a corner near the window.

He could, by raising the curtain, see down both directions of the main road to Ramsey from Peel and Castletown which passed the front door.

The landlady attended to him herself. She looked a bit scared. She daren't ask any questions, but she seemed as if she would have liked to. For days, there had been terrible news from the curraghs and now, here were the police from Scotland Yard.

"I hope you find the fowl to your liking, sir."

It was lovely, but she said it in a voice which implied that she feared arrest if it wasn't.

"It's beautiful. No wonder you're full every summer, with cooking like this. What do people do when they come to stay here?"

"They walk, sir, and there's good fishing in the river.

Salmon and trout. Would you like trout for breakfast?"

"I certainly would."

She went away a changed woman. She looked proud.

What queer goings-on! After years and years of peace and quiet and nothing much to relieve the monotony, suddenly drama and mystery had invaded the little place. Real murders and a London detective. Things you read about in paper-backed novels which visitors brought for rainy days and left behind. Every time she entered she smiled and cast a look of complicity across at Littlejohn.

"You'll take a liqueur with your coffee, won't you?"

A car drew up. A little fast two-seater, and a couple climbed out. Littlejohn could vaguely make out the pair of them. They were dressed in tweeds. A tall full-bodied woman and a man a few inches smaller, or that was what he looked.

The landlady was clearing away Littlejohn's dishes and serving the coffee.

The voices of the newcomers sounded in the hall, loudly calling for drinks.

"Who are those?"

"Mrs. Vacey and Mr. Kinley from Ramsey, sir."

"Don't tell them I'm here, please. Don't even mention my name."

The woman gave him a mysterious look and nodded knowingly.

"I understand. She was a big friend of Sir Martin, wasn't she?"

"So I heard. She seems to like them smaller than herself."

"Yes, come to think of it, she could give Sir Martin a couple of inches. She's a bit big for a woman, but they always look taller than men. Every inch taller than a man makes them seem three or four. Or that's how it seems to me."

"Do they often come here?"

"Now and then. When they're passing. They've probably been to some sale or other. She attends all the sales. She collects antiques."

"Just friends?"

"If you like to call them that. She's always some man or other with her. They're coming in here."

A dark-haired, good-looking woman with a lovely face, sensual lips and hard, insolent eyes. They said she was a widow of just over forty. She didn't look her age, except there were tiny lines round her eyes. She looked as though she was always wanting something she couldn't get. Sir Martin had, from all accounts, been that way, too.

"Ask about the sandwiches, Charlie. I'm starving." Charlie was a fair, mild, easy going chap with a receding chin who danced attendance on her like a dog. She treated him like one, too. In his hurry to please her, he even brought in the plate of sandwiches himself, set them before her, and then rushed off again for the drinks.

"You said whisky, darling?"

"I didn't say anything, but you know I never drink anything else."

She eyed Littlejohn over as soon as they were alone. "Good evening," he said.

"Good evening."

That was all. She took off her tweed jacket, revealing a yellow long-sleeved jumper which accentuated her breasts brazenly, like some self-advertising film-star. She examined herself in the mirror over the fireplace, titivated her face with powder, and savagely applied lipstick.

Charlie was back with the drinks and a syphon.

"Put me some soda in and give me a cigarette."

It was a wonder Charlie stood for such manners, but he was apparently delighted with them. He was revelling in the fact that, with Skollick out of the way, the field was now his own.

Littlejohn filled his pipe and started to smoke. There was an old copy of the *Times* there and he read it casually. Now and then, Mrs. Vacey looked across at him as though she ought to know him. He took no heed.

They drank whisky after whisky. After the third, Mrs. Vacey seemed to make up her mind about something and rose and crossed to Littlejohn.

"I knew I'd seen you before. You're the Superintendent from Scotland Yard, aren't you? I saw you once at the airport with the Archdeacon."

Littlejohn rose and put down his paper. Charlie stood in the background. As far as Mrs. Vacey was concerned, he might not have been there at all.

"That's right, madam. And you are?"

"My name's Vacey. Gillian Vacey. You'll have heard of me, no doubt."

"Yes. You were a friend of the late Sir Martin." She smiled a slow, sultry smile.

"That's right. But tell me this. Why have they sent for Scotland Yard when they've arrested the parson? The mad parson, we call him. The eccentric from Mylecharame."

"They've not sent for me, Mrs. Vacey. I happen to be here staying with my friend, the Archdeacon."

"Jolly old chap, the Archdeacon. Good scout. All very fond of the old boy."

Charlie thought he'd better chip-in with a message of good will. He smiled all over his face and offered to buy Littlejohn a drink.

"I'm just going out, sir. Thanks all the same."

"Don't mention. Perhaps another time. Time we went, too, Jill, isn't it?"

She might not have heard him.

"Are you staying here, Superintendent?"

"Yes, for a day or two."

"Why? There's nothing much here for a man from London, is there? Or perhaps you're a fisherman."

"No. I'm not fishing just now."

"Interested in bigger fish? Well, I've nothing to hide. As I told the police, he left me dead on twelve o'clock the night he died. That was the last I saw of him. It's put my lights out, I can tell you. He was such a decent sort. And to go and get himself killed by a wretched half-wit of a parson. It just doesn't bear thinking about."

"His car gave-out for petrol at Lezayre, I hear, and he had to walk home. Was he usually forgetful like that?"

"Not he. He was always most particular about his car. I just can't understand it at all. Think somebody syphoned it off deliberately? It was standing outside my place for a good two hours. We'd been to Peel and found it a bit boring, so I suggested we went home for a drink or two. I'm sorry I did, now. He might have changed his programme and gone straight to the manor. In which case."

She shrugged her shoulders.

"Get my coat, Charlie. It's cold, and we'd better be going."

Charlie trotted to where the coat hung over a chair, trotted back, and helped her into it, giving her shoulders a squeeze as he did so.

"Don't do that. Don't maul me."

"I was only."

"Well, don't. I'd like another drink for the road." She was all keyed-up, a bundle of nerves, and Littlejohn wondered why. Her face had grown sulky from too many drinks and she kept looking Littlejohn straight in the eyes as though somehow they shared an important secret. They were fine eyes, but she squinted slightly from a surfeit of whisky.

"Well, if I can be of any use, call to see me. In any case, you can call. My address is in the telephone book. Don't forget."

She gave him a nod and a good-night and Charlie followed her to the car. One minute, they were there; the next they had vanished with a roar.

So that was Mrs. Vacey. The last person, except the murderer, to see Skollick alive. And, judging from her treatment of Charlie, she hadn't yet found a replacement for Sir Martin and was still either grief-stricken in her own selfish way, or else badly scared. The whisky, the twitching fingers with their long, pointed reddened nails, the effort to control her nerves behind a mask of indifference and impertinence, all told the same tale.

Littlejohn left the hotel and strolled along the road, smoking his pipe. Night was falling fast and the last of daylight was shining from across the sea behind Jurby, the church of which was silhouetted against the red of the evening sky like a fortress. Everything was still and the landscape over the curraghs was set against the background of the coming night like a great etching. An odd blackbird was shouting his final challenge before going to roost.

A group of people stood gossiping in front of the village stores which had a petrol pump hanging over the front door. There was a week-night service at the Methodist church on the opposite corner, where a few cars were parked. From where Littlejohn was standing, he could hear the organ playing and voices singing.

He felt he ought to be doing something; but what, he didn't know. It had been a day of indecision, of collecting bits and pieces of information, of chasing here and there for nothing at all. Now, when perhaps he ought to go walking in the curragh and find out what it was like there after dark, somewhere near the time when the murder had been committed, he felt drowsy and lazy, anxious to idle about, to enjoy the peace of the melancholy twilight. Perhaps drink a final glass of beer with the landlord, and then go early to bed.

Across the road at the church, they were singing a hymn he knew before they broke-up. It brought back memories. He thought of himself singing it in the village choir, clad in a surplice which was too big for him, ashamed because the sleeves came over his hands and impeded him when he wanted to turn over the page.

"You the policeman from London?"

Littlejohn turned to find a large powerful man at his elbow. In the remaining light he could make out that he hadn't had a shave for several days. He was half-seas over, too. Otherwise, he probably wouldn't have had the nerve to accost Littlejohn.

Two or three men were standing at the door of the hotel watching them. It was obvious that the man at his side had been dared to speak to him.

"Yes. What can I do for you?"

"My name's Casement."

"The poacher?"

"Who's been talkin'?"

"Nobody, You're well-known, Casement. You don't make a secret of your poaching, do you?"

"No. It's a trade like any other. I could name a policeman or two who."

"What nice dogs you've got."

They *were* nice, too. A pair of sheep-dogs, long-haired collies, quite unlike the usual lurchers favoured by poachers. One was huge, the largest of his breed Littlejohn had ever seen. The other was of normal size, which made the big one seem larger than ever. They stood at Casement's heels, quiet and serene, the large one confident in his strength, the smaller with his eyes fixed adoringly on his master, hanging on his every word.

"Aye, master, they're a grand pair. You see, I earn an honest livin', as well. I'm a shepherd in Druidale. Many a prize these two have won me. The big 'un never misses a win. When he shows himself at a trial, the rest of them as owns dogs starts to groan or shed tears. They know they've not got a chance. You know any thin' about dogs, master?"

"I've one of my own. An old English bobtail."

"Have you, now? They're a grand breed, but too long in the coat for rough work, leek we have over here. I do believe they used to be good on the English short grasslands downs, don't they call 'em?"

"That's right. What are the names of these?"

"I call 'em the Moddey Mooar and the Moddey Beg. Know any Manx?"

"Only a word or two."

"Moddey Mooar means the Great Dog and Moddey Beg the Little 'un."

"It's a good way of naming them."

"I jes' came over to tell ye not to believe what you'll be hearin' about me takin' a shot at Sir Martin. I hated him, that's true.

Hounded me all about the place, he did. Had the police out on me. Me, that, till he came, had the free run of the curraghs and was the friend of everybody. What did they care for a rabbit or two, or a hare now an' then? But to hear Sir Martin, you might 'ave thought I was robbin' his hen-runs or his pig-styes every night in the week. No, I wouldn't have wasted a cartridge on him. It's with me two fists I'd have let him have it. Don't you be believin' any thin' about me firin' off two barrels of a gun at once."

"Thanks for telling me. I'll bear it in mind."

"See that ye do. And while we're together, let me say I'm glad to be meetin' ye, you're not the sort I thought you were. One of these nights I'll stan' ye a drink. I spoke to ye out of swank, because the boys there dared me to do it. Now I'm glad I spoke to ye at all, because I feel ye'll give me a fair deal and not be takin' heed of all the gossup. Good-night."

At least the man was honest! Littlejohn felt he'd helped to eliminate another possible suspect. One who'd despise himself ever after if he fired two barrels of his gun at once.

In the distance the two dogs hung on their master's heels, the shadow of Great Dog looming like that of a wolf in the sad evening light, which brought back vague remembrances and regrets for another day gone.

There was nothing more to be done. Littlejohn asked to be called at five-thirty.

"Five-thirty, sir! Will you want breakfast then?"

"No. I'm off for a walk in the curraghs before I have my trout."

"I'll put the alarm on then."

He was asleep not long after ten and the last thing he heard was a drunkard singing on his way home and a dog barking somewhere in the wilderness behind the hotel.

6
ENCOUNTER IN THE CURRAGH

"It's half-past five."

A voice Littlejohn hadn't heard before, perhaps that of a maid, awoke him from a deep, dreamless sleep. At first he didn't quite know what it was all about. Then he slowly gathered his consciousness together, became aware of the dawn, and realized it was time to get up. The mattress creaked as he sat up and gave the room a surprised look. The curtains were drawn and daylight was creeping in between them. Under the window a thrush was singing.

He walked to the door, his bare feet sinking in the carpet.

The maid had left tea and some biscuits outside for him. She had been terrified when, the night before, they'd told her there was a Scotland Yard detective staying in the house. Her education about such notables had been gained by weekly visits to the cinemas at Ramsey. They were usually handsome, overpowering men and the thought of entering the bedroom of one of them had filled her with fear.

The girl was returning from putting a match to the fire in the dining-room and was only half-dressed. A buxom wench whose white flesh seemed to be trying to pour itself from her tight underclothes. She squeaked and fled downstairs and after Littlejohn had closed his door and was drinking his tea, he heard her creep past and scutter up to her own quarters overhead.

It was cold. Cold enough for frost, although when he opened the curtains there was no sign of it. The smoke from the newly lighted fire below was drifting on the breeze, which was in the north-east. There was a ground mist rising from the curraghs behind the hotel and all the buildings visible seemed to be floating on it. The glow across everything indicated that the sun was somewhere behind the hills in the east and would soon be making an appearance.

Littlejohn washed and shaved, and then lit his pipe.

It tasted good after the strong tea. He quietly let himself out.

There was a solemn stillness over all the countryside and an odour of damp leaves and grass. The village was completely deserted and so silent that he could hear a stream rushing over stones somewhere in the near distance. He could not feel the wind now. Only the sting of cold air on his freshly shaven cheeks. He turned up the collar of his raincoat and thrust his hands deep in the pockets.

He had studied the ordnance map of these parts so closely that now he knew its main characteristics by heart. Knell had filled in a lot of other details, too, and the map in his pocket was pencil-marked to show Myrescogh Manor, Mylecharaine, and the best ways of reaching them. Littlejohn turned to the right at the door of the hotel and after ten minutes brisk walking, reached the first road into the curraghs.

To the Curraghs. It was signposted, but was obviously not a motor road for anybody with respect for tyres and springs. The surface was of loose sharp flints, most of them about the size of an egg. After the first fifty yards the track crossed the railway. The crossing-gates were open and the cottage of the man in charge of them was quiet, with the blinds drawn. At the back, the hens in a wire-netting pen were standing in a cluster watching the door and waiting to be fed. Thence, the road, disappeared into the deepness of the marshes. Littlejohn walked across the line, a narrow-gauge affair which ran straight as a die until it vanished over the horizon at both ends.

A wall of shrubs shut in the road to right and left and nothing was visible through it. A slim grass verge bordered it on each side, and there were narrow ditches which kept the surface drained. The summits of tall trees met overhead and the road unwound mysteriously onwards. Now and then a gate broke the thickets and Littlejohn could see flat fields in which sheep and cattle were feeding, with here and there a sheet of water surrounded by tall twisted trees, which hung over it menacingly.

He was well shod, but the flints hurt his feet and he could feel them through the soles of his shoes, as though he were walking barefoot. It took him almost half an hour before the track joined a properly metalled road, with the sun shining on it and a farm set back at the end of it-a "street" in the Anglo-Manx dialect. Littlejohn stopped to admire the scene, for the house was whitewashed and solid, and the rising sun was casting the shadows of the surrounding trees across the vast unbroken gable-end. Not a human soul about. Cattle in the yard, waiting for milking. An appetizing smell of stables and hay on the air. A flock of geese appeared, and the largest one, which was leading, opened its beak and hissed furiously at him.

The road began to twist through open country, and sod hedges, topped with gorse and covered in brambles on either side, still obscured the view. The mist had vanished, the trees and houses had become detached from the early morning vapour and were beginning to stand out solid and clear. Littlejohn looked over another gate. Beyond, the chain of graceful hills which form the rugged centre of the Island, purple and green with the colours of Spring. In the foreground tilled fields, pastures, a few houses dotted about, copses of bog-oak or willow, and now and then, the glaucous water of a little mere.

Littlejohn realized that he was lost. With the hills running approximately from east to west, it wasn't difficult to judge direction or distant places, but the intimate details of the curragh were now confused to him. He was just taking out his map again when he heard the sound of grinding heavy wheels and a cart appeared carrying a load of manure. A man of magnificent physique was walking beside it, with a little sheep-dog at his heels. He looked at Littlejohn with calm eyes, quite unperturbed at the sight of a stranger there so early in the day.

"Good morning. Am I right for Mylecharaine?"

"Good mornin', master."

The man stopped the horse and came over to Littlejohn.

He wore a suit of soiled blue overalls and a cloth cap. Tall, broad, fair, with a fresh complexion and blue eyes. He pointed along the road behind him.

"You go back till you come to another road which crosses this leek a T. Keep left. It'll bring you to Mylecharaine."

A slow drawling voice with a lilting brogue. The dog, his tongue hanging out and his eyes glued on his master, took in every word as though he understood what it was all about.

"You the policeman from London on the murder?"

"Yes."

"News got round, leek."

Littlejohn offered him a cigarette and they both lit-up.

The farmer made for a gate in the hedge and leaned across it. Littlejohn climbed the bars and sat on the top one. It was a relief to get his feet off the ground after the punishment of the flints on the old road. The horse drew into the hedge and started to chew the grass.

"Did you know Sir Martin?"

"Aye."

There was a look in the eyes and a tone in the single word which implied more than a casual interest in the dead man. Littlejohn waited. The farmer looked ahead of him at the distant hills, his eyes steady and a lost look in them. When he spoke, it was as if he were talking to himself.

"Funny thing, Myrescogh died somewhere near the same time as my grandfather."

He was speaking of Skollick in the old Manx fashion of giving him the name of his home.

"Old chap died just as the bell started. The one the parson from Mylecharaine rang in the dark when he was found with the corpse."

"Did your grandfather live in the curraghs?"

"At the farm there you just passed. Eighty-four, he was, and, leek as not, would have reached a hundred but for Myrescogh. That broke the old chap's heart."

"Trouble about land?"

The farmer drew hard on his cigarette and then threw the stub at his feet and ground it in the soft soil of the gateway.

"No."

Another pause. Littlejohn wondered whether or not his new friend was going to tell him the whole story. The cows were waiting for milking and it was probably time for breakfast at the farm.

"The old man was buried last week. A Methodist, he was, but grandmother lies in Mylecharaine churchyard, so he went there, too."

Traa dy Lioor. Time enough. The whole story was on the way if Littlejohn would give the man time.

"The old fellah was goin' fast, when the bell started to ring. Them'll be the bells o' heaven' he sez to my sister. He'd heard it in spite of his bein' a bit deaf. Then he went out with the tide. People in these parts always go out with the tide at the Lhen. The waters from here reach the sea through the Lhen and the Killane River. Grandad's farm is on the Lhen waters."

Cocks crowing, a lark singing in the air, and in the farm along the road a cow mooing and then a lot more echoing.

Across the fields the smoke from a cottage chimney trickling slowly over the marsh as somebody lit the fire.

"My sister had gone over to England but got back in time to see the old man before he died. It pleased him a lot. He always liked her the best. Left her half the farm along with me the other half. I'm not married and she promised him that she'd settle down here again with me. If anybody says a word about her."

He might have felt like the elder brother in the Prodigal Son, but he didn't act like him. He raised a fist as large as a ham and crashed it down on the top bar of the gate with such force that he almost dislodged Littlejohn.

"Was it Sir Martin's fault?"

The man didn't seem to hear the question, but the silence was enough.

"She was always the clever one of the family. Never took to farmin', leek, though now she'll have to settle to it. She got herself a job in Ramsey, in a lawyer's office. Myrescogh used to call and she must have caught his eye. He got to goin' there and bringin' her home in his car. I told her what I'd do to him if it didn't stop. He was up to no good. But you know what women are. What I said seemed to make her more stubborn. One day she went to Ramsey and didn't come back. She wrote from England. There was a baby on the way and she was with her aunt in Liverpool."

He paused and then turned and gave Littlejohn an angry look as though the Superintendent were somehow forcing him to speak.

"I'm tellin' ye all this so that you'll get it true and first hand. Everybody knows all about it, but they'd add to it to suit their own evil tastes if you was to ask 'em."

Littlejohn handed out more cigarettes and they lit them and puffed in silence.

"It might easy have been me as shot Myrescogh. When Ellen wrote, I took the gun and was off to the manor. I knew it was him. Grandad stopped me. Our mother and dad died years ago, and grandad brought us up. He was a powerful religious man. Preached in the Methodist churches on the Plan. A big strong fellah, he was. He said the Lord would have His vengeance, and repay. It looks as if he was right, though I didn't think so at the time. Now the child, he's only a few months old-has come over to live here as she promised grandad before he died."

"Did you never take it up with Sir Martin?"

"I never seen him since Ellen ran away. He went off the Island, too, about the same time, and didn't come back till a month or so ago. By that time, I'd cooled-off and didn't want to upset the old man, who was dyin' by then. He started to die slowly from the day he heard about Ellen. It broke him up. He was that fond of her. Leek as not, it was the rage he had inside him that burned him out, but he was never a one for revenge or spite."

"There were other girls in trouble through Skollick?"

"Not like Ellen. One in the village was seen ridin' in his car a time or two, but her dad went to the manor with his gun across his arm and sent the girl to her aunt's in Bristol. I ought to have done the same. Anyhow, it's worked out right, as the old fellah said it would, though he's not here to see it."

"You were awake at the time the big explosion was heard?"

"Yes. Me and Ellen and some cousins from Regaby was all with grandfather. We knew he'd go with the tide. The vicar said he'd last till mornin' and went home around one o'clock."

"The vicar?"

"Yes. The Reverend Lee. We sent for him at midnight. There's no Methodist parson near, but grandad was broadminded. Mr. Lee stayed over an hour."

"Did he seem upset about anything?"

"No, except the old man dyin'. He prayed a lot and tried to comfort us all with promises of where the dead went to."

"And the rest of you stayed up until he died?"

"Long after it. There were things to do, you see."

"Yes."

"It's funny that our family should be mixed-up in a murther again. Myrescogh and the vicar, this time. I said when they arrested the parson, they'd got the wrong chap. Rev. Lee wouldn't hurt a fly. You'll see. When he comes before the Deemster, he'll get off."

"You've been mixed up in murder before, you say?"

"Aye. Over three hundred years ago. Only other murther I remember ever happenin' in the curraghs. A forefather of mine. same name as me, William Fayle, was killed for the same old reason, covetousness of his land and his woman."

He smiled slyly at Littlejohn.

"And they didn't bring anybody from across to detect who did it. The parish lockman and the jury caught him. Now, with Myrescogh havin', as they say he has, had his face shot away, they won't be able to use the same way of findin' out who killed him."

Littlejohn looked hard at the man. There seemed to be a lesson in crime investigation in the offing.

"How did they find out?"

"It's well-known that if a man's murthered and the one that has done it is made to touch the corpse, the dead will bleed from the mouth and nose. That's how they knew that Gilnow Casement killed William Fayle. All the suspected were made to touch the body of the dead."

Along the road a woman was approaching and when she saw the two men she slowed down her stride. She wore a beret and raincoat and was smoking a cigarette.

"William. It's taking you a long time to carry the muck. I've had to get the cows in for milking and breakfast's ready."

She spoke well, without a trace of brogue or accent.

Evidently a well-educated girl. She looked hard at Littlejohn. Dark, with black curls escaping from under her cap, tall and strong, and obviously of farming stock, she had the prominent cheek-bones and clear dark eyes of the celtic Manx. An almost impudent retroussé nose and a determined chin. She was a beauty which, with her poise and self-confidence, would certainly have challenged Skollick's predatory tastes. Very different from her Scandinavian-looking brother with his blue eyes and almost red hair. In the partnership which was beginning, she would obviously provide the drive and adventure.

"I'd better be comin' along, then. This is the detective from London."

He didn't mention Skollick.

"So I see. I'm pleased to meet you. It was in yesterday's paper about you."

"My name's Littlejohn, Miss Fayle. Superintendent Littlejohn."

"So it said in the paper."

Her brother looked at her uneasily. Her self-possession seemed a bit like cheek in his eyes, but he was obviously proud of her.

Littlejohn climbed from the gate and began to fill his pipe.

"I'm sorry, sir, we can't ask you to breakfast. You'd have been very welcome, only, well, with grandfather just dying, everything's upset at the farm."

"I quite understand, Miss Fayle. I'm expected back at my hotel about half-past eight or nine. I must be going, too."

The farmer made a clicking noise with his tongue, whereat the horse ceased his eating and drew himself up, ready for off. The dog came to heel, too, from his foraging in the hedge-bottom.

"By the way, Mr. Fayle, did the doctor come to your grandfather on the night he died?"

"We sent for him. The old fellah took the turn about ten. We're on the telephone. So Ellen rang him up. He was out, but got here not long after the parson left."

"Before or after the explosion?"

"He'd got in just after it happened. I remember him saying he wondered if it was poachers. However, he was too busy to bother when he saw the old man. He was like the parson. Didn't believe he'd go with the tide. He left around quarter to three."

"It was Dr. Pakeman?"

"Of course."

They all said good-bye and brother and sister invited Littlejohn to call on them whenever he might be passing. He watched them disappear round the corner side-by-side. He felt he'd have liked to meet grandad before he'd died. A man who had kept vengeance and violence out of his family tragedy and had been prepared to wait. And, as he died in peace, his faith had been justified.

The way, too, William Fayle's murder had been solved three hundred or more years ago. That was a new one! Littlejohn could imagine himself trying it out on one of his cases. They'd think he'd gone completely round the bend!

He walked to the cross-roads. One of them, to the right, led to a dead-end, another farm, set among willows and twisted sycamores. He took the left fork and arrived at Mylecharaine. The village was quiet. A woman feeding poultry; some children playing about in the road, waiting for the bus to take them to school. Another woman pushing a wheelbarrow loaded, for some reason, with plants in pots. A motor-cycle went past, ridden by a rather elegant young man on his way to work.

Littlejohn lit his pipe again and looked round taking in the scene. One or two of the houses, whitewashed, single storied affairs, were reached by little bridges across a dyke. Others sprawled here and there on high land. Gardens were ablaze with wallflowers, and the flower-beds and even the wild hedge-bottoms were yellow with primroses. In the orchards which seemed to cling round the houses for protection, apple blossom was just breaking.

The church was reached by a short path closed by a large white-painted iron gate, shaded by a large cypress and a huge red fuchsia tree. Littlejohn opened it and walked to the churchyard. A small area, just suitable for the size of the community. The stones of the surrounding wall were overgrown by ivy. Gravestones old and new, with one or two elaborate headstones, and some without even a name. Just slabs of undressed granite. Two large vaults on which he read the almost indecipherable names of Mylecharaine and Myrescogh. A huge granite block beneath which, Littlejohn was later informed, reposed the bodies of five generations of Costains, who had lived at a large farm nearby. Faded wreaths and everlasting flowers under glass shades. The hum of bees on the air. The severity and melancholy of the place softened by daffodils and wallflowers in full bloom.

And then a newly filled-in grave, with withered wreaths and flowers ready to be cleared-up and wheeled to the rubbish heap. A headstone lying beside it, waiting for another name. *Here lies Mary Fayle, wife of William Fayle, of Ballagonny.* Other names, probably those of children, inscribed above the dead woman's. It now awaited, like the closing of a chapter, that of the old man, who had been content to defer vengeance, the repayment of the debt which had burned him up and killed him in the end.

The church was closed and locked. He strolled across to the vicarage, past a number of plain graves which, he was surprised to find, were those of men of the R.A.F., stationed there during the war. Some of the dead had come from as far away as Canada.

The vicarage was closed, too. A depressing place with dark windows, some of them devoid of curtains which emphasized the blackness within. It was like an empty sepulchre. A couple of water-hens swimming with their chicks on a dark pool in one corner of the garden. At the sight of Littlejohn they all vanished under the water. He peeped through one of the downstairs windows, which, had he known it, gave a view of the room in which the constable had found the Rev. Sullivan Lee on his knees just after the crime. It was shabby and gloomy. Makeshift furniture, like a job-lot from a saleroom. An old armchair, a table on which books were stacked, leaving a small corner for feeding on. The fire-grate was an old cast-iron thing in which the bars held an overflowing load of ashes dribbling out into the hearth. On the mantelpiece a photograph of a woman was just visible. She was young and dressed in an old-fashioned full-length skirt and a blouse of the type which had a collar held up by whalebone supports. One hand was placed on an open book on top of a cardboard pillar painted to look like marble. There was a small sanctuary lamp in front of it, with a half-burnt candle sticking out from the top. The room was cold and forlorn. Far less tempting than the cell now occupied by the tenant of the place.

Littlejohn turned to see a small red van appear from the tunnel of trees at the end of the hamlet. He made for it. The postman was delivering the slender mail of the community, whistling as he did so and shouting news and greetings. He saw Littlejohn and waved a hand. Littlejohn waved back.

"Going my way?"

He felt hungry and depressed and in no mood for a further lonely walk through the deserted secret roads back to civilization again.

"Sulby."

"Right, sir. Jump in."

The chatter of the postman cheered him up. He was a Ramsey man and his hobby was rifle-shooting. He had won cups and a lot of useful prizes for his skill. He showed Littlejohn a gold watch and an expensive propelling pencil.

They passed a Methodist church miles from anywhere.

It was well-kept and obviously in constant use. The postman said it was there that William Fayle attended.

"Did you ever know him? A grand old man. A great loss to the community. He often preached at that church. Well read, he was. And, would you believe it, he used to say he'd never been off the Island in his life. Not even to Liverpool. Only been three times to Douglas."

William Fayle had done all the good in his life to his own neighbours and friends.

They arrived back at the hotel just before nine. It seemed days since Littlejohn had left it in the early dawn. There was a smell of bacon and eggs on the air which made him hungry.

At the door, a man with a handcart was selling fresh fish.

A cat was standing on its hind legs mewing loudly, and he gave it a cod's head so big that the animal was bewildered and couldn't think what to do with it.

7
TWO WOMEN

It was the sight of Fayle, of Ballagonny, passing the hotel in an ancient Austin in the direction of Ramsey which made Littlejohn take the rocky road to the farm a second time. He had just finished his late breakfast and was filling his pipe, when, through the window, he spotted the farmer, obviously on his way to the mart.

The Superintendent had no wish to torture his feet in the flinty track through the curragh again, but it was obvious that the two Fayles, brother and sister, mutually restrained one another in conversation with the police. Her candour would annoy him and his caution and lack of sophistication would tire her patience.

It was even hotter following the damp way through the marshes under the morning sun. Littlejohn took off his jacket and slung it over his arm. He walked alternately on the flints of the path and the grass verges. When his shoes were soaked with the dew of the latter, he took to the former, and reversed the process when the pointed stones had punished him enough.

Ballagonny came into view, white in the sunshine at the end of the trail. The cattle had vanished from the farm-yard and instead a wiry little woman, clad in black and wearing a large apron, was occupying almost the whole of it with the job in hand. Spread all around her were the contents of a bedroom which she was turning out and cleaning. A dismantled bed with a large mattress, a chest with all the drawers out, and blankets, quilts, window curtains, a carpet and a hearthrug spread along a clothes-line and flowing in the breeze. She was beating the rug when she turned and spotted Littlejohn.

"Is Miss Fayle in?"

The woman seemed surprised and a bit put-out by this interruption of her mighty task, and merely nodded in the direction of an open door, set between two windows with small leaded lights.

"She's through there."

Ellen Fayle came to the door to see what it was all about.

"I thought you'd be back, Superintendent. Won't you come in?"

She was as self-possessed as ever and, without her beret, even better looking than when Littlejohn had first seen her along the road. She led the way indoors, through a low ceilinged, whitewashed hall.

"Won't you give me your hat? I'm sorry, but we have nothing to offer you to drink, except milk and buttermilk. Grandfather was a strict abstainer and wouldn't have alcohol in the house."

"Buttermilk will suit me splendidly."

He looked round the room during her absence. A large raftered farm kitchen with a big hearth and plenty of windows through which shafts of sunlight, penetrating through surrounding trees, made the air shimmer and sparkle. It bore signs of modernization. A new red-tiled floor with mats here and there, a great welsh dresser with blue plates on the shelves, straw seated chairs and, in the middle, a huge oak table, black with age. On one of the chairs stood a large open work-basket.

She was back and handed him his drink. It was ice-cold and refreshing after his unsteady trek through the hot curragh. He sipped it gratefully. He hadn't drunk buttermilk since he was a boy and used to go with his father to farms around his home.

"Sit down, Superintendent. How did you know William was out?"

She seemed to sense the reason for his visit, and, as he was smiling and ready to reply, she took him up with a laugh.

"I was always one for asking questions and wanting to know the reason why."

"I saw your brother pass the hotel in his car."

"He's gone to see the lawyer about grandpa's estate."

"I wondered if we could perhaps speak a little more freely in his absence. He is so protective towards you that certain questions might anger him."

"You're quite right. I'm glad you came back."

"Why?"

"Because I want you to find out who killed Sir Martin. It was a shameful business and an end he didn't deserve."

"So you don't think the Reverend Lee committed the crime?"

"Of course I don't. Do you?"

"May I ask why?"

"He wouldn't do such a thing. He's a mild man. As for using a gun. It's ridiculous."

Littlejohn drank the last of his buttermilk and lit his pipe. Ellen Fayle filled up his glass again from a jug. Upstairs, the daily help was taking back the contents of the bedroom, bumping and lumbering, and finally, a tall gangling man in overalls and a misshapen old hat, appeared from some outbuildings and began to help her carry up the furniture.

"This will be a new life for you, Miss Fayle. I mean, farming with your brother."

She nodded.

"Yes. I was brought-up here, but I never took to farming. I was always one for books and reading, and, as I told you, asking a lot of questions. My mother was English. Her father was an ex-army man who retired to Ballaugh. Father and she made a love-match of it, they say. When we were children, she persuaded him to go for a holiday on the Continent. They were drowned in a boating mishap at Aix-les-Bains."

That explained quite a lot. The girl had obviously taken after her mother in a craving for things beyond the quiet life of the Manx countryside. And her brother, William, probably like his father, had inherited a Manxman's deep love of his own land and yet, had in him some of his mother's temperament. Otherwise, he would not have talked so freely with Littlejohn earlier in the day. Manx caution had been leavened by more easy going English ways.

"You have always lived here?"

"I went to a school at Cheltenham for two years. Otherwise, I've been brought-up here. When I came back from school, grandfather said I needn't stay at home if it didn't suit me. He was always so sweet to me. And now, my brother is just the same. To hear him talk, I'm to be the lady of the house and he'll do all the work. Which is rather silly. I shall do my share here, now."

"You were in a lawyer's office?"

"Yes. If they'd allowed women at the Manx bar, I think I would have tried it. As it was, I wanted to train as a law clerk. I found it very interesting."

"And there you met Sir Martin Skollick?"

"Yes."

A pause. Upstairs, the noise continued, as though the pair renovating the bedroom, were pulling it down first.

"Were you in love with him?"

"Yes. And he loved me."

Her self-control was wonderful. No sign of tears or emotion. She kept her feelings hidden and well in hand.

"I don't know what you are thinking, Superintendent.

You've probably been told a lot of strange things about Sir Martin. Most of them are legendary."

"His fondness for women, his inability to get on with his neighbours, his love of money. Are those what you mean, Miss Fayle?"

"I don't care what reputation he had. I only remember him as I knew him. You must think me a hard woman remaining so calm in the face of recent happenings. I can only say that when he was alive, I lived through such events in imagination over and over again. He used to say he was a doomed man, and would come to a bad end. Everyone seemed against him. Well, he was right, in spite of my efforts to convince him otherwise by pretending I took it all as a joke. I seem to have wept until I've no more tears. I have the child. He's asleep upstairs. I can't realize yet what has happened. When the delayed shock breaks upon me, I suppose then."

Her face was hard and drawn as she rose and took away the jug and glass to hide her feelings. When she returned, Littlejohn saw her eyes were bright with tears. She sat down and calmly faced him.

"Were there any questions you wanted particularly to ask?"

"Did Sir Martin visit you in England after you left home?"

He asked it as kindly and objectively as he could, and she seemed to appreciate his manner.

"Yes. He made arrangements for me at a nursing-home and he visited me at my aunt's. My aunt is my mother's sister and although the news came as a great shock to her, in the circumstances she was very kind."

"Circumstances?"

"Yes. Sir Martin and I were going to be married as soon as he could get a divorce."

Littlejohn nodded. "I see."

"I hope you do, Superintendent. I hope you realize that this wasn't just another of what have been locally described as Sir Martin's wicked ways. I know he had a reputation as a philanderer, or worse. But this time, it wasn't the same. There was the child, you see."

"You mean?"

"He had no children of his own. He wanted children, but his wife, it seems, didn't. She was, in her day, a famous opera singer, a coddled artist, a woman of temperament. Sir Martin was very fond of children."

"And intended to marry you in course of time and make your son legitimate."

"That's right."

"Had he approached Lady Skollick?"

"Yes. She refused. She said it was against her principles. Besides, I believe she asked what was going to happen to her. She said she had sacrificed her career for Sir Martin."

"In such case?"

"If he could not persuade her, we were leaving the Island and going to live somewhere together, probably Italy."

"Did your family know this?"

"No. The divorce wasn't mentioned to anyone except my brother. I told Sir Martin that until the future was settled one way or another, my grandfather was not to know."

"And before anything further was arranged, Sir Martin and your grandfather were dead."

She nodded, as though not trusting herself to speak.

"Forgive the next question, but you know of the existence of Mrs. Vacey?"

"I do. It was purely a superficial love affair."

Littlejohn admired her loyalty and her way of brushing Mrs. Vacey aside, but…

"You know he was with her until midnight just before he died?"

"I know that, too. He promised to break with her. No doubt he'd been that very night about it."

"How long had he known about the child?"

"A month before he was born. I'd left for my aunt's before that. Sir Martin came over to see me. It was then I told him about the child. He said he loved me and reproached me with leaving the Island without telling him and for giving him all the trouble of finding me. Then he said he'd ask his wife for a divorce and marry me. He had been off the Island when I left and only discovered that I'd gone when he returned. He'd found out my whereabouts right away from the post office and came to me without delay."

"So, he really wouldn't have much chance of seeing and settling matters with Mrs. Vacey until very recently?"

"That's quite true."

"Do you think Sir Martin had any enemy who hated him enough to want to kill him?"

"I don't know. He had a bad financial crash in England some years ago. Several people were ruined. He had to go to prison in connection with it. I don't know how badly those who lost money would take it."

Littlejohn felt she was putting it mildly. Perhaps Skollick had softened the tale in the telling. The financial crash had been a pure swindle, and Sir Martin had been sent to prison for sheer roguery. No use, however, washing ancient dirty linen. He rose to go.

"You don't think anyone on the Island, anybody locally, would hate him enough to shoot him?"

She shook her head in a bewildered way.

"My brother might have felt that way, but, for my sake, would never have done it. I told him everything. The idea of a divorce horrified him. He said he'd never agree. But William was here, at grandfather's deathbed when Martin was killed. Quite a lot of us can testify to that. The vicar, of course, didn't approve of Martin at all."

She had a way of understating things, of playing them down, which Littlejohn observed. Even her own emotions were held in check, damped down under her quiet, calm exterior. And now, as she found it easier to confide in Littlejohn, she had turned to calling Skollick simply by his Christian name, as doubtless she'd done when he was alive.

"Who then could have been responsible?"

She paused and then in a deliberate, icy voice.

"Have you thought of Lady Skollick? How she must have hated him for the idea of divorce. A temperamental, violent woman."

"All the same, she could hardly have burgled the schoolroom and stolen the gun. In any case, how did she know of its existence?"

"Someone might have told her. One of the women there."

"It's very unlikely."

"I only thought of her because she hated him. He told me she said so when he mentioned the divorce."

"Has she any friends?"

"Very few. She thinks herself a cut above most people round here. She's connected with the church and subscribes liberally there, but she's not sociable about it. She's friendly with Dr. Pakeman. I believe she's very neurotic and sleeps badly. The doctor's frequently there. Martin told me the doctor was a great admirer of Lady Skollick during her operatic days. He's a musician and often crosses to England for concerts and opera seasons."

"Well, I must go. I'm keeping you from your work, Miss Fayle. I'm very grateful to you for being so frank and helpful. If I think of anything else, perhaps I might call again?"

"Certainly. Thank you, too, for being so kind and sympathetic. With the exception of William, not very many people approve of me just at present. I'm the kind of woman whose photograph is removed from the family album. And I think that perhaps if grandfather hadn't been so good and made his wishes understood to my brother, things here at Ballagonny might have been much more difficult."

They parted with a handshake. In the room above, the noise

suddenly ceased as the domestic helpers paused to watch Littlejohn off.

From the road beyond the farm, the chimneys of Myrescogh Manor were visible. A thread of smoke was rising from one of them and slowly mounting to the pale blue sky. Littlejohn lit his pipe and strolled in that direction. He didn't meet a soul until he reached the gates of the manor. There, a man was weeding the drive, the metallic sound of his rake and the rattle of the gravel sounding loud on the still air. He was small and almost hunchbacked from rheumatism and bending at his eternal task of tending the earth. He raised his small spiteful eyes as Littlejohn approached and presented a face like that of a ferret emerging from a burrow.

"Is Lady Skollick at home?"

"Better go to the 'ouse an' ask."

He resumed his work without another word, following Littlejohn with his eyes all the way to the front door. Jinnie answered it. She had the same frozen face as before and made it obvious that the police weren't welcome there.

"Is Lady Skollick at home?"

"Yes, but she's not well."

"Please take in my card and ask if I may have a minute or two of her time."

"Very well, but I don't think. You'd better come in."

She left him standing in the hall whilst she went upstairs.

There was an extraordinary silence in the house. A delay of a minute or two and then Jinnie was back.

"She'll see you. This way."

There was nothing much wrong with Jinnie. An honest-to-goodness countrywoman, hard-working and doing her best. She had had no training as a servant and had survived there when the rest had gone to seek work where there was more excitement. Miles from anywhere and lost in the curraghs, Myrescogh Manor was no place for anyone who wanted high-life.

They climbed the staircase, large and yawning, crossed the broad landing and Jinnie opened the door to let him pass. Littlejohn entered a huge room lit by two windows, situated over the front of the house, with an outlook across the vast sweep of the Manx hills from the coast at Ramsey to far inland. It was a mixture of a study and a boudoir. Books on shelves, a grand piano in the middle of the floor, a large, antique desk covered with papers, a huge cabinet along one wall filled with what appeared to be musical scores of all shapes and sizes. And on the walls, photographs of every phase of opera, from singers to the insides and outsides of opera houses and stage sets. The place was stuffy and two electric radiators supplied the heat. There were expensive Persian carpets on the floor and, were it only known, the furniture was the very suite used in the production of *Tosca* at Vienna in 1904. Littlejohn paused a moment to sort out the occupant from the mass of furnishings, papers, bric-à-brac, souvenirs, and photographs, including those of Chaliapin and Caruso autographed in affectionate terms. She swept to the door to meet him as though his were the next entrance and, like a villain in the best Italian tradition, were about to sing affectionately to her and then assassinate her.

"Good morning, Superintendent. It is good of you to call."

The whole place had a theatrical, unreal style. Even Lady Skollick herself looked like a younger woman made-up to take the part of an ageing marquise. She was tall, slim and melancholy. She wore an expensively tailored grey costume. Why, Littlejohn couldn't guess; she was supposed to be confined indoors and unwell. She was beautifully turned out and one almost imagined she kept a coiffeur and a beauty specialist hidden somewhere in the manor. The photographs in the room below and here, and even the picture at the horse-show taken by the newspaper, made her look younger and better preserved than she really was.

And yet, much beauty remained in her. The high cheekbones and fine arched nose were there, the well-preserved figure, the pointed chin and the fine eyes, now seeking sympathy from Littlejohn. The thin lines of middle-age showing on the skin, the dryness of the proffered hand, the sagging of the muscles of the neck had been missed by the camera.

She waved him to a chair and sat down herself.

"Help yourself to a drink, Superintendent, and I'll join you."

She waved again, this time to whisky and soda standing on a tray on her desk. Littlejohn rose and mixed two drinks.

A grey cat with golden eyes on a red cushion on one of the chairs slowly opened them, regarded Littlejohn casually, and then settled down again.

"I'm sorry I wasn't well enough to see you when last you called. I've had a lot to go through of late."

The voice was quiet, natural and relaxed. In fact, the ease of it was out of character. Littlejohn realized it was probably alcoholic.

"I'd like to offer you my deepest sympathy, Lady Skollick. I called to see if you could help us in the investigations about the death of Sir Martin. I'm not in charge of this case, but I'm a friend of the Manx police and am rendering what help I can."

"I shall be happy to answer any questions you care to ask, Mr. Littlejohn."

She took a good drink of her whisky and soda. She was used to it and relished it. She re-filled her glass.

"You'll excuse me, Superintendent. I haven't been well and a little whisky is a tonic."

"What made you and Sir Martin come to live here?"

"That's an easy question. To keep up our standard of living. My late husband lost most of his money several years ago. I had a little of my own which, on the mainland, after taxes, would have meant considerable economies. Here we managed and, besides, we were not pestered by friends and callers much. We couldn't afford the lavish entertainment we once indulged in."

So, it had been a bit of each. Reduced taxes and avoiding awkward encounters.

"I believe your husband's financial troubles in the past caused ruin to quite a lot of people. Has he ever been threatened?"

"You mean, in danger of his life? No, certainly not. People don't shoot one another these days when speculations prove unlucky."

Here was another playing down Sir Martin's financial swindles! He seemed to command the loyalty of his women, at least.

"Were you at home when Sir Martin met his death, Lady Skollick?"

"Yes. I was asleep in bed. I sleep badly. On that night I took two of Dr. Pakeman's tablets and fell off around eleven. Jinnie, the maid, will confirm that, if you wish. She was indoors all the time and attended to my needs till I fell asleep."

"Dr. Pakeman is a great friend of yours, my lady?"

"A very dear friend."

"Your husband was, of course, out all the evening?"

"Yes. He often spent the evening in Ramsey. I never waited up for him."

This was just fencing. Littlejohn would have to be blunt, and, as she was again filling-up her glass with whisky and soda, time was precious.

"Was there any talk of divorce between you, Lady Skollick?"

A pause. She remained silent and calm, and then took a slow drink.

"I'm sorry to have to put questions which might pain you, but they are very vital."

"There was no talk of divorce."

"Are you sure, Lady Skollick?"

The fine eyes opened wide and the chin lengthened. "Are you suggesting…?"

"I have been told there *was* talk of divorce."

"That may have been outside this house. Tittle-tattle among other people. Never between my husband and me."

"Again, I fear I must be frank with you. We know that Sir Martin has given you ample grounds for a divorce."

"This is pure gossip, Superintendent. I'm shocked and surprised that you give it any credence."

"You are fully aware of Sir Martin's relations with Mrs. Vacey? And of the existence of a son by another woman?"

Lady Skollick was on her feet in a fury. Her face grew mottled and her breathing laboured. She looked about to create a full-blown theatrical scene. Then she calmed down and faced Littlejohn, who was also on his feet waiting for the storm to burst.

"Whatever happened and I admit nothing, whatever happened, I would never have divorced him. He was a weak, sometimes pitiable man. He had ideas of his own about things. He was even unfaithful to me now and then. But he needed me, and he knew it. He knew I loved him, and he loved me. Without each other's support we would have been lost. We'd have died of boredom. Here, shut up, away from the old life we loved, all that remained to us was each other."

Littlejohn remembered that during Skollick's years in gaol this woman had stood by him and waited for his release. Then she'd followed him to the Isle of Man to get out of the way of accusing old friends, creditors, and taxes, and exiled herself for his sake. Now, she was watering down his conduct and the wretched way he'd treated her, dramatizing the situation, gesticulating about it, waving her arms about.

"Your late husband was making a large estate here, I believe."

"He wanted to extend the grounds and have it private and remote. He met with little success. The local landowners took it amiss, opposed him, and quarrelled fiercely with him for trying to corner land, as they called it. Much of it is wasteland, but that they would not admit."

"Were you aware, Lady Skollick, that your husband had enemies locally, men he had quarrelled with about land and other matters?"

Another glass of whisky. She brooded over her drink and almost gaily reproached him for being a slow drinker.

"Are you sure you won't fill-up your glass, Superintendent? No? Then, you'll excuse my taking another. My nerves have been thoroughly upset since my husband's death and I must confess that I find an odd glass of whisky now and then does me far better than my dear old friend's drugs. Besides, the drug habit isn't a good one to get into. A friend of mine, a Harley Street man, always said a toddy of whisky now and then. Oh, I beg pardon. You were asking?"

"Your husband's local enemies?"

"Negligible."

She dismissed them with a wave of her glass.

"None he couldn't deal with. Certainly none who would want to pull a gun on him. But I do want to emphasize, Superintendent. I do want to emphasize."

She made an energetic gesture with her free hand, and declaimed the words like a tragic actress busy with a funeral oration.

"...Emphasize that he loved me and I loved him to the end. Divorce? Never! Apart, we'd have died of boredom."

Judging from her present state, she wasn't far from right.

At this rate, with Skollick gone, she'd slowly degenerate to a sordid finish. No wonder Pakeman had hurried ahead of Littlejohn and Knell on their first visit and then said it would be as well if they didn't see her for the time being.

Jinnie came back to see him out. Lady Skollick in a dash of bravado insisted on checking in front of Littlejohn her movements on the night of her husband's murder. The maid seemed amazed at her questions.

"Of course you were in the house, *and* in bed by eleven! You know very well you were. Didn't I give you your pills and weren't you fast asleep when I came to wake you about three o'clock and tell you about Sir Martin's bein' dead? I'm surprised you need remindin'. I'll never forget it. I have nightmares about it every night."

As they made their way down the stairs together, Jinnie turned back for a moment and he could hear her speaking to her mistress.

"Are you goin' to eat up the liver I cooked yesterday for your lunch, or shall I give it to the cat?"

8

THE MAN WHO LOST HIS FAITH

It was a relief to be in the fresh air again after the sultry faded atmosphere of the manor house. Littlejohn had a feeling that had he not kept the interview well under control he and Lady Skollick might have held a sympathetic session over the whisky bottle, grown sentimental, and ended by slapping each other familiarly on the back.

He wondered what was happening in the room upstairs now that his back was turned. Was she still smiling languidly over her re-filled glass? Or, alone with Jinnie again, had her temper changed and was she raging about yesterday's relics of cold liver or the impudence of the police in asking her for an alibi?

He made his way to the main road again so deep in thought that he had passed through the curragh lands and was almost back in Sulby before he realized that he had walked so far. A small police-car was standing in front of the hotel from which Knell was emerging. The door was not visible from where Littlejohn stood and Knell appeared to walk through the wall. His face lit-up when he saw the Superintendent.

"Everything all right, sir?"

It was obvious from his expectant smile that he thought the case was in the bag!

Littlejohn was glad to see him. His early rising had made the day seem very long already and his solitary investigations had made him very much on his own. He longed for the company of the Archdeacon.

"I'll be coming back with you, Knell. I've done all I wish to do here for the time being."

"I'm very glad to hear it, sir. What about lunch?"

"We'd better stay and take it at the hotel. It's past noon and we may as well."

"There's the Venerable Archdeacon, though. I left him at Maughold, sir. He rang up this morning and seemed anxious to be putting a sight on you again. Said it was a bit lonely, like, without you. I told him about Mrs. Joughin, the woman who used to be Dr. Pakeman's servant, and how you wanted a talk with her about the doctor. The reverend said he knew her well. In fact, he married her to her now deceased husband when he was vicar of Andreas. So, I picked him up this morning and dropped him off on the way here. I hope that's all right?"

He looked desperately anxious about having done the right thing.

"Good! I want to call on the doctor again on our way and then we'll pick up Archdeacon Kinrade at Maughold and lunch in Ramsey. That do, Knell?"

It was a matter of minutes paying the bill and thanking the landlady for her hospitality. She was disappointed at the curtailing of the stay and said so. The hotel had been for a short time the metropolis of the case, the headquarters of Scotland Yard. Many callers had turned-up for lunch or for drinks on the off-chance of seeing the famous detective 'from over' and now the excitement would die away.

"I'll be back," said Littlejohn.

"See that you are, sir."

"We heard from London, sir, about Skollick and the Reverend Lee. Nothing we don't know already. Sir Martin had been share-pushing, they said, and went to gaol for selling stock in a company that didn't really exist. As for Mr. Lee, he seems to have led a perfectly normal and good life in his London parishes. An exemplary man. Lost his wife in the bombing and was sent to the Island after a breakdown. Nothing to help us there. Sir Martin, as we know, ruined quite a number of people by his frauds, mostly small investors."

"Who probably never thought of murdering him when he came out after serving his sentence."

"If they did, sir, it's taken them long enough to trace him and make up their minds to kill him. It's years since he left gaol."

They pulled-up at the door of Pakeman's house in Lezayre.

"He's in, sir, but he's in the surgery at present seeing a patient."

"We'll wait, Mrs. Vondy."

"He won't be long. I'll tell him you've called."

As she spoke, the door of the conservatory which led into the patients' department opened and a large pregnant woman like a farmer's wife emerged holding a small boy by the hand. His head was bandaged, but he was not too sick to smile and show his mother the shilling the doctor had given him for behaving himself.

The doctor appeared at the front door almost at once.

"Come in, come in. Glad to see you again. Stay to lunch with me?"

"I'm sorry, doctor, we've arranged to meet the Archdeacon and are already on our way. I just wanted to ask you another question or two."

"You'll have a drink, then."

The same room overlooking the garden and the same delicate scent of wallflowers on the air. The doctor produced whisky and glasses.

"Good health, Superintendent, and yours, too, Knell. I'm sorry you can't stay. I hear you've been at the manor."

He said it casually, as though he didn't mind one way or the other, but somehow the atmosphere seemed to grow more sombre. It may have been Littlejohn's mood, or it may have been the fact that the sun had gone in and the tall trees of the garden were adding to the gloom.

"Yes. You didn't tell me, doctor, that Lady Skollick was somewhat of an alcoholic."

Littlejohn said it blandly, without a trace of challenge, but Pakeman lowered the glass from which he was about to drink and gave him a queer look.

"Lady Skollick rang up for some more tablets when next I am near the manor. She said you'd called. She's been a bit overwrought since Skollick was murdered. It's natural, isn't it? It's made her drink rather heavily."

"She didn't drink much before?"

"Not so much as now."

"She described you as her dear old friend, doctor. Do you feel you can tell me something about her without betraying friendship or professional secrecy?"

"Try me and we'll see. Another drink."

He filled up the glasses and splashed in the soda. "Your very good health, both of you."

He sat down again and crossed his legs, looked expectantly at Littlejohn, and pulled out his pipe and began to fill it.

"Is Lady Skollick quite normal?"

"Mentally, you mean? Well, Littlejohn, you must confess that this is a bad time at which to meet her. She's been through quite a lot of late."

"So she told me, doctor, and I agree. Did she and Sir Martin get on well together?"

"I think I told you when you were last here that when he was sober, he was most kind and considerate; when he was drunk, he was somewhat of a handful."

"There was talk of a divorce, however."

The doctor sat upright and stared hard at Littlejohn. "Did she tell you that?"

"No. She denied it."

"I'm amazed that you asked her. She was devoted to him and such a thing would be quite out of the question for her."

"He wished for a divorce, however."

"I never heard of it. Who told you, if Lady Skollick didn't mention it?"

"Is Ellen Fayle a patient of yours, doctor?"

"Ah! I see."

"Let us put it briefly, doctor. Sir Martin liked and wanted children. His wife did not."

"Excuse me, could not. A major operation some years ago made it impossible and also cut short her career as a singer."

"Whatever the reason, they had no children. Then, after a lot of philandering, it seems Skollick found a girl he loved, a child was born, and he promised to obtain a divorce and marry her."

"He may have done, but as far as I am aware, whatever Skollick promised Ellen Fayle, he hadn't got round to discussing it with his wife before he died."

"So, he was a cheat to the last."

"Exactly. I know about the affairs of Ellen Fayle, although I had nothing to do with them medically. I suppose you know she went to the mainland."

"Yes. And Skollick followed her there with his promises.

He may have made them. He may even have approached his wife about a divorce. It is likely that Lady Skollick would now deny it. Neither of them may have wished to confide in you about the matter, doctor."

Pakeman winced slightly; just enough for Littlejohn to notice it.

"You have known Lady Skollick for a long time, doctor?"

"Yes. I knew her before Skollick met and married her. I have always been very keen on opera. I practised in London years ago before I came here. I heard her sing often then. A glorious voice. Jean Calloway, she was then. I met her through a mutual friend. We became friends, too."

"Had you anything to do with their coming to live on the Island, doctor?"

"She wrote to me when they were seeking a quiet place to retire to and where their money would spin out better than on the mainland."

The doctor was showing signs of irritation and Littlejohn realized that it was the presence of Knell which was preventing his talking freely.

"Would you mind, Knell, running into Ramsey and arranging a meal for us?"

"But you could dine here with me, Littlejohn."

"We have someone to meet there, so please excuse us this time, doctor. Knell, you don't mind, old man?"

And Knell suddenly twigged what it was all about, excused himself, and made off with great dignity.

"Thank you, Littlejohn. I tan speak more freely now." Littlejohn understood. They were men of the same age and who instinctively liked each other. Thrown together a lot, they could easily have become good friends.

"Could you now tell me something of the past life of the Skollicks together, doctor?"

"She loved him very deeply. Why, I don't know. He was always a rotter. When he went to gaol, it almost killed her. But she was waiting for him when he came out. He was beggared, himself, but had invested money in her name. She gave it back to him, although she would rather have divided it among his creditors. It wasn't enough to enable them to live as once they'd done. Besides, everybody cut him dead. He was a condemned swindler. She followed him into exile here."

"Her grief turned her to drink. Shall we put it that way?"

"Put it any way you damned well please. The life of a famous prima donna tends to champagne and the like. When he went to gaol, she drank more. When he returned to her, she was an alcoholic. I must say, he didn't like it, and he did his best to stop her. She tried, and when they came over here and we met again, I joined in and managed to break her of the habit. Now, all this shocking business has started her off again. I don't know where it will end now. Without Skollick, she doesn't care. In that great lonely place on her own, she'll drink herself to death."

"Unless you intervene, get her out of Myrescogh, and help her to start afresh. You were once in love with her?"

"I still am."

He said it in a voice so quiet and sincere, that he reminded Littlejohn of a young man talking of his first love.

"I'm sorry."

"For God's sake, don't apologize. In any event, what the hell has it to do with you, and why the hell am I telling you? Enough to say that I didn't murder Skollick. Although I've felt like it many a time. I could have strangled the swine. Let's change the subject. It has nothing to do with your case."

Littlejohn's glass was almost untouched, so Pakeman filled his own empty one again and drank it off hastily.

"You didn't tell me, doctor, that you were abroad in the curraghs when Sir Martin was killed."

Pakeman was himself again and looked up sharply.

"Yes, I was. I was called-out to Fayle's place. The old man was dying."

"May I show you my notes on the night's events?"

"I'll be most interested in them."

Littlejohn produced the usual plain envelope on which he made his notes and the doctor rose and looked at it over his shoulder. He even put his arm across Littlejohn's back and his hand on the other shoulder as he did so. They could have been very good friends if only.

10.0 p.m. William Fayle of Ballagonny dying. Dr. Pakeman sent for. Not at home. Message left.

11.00 School 'tay' ends. Rev. Lee locks up.

11.30 Lee at home.

12.00 Skollick leaves Mrs. Vacey. Lee goes to William Fayle's deathbed.

1.30 Lee leaves Fayles'.

2.00 Shots fired.

2.10 Dr. Jakeman arrives at Fayles'.

2.15 Church bell begins to ring.

2.45 Dr. Pakeman leaves Fayles'.

2.50 Doctor arrives at Church.

"Now, doctor. You were at the church five minutes after leaving old William Fayle's deathbed. Did you go that way home?"

"When Skollick's body was found, about 1.30, they telephoned my house from the call-box in the village. I was out, of course, but Mrs. Vondy knew where I was and rang me at Ballagonny."

"And you left right away."

"I did. I was sure the old man would rally and last until the morning. But, as they say in these parts, he went out with the tide, just after I left. A very strange business and, to me, quite inexplicable, unless you believe that superstition can kill a man. or make him live in spite of a death sentence."

"I have often come across such things. And you went right away to the church?"

"Yes. The body was there and past helping. I didn't even move it, but left it for the police surgeon who arrived soon afterwards. Sullivan Lee was half demented. We took him to the house of one of his parishioners and put him to bed. We even had to undress him. I gave him a shot in the arm and left him ready for sleep. When the Cellings, who gave him hospitality, went to see how he was next morning, the vicar had got up and gone. I believe the police arrested him trying to board the morning boat."

"May I ask about your movements on the night of the crime, doctor? You arrived at Ballagonny just after two. What were you doing, say, between ten o'clock and your arrival at the Fayles'?"

"Am I suspect, then?"

"Not at all, sir. This is just a matter of routine." Pakeman sat down again and poured himself another drink.

"Have another, Littlejohn?"

"No thanks, doctor. It's getting past lunch-time for us both. If you'll just."

"Very well. You can add this schedule to that you've already got. At ten, when the message arrived from Ballagonny, I was in Andreas. Baron, of Ballabreeve, Andreas, will confirm it. I'd called to see him about some shooting. I got back here at about a quarter to twelve; Mrs. Vondy was in bed. She had left a message about the call from Ballagonny. I must confess I was tired out. I'd been for a walk with Baron over the fields, following a busy day, and I'll be quite candid about it, I fell asleep in this chair over a glass of whisky. It was half-past one when I awoke. I went off hell-for-leather to the Fayles' place. I got there just after two."

"Thank you, doctor."

"You see, I've no alibi between leaving Baron and arriving at the Fayles'. I was at Ballagonny just after the shot was fired and just before the bell started to ring, and that gives me no alibi at the time Skollick was murdered. But who *could* give anyone an alibi at that time of night in pitch darkness?"

"I quite agree, doctor. You just happened to be abroad at the time, on your way to a case."

Knell was back, tactfully strolling in the garden, smelling the flowers and examining the fruit trees with an expert eye.

"It's time to go, doctor. We'll meet again soon, I hope, and by then, I trust all this unhappy business will be cleared up."

"So do I. You've no idea who did it?"

"None whatever."

"Not suspecting poor old Sullivan Lee, are you?"

"It's not a question of suspicion, doctor. Mr. Lee has, by his conduct in the affair, almost confessed. He's piled up circumstantial evidence against himself and won't even explain or tell us what happened on the night of the crime or how he came to be praying over the body at that unearthly hour. He's not the type, and I hope he comes to his senses before his trial."

"It's ridiculous. He wouldn't hurt a fly."

Knell decided to ring the bell and the interview ended.

"I took the hint, sir, and not only booked us a lunch in Ramsey, but went and gathered up the parson as well from Maughold."

"I'm very grateful, old chap. The doctor was a bit overwhelmed by the two of us."

"Did you get any further, sir?"

"Yes, thanks."

The parson was waiting for them in the car along the road. The very sight of him lifted the gloom from Littlejohn's mind. They were soon in Ramsey for a late meal, awaiting which Littlejohn brought the Archdeacon and Knell up-to-date with all that he'd done since last they met.

"And now it's my turn," said the Rev. Caesar Kinrade just as the meal arrived. They were dining in a tastefully converted cellar of an hotel on the promenade at Ramsey. Through the windows, which were level with the road outside, they could see the sea, with ships on the far horizon. The sun was shining again and the sky was clear blue. The meal consisted of large helpings of grilled plaice caught that morning off the sandbanks beyond the pier.

"I've had a good talk with Martha Joughin. Pakeman's a strange fellow from all accounts."

The old man looked thoughtful and there was a look of compassion on his face.

"He was trained as a medical missionary and lost his faith."

Outside, a coal boat was blowing to enter the harbour.

A procession of legs passed the windows which, on account of their height in the wall of the cellar, cut off the bodies at the thighs, revealing only the skirts and trousers of anonymous strollers whose footsteps rang on the pavement.

"I called on Mrs. Joughin, at Maughold. It was difficult getting her to talk of her former employer. She is still so overwhelmed by her large legacy that she can do nothing but eulogize her dead benefactor. In addition, she's deaf. However, eventually."

The owner of the restaurant arrived to enquire if they were enjoying the meal and had all they wanted.

"I have some fine old Cognac, gentlemen. You'll take a glass with your coffee, I hope. On the house, of course. And by the way, there's a reporter in the bar upstairs. He wants to know if you can give him anything fresh on the case."

Knell made a hasty exit and they could hear him in indignant conversation with someone unseen, who was apparently excusing himself but asking for fair play.

"Give us a break, Inspector. Give us a chance." Knell returned after telling the landlord they wished to be private, and closed the door of the room after him. He looked like a man who has done a job well and sat down and helped himself liberally to cheese.

"Mrs. Joughin was with the doctor for many years and naturally she saw a lot of him, knew his history, and also many of his secrets. These she found out for herself in ways I didn't ask her to detail. But she said that he still has a simple cross nailed to his bedroom wall. Sometimes he prays before it and at others he hurls taunts and abuse at it. He must be a very unhappy man."

"He reminds me a little of Sullivan Lee, Archdeacon."

"I was just going to say the same, Littlejohn. They seem to be a tortured pair and I've no doubt they understood one another very well. To see them face to face. However, Lee's very looks betray the turmoil of his mind, but Pakeman has his feelings very thoroughly under control. He has a sardonic humour quite alien to Lee and is a man of broader mind. I wonder what brought Pakeman to his present state of mind."

"An unhappy love affair?"

"I hadn't thought of that. I was too busy imagining the substance of his faith changing and decaying, like India rubber which, in time, rots and loses its strength and resilience."

"He fell in love with Lady Skollick in the days when she was a prima donna. She was Jean Calloway, then." The parson threw up his hands in surprise.

"Well, well. So she was Jean Calloway. She was very familiar with the Isle of Man in times past. In her heyday she crossed every summer to sing at the celebrity concerts held in Douglas. She knew the Island well. Perhaps that is why she thought of it when it came to her husband's release and the need to seek refuge in some quiet place. Pakeman was once in love with her?"

"She married Skollick instead. She apparently loved him right until his death. He seems to have made her very unhappy. She turned to drink for comfort and is now on the way to becoming a confirmed alcoholic."

"And Pakeman lost his faith through losing her, and fled to the Isle of Man. The whole affair has about it some of the ingredients of a Greek tragedy."

"But, so far, we haven't a clue as to who murdered Skollick. It might very well have been the denouement of a drama which began when Jean Calloway married Skollick instead of Pakeman. Either Lady Skollick or Pakeman might have murdered Sir Martin. But neither of them did. She was asleep in bed at the time of the crime. Her maid confirms that in the strongest of language. The doctor was hurrying to the deathbed of old William Fayle of Ballagonny and the whole of the Fayle family can testify to it."

The Archdeacon sat quietly, his chin on his breast across which also spread the white froth of his beard.

"Old William Fayle. I remember William. A fine man."

"His granddaughter is the mother of Skollick's son."

"Dear me! More and more complications."

"But not more and more suspects. They were all in at the deathbed whilst the crime was being. Wait a minute! *Was* the crime being committed at two o'clock? Were the shots heard at that time, the ones which almost blew off Sir Martin's head? The report of the autopsy said death occurred round about two o'clock in the morning."

"In other words, did the police surgeon assume that the murder took place when the shot was heard, before he examined the evidence? Did he commit the famous logical fallacy of begging the question?"

"Perhaps assisted by another doctor from whom he took over the body. Dr. Pakeman. Who performed the postmortem, Knell?"

"Dr. Rees Whatmore, sir."

"My old friend! He won't like me soon. I challenged his finding once before in a very similar case to this. One which involved a change of time and place, too. I'll ring him up. Excuse me."

There was a telephone-box at the head of the stairs and Littlejohn rang up the police surgeon. Luckily he was in.

"Dr. Whatmore? Superintendent Littlejohn. How are you, sir?"

"Very well, thanks. Hope you're the same."

His voice sounded inquisitive, as though he either expected Littlejohn was about to call him in for an ailment of his own, or else challenge some report or other in his work as police surgeon.

"I'm just helping the local police on the Skollick case. You performed the autopsy?"

"Yes. Nothing wrong about it, is there? I'll stake my reputation."

"You don't mind if I ask you a question or two, doctor? I'm not doubting your findings, but a little more detail will help us."

"Fire away."

There was relief in the voice.

"The head was so badly shot about that a proper examination of it was difficult?"

"If you'd had two shotgun cartridges fired at your head at almost point-blank range, Superintendent, there wouldn't be much of it to be examined. Death was instantaneous and from the obvious cause."

"And occurred at two o' clock?"

"Yes."

"Judged by the temperature of the body and other usual signs?"

"Yes. Look here, Littlejohn, what are you getting at?"

"Could death have occurred sometime before two?"

"I stated in my report that I inferred that death had occurred between one and two o'clock that was in keeping with the time the shot was heard, but fully confirmed by examination of the body."

"You weren't able to be more precise?"

"No, Superintendent. You see, the body had apparently been first out of doors, where the crime occurred. Then, it was carried indoors. The temperature of the interior of the church was considerably higher than that outside. In fact, almost ten degrees. I noted the thermometer by the door.

The stove had been going during the day. It is usual to light it for a day in mid-week at certain seasons in the year. The curraghs are damp, you know, and the interior decorations and fittings tend to mould if the fabric isn't kept dry. The temperature of the dead body, therefore, was quite a problem."

"Which you tackled admirably, doctor. A little before one or just after two might, therefore, be reasonable?"

"Theoretically, yes. Practically, no. The shot was fired at two and the dead body found shortly after. That seems to confirm the expert findings."

"Thank you very much, doctor."

"A pleasure, but I don't quite see what it's all about, Littlejohn."

"I'll call and explain personally very soon, sir. By the way, was there another doctor present when you arrived?"

"There were two. McWinnie, the police surgeon from Ramsey, and Pakeman of Lezayre. Strangely enough, Pakeman was passing at the time the body was found. He'd been to a case nearby."

"Did you and Dr. McWinnie perform the autopsy, sir?"

"I did it with his help. I'm the medico-legal expert for the Island and as it was murder the case was turned over to me."

"Dr. Pakeman was first on the scene, then?"

"Yes. He heard the shot at two o'clock."

"And emphasized the experience?"

"He told us the full story of the night's events, although I don't see how that affects the finding of the criminal. Is that all you wish to know?"

The Archdeacon and Knell seemed surprised at Littlejohn's long absence.

"Been having an argument, Littlejohn?"

"Not really, but death might have occurred before two in the morning."

"But that's the time the shot was fired."

"Yes, sir. And I think the time has now come for us to have another word with Mr. Sullivan Lee. Shall we call on our way back?"

"Yes. One other matter about my interview with Mrs. Joughin.

I forgot to say that she described Dr. Pakeman as morose. Did you find him so?"

"Not at all. He was full of good humour and hospitality, as Knell will agree."

Knell removed his pipe and nodded sagely. Littlejohn drank the last of his cold coffee.

"The death of Skollick made a new man of him," he said.

9
THE FOLLY OF SULLIVAN LEE

"It's a beauty. A genuine antique, but a beauty."
Littlejohn laid down the gun on the table of Knell's office and patted the stock appreciatively.

Almost a century old, it was the work of a London gunsmith whose firm was still in the trade. The barrels, worn thin by long use, were beautifully chased, the balance of the weapon was perfect, and it seemed to rise to the shoulder automatically, as though it had life in it.

"There were only Sullivan Lee's prints on it, you say.

That's a bit strange isn't it, seeing that it was handled by the women at the school?"

"I enquired about that, sir. It seems the women gave it a good polishing-up before they left it. Not that it would make it sell for more. But you know what some women are, sir. Miss Caley, who did the job, said the wood of the stock was so lovely, she couldn't help giving it a good rubbing."

"She was right, Knell. A fine piece of timber, indeed." Littlejohn drew back the hammers of the gun and opened the breach by means of the bolt which lay under the trigger guard; there was no spring action. He squinted along the insides of the barrels.

They were in the state in which the police had found them, and fouled by smoke and powder. The half-empty box of pin-fire cartridges was on the table beside the gun. Littlejohn took two of them and tried them in the breach. They slid easily in and out, the pins held in position beneath the hammers by sockets in the barrels. The gun was now at half-cock, in a safety position, for the triggers could not be pulled until the hammers were put at full-cock.

"This old-fashioned pin-fire idea is a bit complicated. I'm sure Lee didn't know how to manipulate the gun properly. It's a wonder he didn't blow himself up. Is Miss Caley on the telephone?"

They looked her up in the directory. She was there. "Superintendent Littlejohn, Miss Caley."

There was a gasp, and over the instrument Littlejohn could almost hear the palpitation of her heart, like using a stethoscope instead of a telephone. Finally, she managed to speak in a hushed voice.

"Yes. I'm so very glad to meet you. We are very grateful to you for your help. all the trouble."

"I hear you had charge of the shot-gun which was for sale at the jumble."

"Oh, dear."

She sounded to be sniffing smelling-salts.

"Oh, dear. I really didn't."

"Please don't distress yourself, Miss Caley. I simply wish to ask if you and Mr. Lee examined the gun on the night you arranged the things for the sale."

"Oh, yes. Mr. Lee did. You see, he had some doubts about whether we were justified in offering it for sale. It was so old, that he said it might be out of order. However, he opened and closed it and seemed satisfied. It took him a long time. He said he hadn't handled a gun since he was a boy, when his grandfather used to take him out shooting and he used to place his fingers over his ears and fall many paces back behind his grandparent when he thought a shot was going to be fired and..."

"He managed to open and close it all right?"

"Yes. He commented on the beauty of the workmanship, saying that our forefathers worked most lovingly on."

"Did he load it?"

"Dear me, no. But he explained, or tried to explain to me the mechanism for loading it. He spent some time on finding out how it worked. You see, he thought at first, when he tried to set it off."

"Fire it?"

"I beg your pardon."

"Sorry I interrupted. You were saying, Miss Caley?"

"When he tried to set it off, it would not function. Then he discovered how to make it do so and seemed very pleased, because had it not worked it would not have been right to sell it except as defective, he said. I'm afraid I wasn't very interested. In fact, I was terrified of the thing, but I thought that as it was in the hands of a good practical man, no ill would befall me."

"Thank you, Miss Caley. Your information is of great help."

"I'm afraid I can't see how."

"It will probably prove that Mr. Lee is innocent."

"Oh."

He bade her good-bye and left her to recover and think it out. Then, he took one of the cartridges, gingerly cut the cardboard case, and shook the contents out on a newspaper. Knell and the Archdeacon watched him inquisitively.

"Why! It's black powder. The old gunpowder they used when I was a lad, Littlejohn."

"That's right, sir. This type of gun belongs to those days. Let's ring up Dr. Rees Whatmore again, shall we?"

The doctor was still at home. Most convenient for the police; what his patients thought was another matter.

"You again, Littlejohn! What's wrong now?"

He sounded tetchy this time. He had been engaged in a long

post-mortem and was relaxing and enjoying a detective story over a late meal. It was irritating being brought back to realities.

"I just wanted a word with you about the wound in Skollick's head."

They'd shown Littlejohn the photographs of the body and they hadn't been a pretty sight!

"The wound! It was like a combination of all the wounds I've ever seen. What about it?"

"You say in your report that it was made at short range."

"Yes. Any reason for doubting it?"

"No, sir. Not at all. Was it a dirty wound?"

"What do you mean by that? A shocking one, or a filthy one? You must remember that one side of the head and the face had been shot away. Whoever did it must have let him have it good and proper."

"Was it blackened?"

"Scorched, you mean? Not much. The murderer stood too far away to do much of that."

"I'll put it plainly, doctor. Was there any trace of black powder about? The cartridges in the gun fired by Lee were loaded with old black gunpowder."

"Good God! I made no comment in my report. The gun was there with the body and Lee was there as good as saying he'd done it. The load was of 5 shots according to the figures on the cartridges and I extracted 5 shots from the head. I made no examination of the powder, but there were no black or sooty traces there."

"One wouldn't normally expect you to do so, doctor.

This has proved to be a most unusual case. Thank you for your ready help. That's all I want to know."

He turned from the telephone to the Archdeacon.

"That lets out the Reverend Sullivan Lee. Skollick wasn't killed by this gun."

"Thank God! Let's go right away and tell him so."

"I wonder if it will do him much good. We can try, however. The old-fashioned gunpowder would have left traces in the wound. Even if it was only carried on the shots and the wads. Skollick was probably killed by cartridges loaded with smokeless powder."

All was still peaceful in prison. The warder was reading his paper again, sprang to attention, and put his hat on. Littlejohn observed that murder had taken second place in the news.

CURATE, 56, ELOPES WITH CHOIR GIRL OF 17.

Police have Clue in Curragh Murder.

The Rev. Sullivan Lee was quietly reading his book on Manx Worthies, a cup of tea at his elbow, a beatific smile on his face.

"It's driven him off his chump," whispered the warder to Knell as he turned to leave them.

Lee rose to greet them.

"So good of you to call again. Please sit down." The Archdeacon went in to the attack right away.

"You've been in gaol quite long enough, Lee, and it's time you answered the questions of the police sensibly." Lee gave him a startled look, and the old stubborn, almost mulish expression drove the smile from his face.

"I have nothing to say, Archdeacon. I'm so sorry. Please don't think I don't appreciate."

Littlejohn lit his pipe, the fumes of which quickly dispelled the smells of disinfectant and peppermint which mingled in the cell. Mr. Lee was an addict to curiously strong peppermint lozenges and the warder had supplied large quantities of these as required.

"If you won't answer questions, Mr. Lee, let me tell you a story. All you need to do is listen, for the time being."

Lee looked puzzled, took out his peppermints, offered them round, drew a blank, and apologized for taking one himself. This he immediately disposed of by furiously crunching it.

"On Tuesday April 13th, you were at a social evening in the Mylecharaine schoolroom preparing for a jumble sale next day.

All was ready at eleven o'clock, and you and some of the ladies locked-up the school and you put the key in your pocket."

Lee nodded his head in agreement. He was so interested in the tale that he forgot to chew his lozenge and listened with great attention.

"At that time, old William Fayle, of Ballagonny, was dying."

"*Requiescat in pace,*" murmured Mr. Lee.

"You arrived back at the vicarage at half-past eleven. At just before midnight, you received a message asking you to go to the bedside of the dying man. You answered it at once by hurrying to Ballagonny, where you arrived at about midnight."

Mr. Lee was now looking alarmed and it was not because the truth was unfolding, but because he had been caught-up in Littlejohn's account of the fatal night and was living it again. He saw the nightmare relentlessly approaching him. He sat still and wide-eyed as the horror paralysed him.

"You stayed at Ballagonny over an hour and then, being of the opinion-which, by the way, was shared by the doctor-that the old man would last the night out, you left for home at one-thirty."

The darkness of night was gathering in the imagination of the Rev. Sullivan Lee. He could hear the wind in the trees along the roadway and, in the distance, just make out the glow of the candle in the front room of his vicarage, the candle which burned before the little shrine to his wife. He sighed deeply, a noise like a sob. He was like someone without hope, at the end of his tether.

"You occupied yourself in prayer and getting ready for bed, sir, until about a quarter to two. Then you looked out of the window across the curragh and saw a faint light near the schoolroom."

Lee's terrified jaw dropped and a bead of saliva formed and trickled over his bottom lip and down his chin.

"You went off to explore. You thought someone was trying to break in and steal some of the goods from the schoolroom."

Still the vicar of Mylecharaine did not speak. He sat like one who sees death or worse approaching in a nightmare and cannot move a muscle or cry out. He saw himself walking through the mists rising from the dark marshes and heard the dogs barking as he passed the sleeping cottages.

"You arrived at the school, but found nobody had entered. But something else scared you. It caused you to take up the gun lying there for sale, load it, and go out into the darkness. What was it, sir?"

It was plain to see that the details, step by step, of the priest's night of horror, were reducing him to the state of a man undergoing a third-degree and when Littlejohn's final question, gently asked at the end of a narrative, suddenly arrived, Sullivan Lee's answer came before he could think what he was doing.

"The dog! The dog!"

"What dog?"

"The Moddey Dhoo."

"You mean Moddey Mooar. Casement's dog. Did you see the dog?"

"It was the Moddey Dhoo." The Archdeacon intervened.

"Several places on the Island have their spectral black dog, the Moddey Dhoo, the appearance of which is said to foretell disaster. Mylecharaine is not without its hound, either. You saw a dog, Lee?"

"I have never believed the story. Such things do not happen. But there it was, outside the door, eyes ablaze, horrible."

It was the first sensible thing Lee had said for days, but he mustn't have thought so. He wrung his hands.

"I beg you to believe me."

Littlejohn turned to Knell.

"Please telephone the Ramsey police, and ask them to bring in Casement, the poacher. I think he's a shepherd in Druidale."

Knell hastened out, like someone in a trance. The story bewildered him. He wondered if Littlejohn had dreamed it all.

"You saw the dog, and were afraid, Mr. Lee. You loaded the gun."

"My faith faltered. I sought something to defend me. I sinned in turning to the weapon."

"You went out into the dark."

"The dog had gone."

"You locked up, and went, taking the gun with you in case you encountered the dog again."

No answer from Lee. He had slumped in his chair, his eyes fixed unseeing ahead of him, his mouth hanging loose and open.

"You met the dog again and shot at him."

"No, no. I saw no more of him. He had vanished. Such things cannot harm the righteous."

"But you fired the gun all the same."

"I stumbled. I staggered forward a few paces, trying to right myself. I must have had my fingers unconsciously wound round the triggers. The gun went off and cast me flat on my back."

"You picked yourself up, went ahead again and..."

"No. I have said enough. You have made me say too much already."

"You went ahead again and stumbled over the body of Sir Martin Skollick lying dead by the roadside."

Lee covered his face with his hands, but still said no more. He was in sorry shape. His colour had drained away, leaving his features pale but lined with livid veins. Littlejohn felt compassion for him but was determined to pursue the enquiry to the finish.

"You thought you had killed him."

"God forgive me! I..."

"You picked up the body, took it and the gun to the church nearby, and prayed for forgiveness. You had no need for that. Your shots were too late, even if they had hit Sir Martin. He was dead before you appeared on the scene."

Lee's hands dropped and his face suddenly grew suffused with blood. He looked ready to have a stroke. At first a ray of hope came in his eyes. Then it died out and he sagged back in his chair.

"That is quite untrue. Nobody could have done a fellow human being to death in such a manner except through an accident like mine."

Littlejohn shook his head gently at Lee. It was almost a gesture of rebuke. A man who had gone through the bombing of London and seen deliberate slaughter in such a fashion must be hard-pressed or wool-gathering to make such a statement.

"We can prove scientifically that the gun you used could not possibly have killed Skollick. And now, sir, let us be done with all this nonsense and hear a proper account of your share in the events of the early morning of April 14th."

Lee was thinking hard. The shock of Littlejohn's story had come to him like a revelation.

"But who told you all this? You could not have been present. It is, with a few minor and irrelevant corrections, a true account of all that happened. I went to the schoolroom not because I saw a light there, but because I had left my reading-glasses behind and did not discover it until I got to Ballagonny. I had a key and a torch and went to get them. I turned and saw. I saw the…"

"You saw Casement's big black dog, Lee, and let us have no more nonsense about the Moddey Dhoo. It was a living poacher's dog. Do you hear? A living dog."

The Archdeacon struck the table with his hand to emphasize his words. Knell crept in, nodded to Littlejohn to let him know matters were in hand, and sat down.

"He was standing there, his jaws open, his eyes blazing, just on the edge where the light met the dark."

"Dogs do pant and their eyes shine when they've been running, Lee. For the rest, the Superintendent's reconstruction is correct?"

"Did you meet anybody else, hear any cars about, see any lights whilst you were abroad, sir?"

"Ballagonny was lit-up, of course, and I could see the light of my home, the little lamp before the picture of my dear one."

He broke down now completely and sobbed openly, making no effort to conceal his emotion, the tears running down his cheeks, his body writhing with his grief and, perhaps his relief, too.

"We shall take steps to have you released at once, sir, after you've made a statement, but there are one or two things you must clear-up first."

Lee looked at Littlejohn through his tears. He sat limp and exhausted by his many emotions and indicated by the mere stillness of his features that he was waiting for the next blow to fall.

"Why didn't you tell all this to the police?"

"I was convinced that I had killed Skollick."

"But even then, it was by accident. Why didn't you say so and be done with it, instead of acting like a murderer and getting yourself thrown in this place?"

Lee stiffened and a stubborn look returned to his face.

"When I stumbled over the dead body of Sir Martin Skollick and turned my torch on it, my first emotion was one of relief, almost of joy. It was momentary, of course, but I was for a brief, a very brief time, glad. The appearance did not fill me with horror. I had ministered to the injured in London during the war. I do not wish to speak ill of the dead, but Skollick was a wicked man, corrupting others by his ways. When I suddenly realized that I had felt glad, I felt, too, that in spirit, I was a murderer. I had killed him accidentally, but I had, in my heart, murdered him. I took him to church for my soul's sake as well as his own."

"But why didn't you say so? Why refuse to explain it all.

Why maintain silence and why try to run away and leave the Island by the next boat?"

Lee had now a mulish, self-righteous look, as though he resented his motives being questioned. His voice recovered strength and he began to glare at Littlejohn.

"I had to think it all out. I did not care to lay bare all my thoughts, motives, sins, and feelings before the magistrates. I was not clear about it all in my mind. I preferred to defer my case until I saw plainly where my duty lay. A spell in this quiet cell was just what I needed. In fact, it was very convenient. I had decided to leave the Island, consult my confessor, and then go into a retreat until my course became clear."

The Archdeacon threw up his hands in a gesture of despair.

"Your confessor?"

"I had decided to join the Catholic Church and enter a monastery, the Abbey of Vaux-le-Vicomte. The abbot is at present in London, or rather was at the time I was prevented by the police from crossing to consult him. Now he has returned."

He said it in a tone of annoyance as though he, not the police, had been caused a lot of trouble by the whole affair.

"So, you remained silent. Meanwhile, the real murderer of Skollick is at large, and valuable days have passed, days in which perhaps the trails have gone cold."

"I'm sure I wasn't aware that I was impeding the law, Archdeacon. I thought I had killed Sir Martin. I thought the whole sorry affair revolved round me, and I had to make up my mind whether or not I was, in spirit, a murderer or not."

"The law is here to help you on such matters. I'm sure when the time comes, your confessor will tell you you have committed no sin, but have just been foolish; foolish and, I must add, a trifle ridiculous."

"I fail to see, Archdeacon, wherein the foolishness lies."

"You miss your glasses in the small hours and *must* have them. You ought to have gone to sleep, instead of needing reading glasses. Morning would have been early enough. A poacher's dog looks in at you as you are fumbling in the schoolroom. You load a gun, although I doubt if you know the right end of one. You go out into the night with it and fire both barrels at once, wake the whole neighbourhood, ring the church-bell, create emotional scenes, and then land yourself in gaol because you are more concerned with the rights and wrongs of moral doctrine than telling a sensible tale of what happened. You have failed in your public duty through a piece of wretched sophistry. I sympathize with your mental dilemma, but you surely trusted one of your fellow priests here on the Island sufficiently to ask for his help."

"I am very sorry if I have caused anyone trouble, Archdeacon. The whole business upset me very much."

"Well, sir, all that now remains is for you to make a statement to the police and then steps can be taken for your release."

"Thank you, Superintendent. And I do apologize for all the trouble I've caused, however, the matter is now cleared up, I hope to your satisfaction."

"Yes, sir. Except that we have now to find the real murderer of Sir Martin Skollick, instead of the imaginary one. You are sure you have no recollection of any incident on the night of his death which might 'help us?"

"I fear not."

"He had, of course, many enemies?"

"Yes. But none, I think, who would go as far as taking his life in cold blood. If I think of anything, Superintendent, I'll let you know."

With that, they left Lee, who forgot to thank them for their help and kindness and was eagerly awaiting the warder, for he was feeling hungry and ready for his tea.

10

THE WATCHERS AT MIDNIGHT

"I thought better of you. Bringin' me all the way to Douglas, leavin' my sheep and my dogs. The dogs'll look after them till I get back, but it had better not be for long."

Casement was indignant at being summoned to Douglas police station for questioning. He looked out of place in the town, too, dressed in his old rough tweeds and with a growth of several days' beard hiding his features. He showed no fear about the situation, however.

Littlejohn offered him a cigarette, but Casement was in no smoking mood.

"The sooner I get back to Druidale the better."

"That depends on yourself, Casement. You didn't tell me when last we were together, that you were abroad in the curraghs on the night Sir Martin was shot."

"I didn't shoot him. That's all I'm concerned about. The curraghs is free for a man to walk in at any time of the night an' day. No fault O' mine if he chose to get shot."

"If you want to get away quickly, don't let's argue, Casement. Were you or were you not in the vicinity of Mylecharaine school about two o'clock in the morning of April 14th?"

"That the night of the shootin'?"

"Yes."

"Then I was."

"Doing what?"

"Settin' snares for the rabbits before dawn."

"Your dogs were with you?"

"Never go abroad without 'em."

"Did you know Great Dog met the Reverend Sullivan Lee in the Mylecharaine schoolroom just before two that morning?"

"Aye. I see Moddey Mooar at the school and I whistled him to heel. Didn't want to get mixed-up with nobody messin' about schools at that early hour. I'd my own work to do."

"Did you come across anyone else in the curraghs between midnight and the time you called back the dog?"

"I saw noborry, but a car passed along the Mylecharaine road without lights not long before I whistled the dog. I was two fields away and didn' see it, but I heard it and saw no lights on it."

"Any idea whose it might have been?"

"I said to myself it might be Sir Martin's."

"Can you be more precise about the time?"

"Naw. I don' carry any watch. Between one an' two, and maybe a quarter hour before someborry fired both barrels of a gun off."

"How do you know it was both barrels?"

"If you've lived with guns all your life, you know the sound of 'em."

"You didn't by any chance take a pot at Sir Martin yourself? You say you think it was he who passed in his car. Weren't you sure it *was* he?"

"Now look 'ere, master. I didn' like Skollick. I told you why last time we met. But I didn' hate him enough to waste cartridges on 'im, I told you that, too. Besides, did anybody hear any other shot than the double 'un the vicar fired?"

"You're right there. Nobody did. Where were you when the vicar fired the gun?"

"On my way home to Ballaugh Glen. My night's work was done."

"Were you far from the vicar?"

"Maybe half a mile down the road."

"And you didn't turn to see what was the matter?"

"I didn' want to be mixed up with trouble with guns at that hour. Made me hurry my feet all the more to get home."

"You thought Skollick might be abroad after poachers?"

"The idea did come into my head."

"So you can't give us any help?"

"Naw. An' I hope I've not to get back to Druidale on my own two feet. Bringin' me all this way for nothin'."

"The police will take you back. First of all, cast your mind back again to the night of the murder. The car. It came from the main road?"

"Aye. That's why I thought it was Skollick's, It's on'y the home-comers into the curraghs that drive cars there at that hour. Skollick was offen abroad at one or two in the morning."

"This car without lights. Did it stop at all, or did it drive right on until you couldn't hear it anymore?"

"I got the idea that it stopped for a minute or two, then started off again. That's why I thought it was Skollick. He's got some gal along with him, I sez to myself."

Casement bared his teeth, two of which were missing in front.

"Where did it go on to?"

"I didn' follow it all the way. Maybe to the main road by Ballamooar, or to Jurby. Or perhaps to Mylecharaine. I wouldn't be knowin'."

"You were in the vicinity of Mylecharaine with your dogs and your snares for how long, Casement?"

"Maybe an hour."

"Between one and two?"

"About it. I told ye I made for home when the vicar fired the gun."

"And you saw no other car than the one without lights during all that time?"

"That's right, master."

"Sure?"

"Of course I'm sure. A car with headlights shines all over the curraghs, they're that flat. I wasn't too busy to notice."

"You don't get much sleep o' nights, Casement?"

"Enough for me. I'm usually out between midnight an' half-past two, comin' and goin', and what sleep I miss I teck in the open as I'm mindin' the sheep. The dogs work for me when I'm sleepin'."

"Well, that's all, thanks. I may want to see you again."

"You know where to find me. I'm not the one for runnin' away. Is the motor-car ready to teck me back?"

"Off you go."

Littlejohn slowly filled his pipe and thoughtfully lit it.

"Have you a list of licences issued for shot-guns, Knell?"

"Yes, sir. I'll get it."

Pakeman's name was, - of course, on the list. Littlejohn had already seen his gun. Mrs. Vacey's too. William Fayle, Armistead, Casement.

"In fact, the whole bloomin' lot," said Knell.

"I'm interested in Mrs. Vacey. I think we'd better make a call on her. It's long overdue."

Knell's face wore a look of exaggerated patience. This scuttering backwards and forwards to Ramsey was getting to be a bit of a bore. He wished Skollick had arranged to be murdered in Douglas, or even half-way between the two towns.

"Shall we go over the mountain road, sir? Mrs. Vacey lives not far from where it enters Ramsey and it'll be the shortest way."

The journey was made along the T.T. course all the way, and Knell, like a radio commentator, called out the landmarks so familiar to motor-cycle fans.

"Governor's Bridge. Hillberry. Creg-ny-Baa. Keppel Gate. Bungalow."

It was like taking a bus ride with a garrulous conductor. "Ramsey Hairpin."

The car went round the corner almost on two wheels and they pulled up at a pleasant little villa standing back in a fair-sized garden. The late Colonel Vacey had been in the Indian army and this was commemorated by a label on the garden-gate. *Kashmir.*

The view from the house was magnificent. A sweep of sea right from the Point of Ayre to Maughold Head, with Ramsey Bay a deep blue, shining between. A man in his shirtsleeves and braces was slowly and methodically mowing the front lawn.

"Is Mrs. Vacey at home?"

"Aye. She's upstairs, dressing."

He said it as though he could see through the bricks and mortar and follow his employer's every movement.

Knell rang the front door bell.

Mrs. Vacey must have seen them arriving, for she answered at once. She wore a navy-blue rough-knit jumper and slacks and was smoking a cigarette. She didn't seem very surprised to see Littlejohn and when she spotted the Archdeacon in the car where he had insisted on remaining, she went and brought him in as well.

"I'm just going to make myself some tea. You may as well all have some," she said, smiling, but only with her lips.

The hall and the lounge into which she led them were chock-a-block with relics of the late Colonel Vacey. He must have been an eager traveller in his time. Native weapons from all parts of the globe. Even a Red-Indian tomahawk. Curios, handicraft, bric-à-brac, Chinese ivories and pottery all jumbled about. During his lifetime, the Colonel had meticulously cared for them himself. Mrs. Vacey had then constantly tried to persuade him to get rid of a lot of them, to turn them into cash. Now, that she could please herself what she did with them, she wouldn't part with a single one.

In half-a-dozen places in the room the photograph of the Colonel looked down on the visitors. In groups of officers, sitting in the front-middle with his legs crossed and his moustache bristling; astride a pony dressed-up for polo; in hunting kit ready for a tiger shoot. And finally, head and shoulders, chest overflowing with medal ribbons, looking scornfully down at lesser mortals from over the fireplace, in which a few embers still glowed among the dead ashes.

It was as if his widow, a woman of easy virtue, either worshipped the one ideal, strong man in her life and wished to be constantly reminded of him, or else insisted on his ubiquitous presence to remind other admirers that whatever else she gave them, her heart had gone elsewhere long ago. Or, perhaps it was just a bad joke.

She left them to admire the confusion of collector's pieces and photographs, one of which showed Vacey with King George V, whilst she made tea and quickly returned with a tray spread with fine china and silver utensils. It was very hospitable of her, but a nuisance. It held up the conversation Littlejohn wished to have with her and made it awkward to enjoy her tea and cakes and ask pointed questions at the same time.

Littlejohn had an idea that Mrs. Vacey was playing for time. There was uneasiness in her behaviour. Her pale face was expressionless. Her eyes were tired too, and although the dark shadows, almost like mist, beneath them gave her a strange added attraction, they might have been due to the strain of sleepless nights.

"You promised to call if I could help. I take it you've some questions to ask."

Knell's mouth was full of plum-cake and he balanced a cup and saucer precariously on his knees. The Archdeacon came to his rescue by sliding to him an ebony stool inlaid with mother-of-pearl, which the Colonel had picked up in Ashanti.

"That's right, Archdeacon. I should have done that myself."

There was a pause. This fussing with food and drink was exasperating and embarrassing, but a start had to be made some time.

"You were a great friend of Sir Martin Skollick, Mrs. Vacey?"

"Yes."

She said it quietly and casually as though it were not of much significance and Littlejohn realized that something in the nature of a duel was about to begin.

"You knew him before he came to live here?"

"No. We had mutual friends and he joined our set not long after he arrived."

"His wife, too?"

"No. She wasn't interested in sport. We did a lot of riding and we even ran a dance-club and a motor rally."

It was easy to guess how this good-looking woman and Skollick had been brought together and thrown into each other's arms.

"He was a frequent visitor here?" She looked Littlejohn in the eyes.

"I think you know all about that, Superintendent."

"Yes, I do. How often did he call?"

"Perhaps twice a week. He was interested in antiques and so am I. I keep my collection in the other rooms; this one is too full already. We used to go to sales in various parts of the Island. There's some fine stuff here in places and it often comes in the market at auctions."

He gave the Archdeacon and Knell a significant look before he asked the next question.

"Could I see your collection? My wife and I are interested in such things. Particularly in ceramics."

"Of course. Come along."

She looked puzzled at first and then, when the Archdeacon and Knell excused themselves and left Littlejohn to go on the tour of inspection alone, she understood. When she and the Superintendent reached the morning-room next door she smiled.

"Very tactful of them. You're now going to ask the really searching questions, Superintendent."

"I am interested in your china, Mrs. Vacey. But I wanted to avoid any embarrassment, too. I hope you'll help me by answering what I ask."

There were three glass-fronted cabinets in the room, all of which were filled with tea-sets, plates, and a multitude of porcelain figures.

"You've a very fine collection."

"Bought at sales over here, mainly at half the price of mainland shops."

He was stooping to examine a couple of Kändler figures of the Tailor and his Wife. She opened the cabinet and gently placed one in his hands.

"Meissen."

He examined and caressed it fondly.

"Sir Martin stayed here very late at nights, didn't he?"

His eyes were still on the figure of the tailor astride a goat, his pistol and his scissors in his hands, and his smoothing-iron held by the animal between its teeth.

"Yes. He was a cultured man, a man of the world. He had travelled widely and was a connoisseur of treasures such as these."

She picked up and fingered a wine-glass with an engraved profile of the Young Pretender.

"That is the last thing he bought. It cost a pound in an auction."

The pair of them might have been doing a deal together instead of grimly fencing about Skollick's last days.

"And Lady Skollick had no interest in this direction, either?"

"No. She was concerned with her past career on the opera stage, and I believe she had a collection of souvenirs of those days. I never saw it."

"You never visited Myrescogh?"

"No."

He laid down the figure and picked up a Ralph Wood Toby-jug.

"His wife's company bored him?"

"I think so. He never spoke of her. In fact, he avoided saying anything about her."

"You were lovers?"

A pause. She seemed to be making up her mind whether to tell the truth or not.

"Yes."

She casually rubbed the glass against her jersey and put it away.

"On the night of his last visit here, did Sir Martin tell you he would not be coming again?"

Her hands were stretched to take up a little terra cotta figure of the Virgin and Child and stiffened without touching it. She turned to him, her eyes bright with rage.

"That is most unfair. Who told you that?"

"Nobody. I wondered, though. Was there not talk of a divorce?"

"He never mentioned it to me."

She took the figure from him, replaced it, and began to close the cabinet. She winced as she slowly turned the key. With a quick gesture, Littlejohn took her wrist and gently thrust back the long sleeve of her jumper. He raised his eyebrows. There were livid bruises between the wrist and the elbow. She tore her arm away and drew down the sleeve.

"How dare you!"

"How did you come by those? Is the other arm the same?"

"That is no business of yours and you seem to be in the habit of taking liberties. Those bruises were caused by a cabinet which toppled over in my bedroom. I don't see how they concern you."

"I'm sorry. Natural curiosity. I noticed that in spite of the warm weather, you have taken to wearing long sleeves, and you did wince as you closed the cabinet, you know."

"Will that be all?"

She was a self-possessed, bold woman, but she was obviously badly shaken by something and anxious to end the interview.

"Just tell me again, when did Sir Martin leave on the night of his death?"

"We're wasting time. I've already told you, midnight."

"He usually had a tank full of petrol?"

"He always filled-up at Perrick's garage whenever he needed petrol. It's on the way here."

"*When* did he fill-up, coming or going home?"

"Either. Perrick lives over the garage and Martin could ring the bell and get a fill on his way back if he'd forgotten on the way in."

"On the night he died, he arrived here with a tank almost empty. Didn't he say anything about getting petrol on his way home?"

"I don't remember it being mentioned."

"Did he seem upset at all?"

"Not to my knowledge. He was the same as usual."

"He hadn't mentioned breaking relations?"

She cut him off. She was furious and on her dignity, wanted to take a high-handed line, and yet apparently was anxious to know to the full, what was in Littlejohn's mind.

"Don't ask that question again! There was nothing of that said between us. Shall we join the others?"

She was eager to end the conversation, but had assumed a nonchalant way which might easily have covered her emotions. Littlejohn noticed the tense stretch of her long fine fingers when she was off guard.

"He didn't speak of danger from enemies?"

"He was just the same charming and undisturbed man he always was. He talked of his plans for his estate, the shooting season, a new dog he had bought."

"Very well. Thank you, Mrs. Vacey. I'm sorry if my questions have been blunt and personal. I'm anxious to settle this affair as soon as possible."

"I thought the vicar of Mylecharaine had been arrested and was awaiting trial."

"He has been released. He did not fire the gun which killed Sir Martin."

She started and turned and looked blankly through the window, frowning as if at her own thoughts, one hand shading her eyes. The view was a fine one, overlooking the rising road across the mountains to Douglas. The evening sun was setting across the west and lighting up the spreading hills which gently unrolled to the south. She did not see them. The gardener, finished for the day, tapped on the window. Mrs. Vacey almost woodenly took a note from her pocket, opened the casement, and passed it through.

"Night, Mrs. Vacey," said the man. She didn't reply, so he said it again.

"Oh, good-night, Cribbin."

She turned.

"So it's all going to begin again at the beginning. You don't know who killed Martin."

"No. Have *you* any idea?"

Her eyes opened wide.

"I? Do you think I wouldn't be the first to tell you if I had any suspicion at all? He was my dearest friend. I'm more anxious than anyone else to see the guilty party hanged."

"You live alone?"

He asked it as they were strolling back to join the others.

"Yes. I have a day-maid. The gardener, Cribbin, acts as house-boy, too. Why? Is that relevant in the case?"

"No."

The parson was explaining some legend or other connected with an ivory figure he held in his hand. Knell looked puzzled about it, but was listening politely.

"Thank you so much for the cup of tea, Mrs. Vacey."

"You must think me very rude leaving you as I did, Archdeacon. The Superintendent is quite an expert."

She said it sharply and then smiled with her lips again, baring her teeth in a feline grin.

"An expert on china, I mean."

There was an atmosphere of constraint as they left *Kashmir*. Mrs. Vacey had grown moody and sulky and wished to be rid of them. She shook hands at the door and held Littlejohn's hand in her own longer than the rest, as her eyes looked full into his in question or defiance. He paused.

"Do you own a gun, Mrs. Vacey?"

The other two were at the gate waiting for him.

"I did once. It was my husband's. He had several. Does that satisfy you?"

"I know you take out a licence. You still shoot?"

"No. I did it because I owned the gun. I sold it some time ago."

"To whom?"

"It went to a gunsmith on the mainland along with several others early this year. I had no more use for my husband's guns. I got rid of them. I hope that is enough. I've to go out to-night and I'm late as it is. Good-bye."

She turned and slammed the door in his face.

"Let's call at Perrick's garage, Knell. Know where it is?"

"Yes, sir."

The pumps were still open and in charge of a lad in greasy overalls.

"Is Mr. Perrick in?"

"He's havin' his tea."

"Ask him to spare me a minute. Superintendent Littlejohn."

The boy gaped and for a minute his legs refused to move.

Then he was off two at a time up the stairs to the flat above the garage.

Perrick appeared quickly, still chewing his tea.

"I just wanted to ask you a question or two about your late customer, Sir Martin Skollick."

"Nice fellah, Sir Martin. Died owin' me a bill for nearly fifty pounds for one thing or another, but I don't hold it against him. What can I do for you?"

"You live over the garage, Mr. Perrick, and after closing will come down and serve anybody who needs petrol?"

Perrick blinked his myopic eyes behind powerful spectacles and passed his hand across his moustache. He was a little slow-spoken fellow who gave careful thought to all he said.

"Not *anybody*. Friends, that's all. They know that two longs and a short on the bell will bring me down: That's the signal, if you get what I mean. Anybody else rings, the missus answers it because people have the 'abit of wantin' things after hours and... Well, a man's got to 'ave his leisure. You agree, don't you, sir?"

He blinked at Littlejohn.

"Of course. Sir Martin was one of the favoured. At what time did he used to take advantage of your good nature?"

"We usually go to bed about midnight. He knew it. The lights are out in our house after that. He'd never think of ringin' if we were in bed."

"He didn't call for petrol on the night he died?"

"No, sir. I wondered why he didn't. I hear he ran out of juice at Lezayre and they found his car there."

"That's so, Mr. Perrick. Was he a careful man in that respect? I mean, he wouldn't be likely to forget to have his tank filled-up any time?"

Mr. Perrick was most emphatic. He slapped a pump so hard in his enthusiasm that he jumped and wrung his fingers with pain after it.

"Never. Never. He was a first-class motorist, fond of his car, careful about oil and petrol and such like. He'd never do a thing like that if he was in his right mind."

"If he'd found out after midnight that he'd not enough petrol to get him home, would he have knocked you up?"

"He wouldn't have forgot it till such a late hour. I've known him come down from, well, ahem, from a friend of his who lives not far from 'ere, fill-up, and go back there. He knew we went to bed about twelve and he came in time."

"So, on the night he met his death, you think if he'd known he was short of petrol, he'd have called for a fill-up before you retired and then gone back to his friends?"

"I'm sure of it. He's done it before."

"Thank you very much, Mr. Perrick. Sorry to disturb you."

"Don't mention it. Only 'ope I've been of help. There goes Mrs. Vacey."

A little fast car shot past them without any sign that the owner recognized them.

The town had grown quiet and a melancholy stillness had settled over everything. The small square was utterly deserted. At the station, which was just visible, a train like a little mechanical toy spluttered to the platform and a few passengers alighted. The engine was disconnected, puffed with a carefree air to a shed, and then calm descended again.

"One last call, Knell. There's a grocer's shop almost opposite Mrs. Vacey's. Let's see if they remember anything on the night of the crime."

The place was a conglomeration of sweets, tobacco, fruit, ice-cream and groceries, as though the owner's boundless ambition to stock everything saleable had finally got on top of him. He emerged from behind a large case crammed with chocolates, boiled sweets and ice-lollies, He was obviously expecting a mighty invasion of holidaymakers any minute. He raised his eyebrows expectantly. John William Entwhistle, according to the name over the door.

"We're from the police, sir, investigating the recent death of Sir Martin Skollick."

"Ah! I thought you might be in the neighbourhood."

A man with a grubby bilious face, shabby spectacles, and a peering look. He removed his glasses and polished them, the better to deal with Littlejohn. Without them, he looked changed, disguised, for, unmagnified, his eyes were like little dark beads far in his head.

"You remember the night Sir Martin was killed?"

"I recollect the date. A proper stir and turmoil it created in Ramsey. Not that I have much to do with him *or* his fancy woman. She's not a customer here. In fact, she's one of those that resents me existin' at all. Thinks there shouldn't be any shops in this neighbourhood. Wants to keep it select. Well."

He was a little man who gesticulated a lot and thought he knew everything. Knell glared at him and looked ready to intervene and slap him down.

"Sir Martin left *Kashmir,* Mrs. Vacey's house."

"Oh, I know the name of the house."

"At midnight. Did anyone hear him leave? Were you up at that hour?"

"Of course I wasn't. Nor was the missus, early to bed an' early to rise is my motto, though it's never made me 'ealthy, wealthy, nor wise, that I can see. Just 'abit. But our Ethel was up. She's courting with a young chap from Bride and such is love's young dream that he can't tear himself away from 'er. Here till after midnight and then 'ome on a motor-bike that rouses the whole town."

"They were up at midnight that night?"

"Yes. As it 'appens, they were. I stopped 'im comin' every night. Once mid-week, Saturday, and Sunday's all that I stand for. It's not decent sittin' in the dark every night.

And, I told 'im, he's a good lad and he'll make a good husband given time I told 'im midnight's the deadline and no later. I'd better get our Ethel and see what she has to say. She's told it all to us before, twenty times, I should think. but she can tell it again now."

Mr. Entwhistle raised his mouth like a hen drinking.

"Ethel!"

"Coming, dad," from upstairs and light feet rapidly descended. A smiling, pretty girl, with a fresh complexion and light brown hair gathered in a pony-tail at the back.

"Tell these gentlemen what happened on the night of the murder, Ethel."

She took it all quite calmly. Her thoughts probably turned to canoodling in the dark in the back room rather than other people's troubles.

"Sid and I, Sid's my boy-friend, were saying good-night at the door."

"At midnight, Ethel?"

"Just after, dad. A car came from the direction of the town, somebody got out, went in Mrs. Vacey's house, and closed the door."

A pause. Dad waited, holding his breath until he couldn't hold it any longer. "Well. Go on!"

"That was all."

"Who was it got out, Miss Entwhistle?"

"Miss Grey. Dad's my stepfather. I don't know, sir."

There was another car there with its parking-light on. It's often there."

"You might as well tell 'em whose it was, Ethel. All the town knows."

"It was Sir Martin Skollick's."

"And that was all?"

"We talked for a while and then we went back in the shop for a minute. When we got to the door again, both cars had gone."

Mr. Entwhistle intervened tartly.

"I suppose Sid was gettin' himself a packet of fags again. We've kept Sid in fags since he took-up with our Ethel."

"He always offers to pay."

"What time would that be, Miss Grey?"

"When we came out of the shop the second time?"

"Yes."

She hesitated and gave dad a sidelong glance. "Just after half-past twelve."

Mr. Entwhistle turned upon her a scorching look. His regulations had been flouted and he'd obviously been kept in the dark about it in the previous reports. Someone was going to have to account for what went on in the dark among the silent lollipops and cigarettes during that illicit halfhour. Ethel gave him a Mona Lisa smile.

People on their way to the cinema were calling in the shop for sweets and chocolates and Mr. Entwhistle was beginning to show signs of uneasiness. In any case, there was nothing more to ask him or Ethel, so Littlejohn thanked them both and the little party returned to the police car.

"We'll call it a day," said Littlejohn.

It had been quite a day. A long tiring one, and it seemed incredibly far from the time he'd risen in the dawn and lost himself in the curraghs.

His head relaxed on the comfortable upholstery of the car, the Superintendent surrendered himself to the rhythm of the moving vehicle. The Archdeacon rescued his cold pipe as it fell from his lips. He was asleep as they passed the curraghs again and awoke to find the parson gently shaking him at the gates of Grenaby vicarage. Dear Grenaby, he thought. as the peace of the place entered his spirit again.

11

REPEAT PERFORMANCE

At one o'clock in the morning the same thing happened again. Someone fired another shot which roused the whole neighbourhood of Mylecharaine.

Mr. Lemuel Armistead sat up in his great bed, switched on the light, and angrily addressed his wife.

"I'm gettin' sick of this. If there's much more of it, we're goin' back to Oldham. This place isn't civilized."

He crossed the oilcloth and looked out of the bedroom window. Judging from the lights in upper rooms dotted here and there, others were doing the same.

It was just such another night as the one on which Sir Martin Skollick had met his fatal charge of shots. No moon, plenty of stars, a faint breeze smelling of marsh and country mists, the whisper of leaves, the beam of the lighthouse at the Point of Ayre punctuating the darkness regularly, and those of the Mull of Galloway across the water twinkling in reply.

There were no lights shining, this time, from the church, a solid mass just visible riding out of the mist. Armistead's eyes grew accustomed to the darkness. The cottages and farms of the neighbourhood were like crouching animals asleep. A dog barked and another answered in the distance. A figure emerged from the shadows, a silhouette wearing a cloth cap and overcoat.

"Did ye hear that gun again, Lem?" said the shadow, looking up at Armistead.

"Yes. I'm not comin' out. I'm fed up with it all. I wonder who it is, this time. Vicar's in prison, so 'e can't be mixed-up in it. Ah'm gettin' back to bed. Not that I'se get to sleep again, but."

He didn't finish the sentence, for from the heart of the curragh rose a tragic, heartbroken wail like the cry of a lost soul.

It was answered by a similar sound from under the bedclothes where Mrs. Armistead, head immersed in the sheets, was taking refuge.

The distant cry was repeated and then for the rest of the night there was silence.

Another wraith passed through the village, entered the telephone-box, and was illuminated, revealing a scared little man in a billycock, whose fingers trembled so much that he could hardly dial the number of Ramsey police station. Half an hour later, the lights of police cars and P.C. Killip's motor-bike twinkled across the curraghs, searching the roads, hedge bottoms, copses and fields. The more adventurous of the neighbourhood dressed and joined them and they hunted until the cocks began to crow and daylight slowly crept across the thin fog which swept over the marshes like steam.

It was then that the wild sad cry sounded for the third time and P.C. Killip, his back hair standing upright, opened a gate and entered a field in the heart of the curragh to find what it was all about. Striding through the mist, he almost fell over Casement's Little Dog. He was standing by the body of his master, who was stretched face downwards in the grass. As Killip approached, he bared his teeth and snarled and the bobby knew he had better go no farther. He tried coaxing.

"Come now, lad. Come, Moddey Beg."

The dog stood his ground and it was a good thing that Killip took the precaution of removing his cape and holding it protectively before he blew his whistle. At the first blast, the dog launched himself at him, teeth bared, jaws foaming.

Killip was a patient countryman with no ill-temper at all and calmly and methodically met the attack. Man and dog struggled briefly, blood spurted from the policeman's hand as the flashing teeth met it, and then the cape fell over the dog's head. There was a stifled yell and Killip held the dog firmly by the collar, his grip tightening until the animal was almost throttled. Then he slipped his handcuffs through his collar and clipped them round the wire of a fence. The dog, anchored there, continued to struggle and then, exhausted, sank on his haunches and emitted again the tragic howl. When the bobby touched the dead body of Casement, he began his tantrums all over again.

Forms appeared through the mist and soon a little party of police and villagers approached the corpse.

"That'll be all for now," said the sergeant in charge, halting them before they reached the body. "Thank you all for your help, but you'd better go home. There's nothing more you can do. On the way back, one of you might 'phone Ramsey and tell them we've found out what it was all about. Casement's had an accident. He's dead."

At first it looked like an accident. Casement had fallen on his gun and shot himself through the chest. The reason for the fall was obvious, too. He had put his foot in a wire snare, probably one of his own planting, and measured his length. It looked as simple as that. No nasty wound, no lamenting clergyman, no tolling bells. Just a mishap to a poacher in the darkness. Those were the first impressions of the police and the experts who were soon on the spot. The ground there was hard and showed no signs of footprints. This time, the experts took particular interest in the powder and shot of the cartridges which tallied with the fatal wound. The position of the wound, too, was in keeping with the way in which Casement had fallen on his gun. Apparently carried loosely in his hand, swinging by his side, it had gone off when he stumbled.

The only queer thing was the gun itself. In the words of P.C. Moore, himself a crack-shot, it was "a smasher". It caused a lot of discussion among the policemen, most of whom were marksmen.

"I've never seen the likes of it before," added Moore. The weapon was an up-to-date hammerless ejector, by Daintree and Hotcher, whose guns cost a fortune. It made the men's mouths water to think of using it. "The sort of gun you can't miss with."

Knell told Littlejohn all about it when he rang him up at the vicarage at five o'clock on a Saturday morning.

"Thank you, Knell. You might please call for us in an hour's time. And ask the northern police *not* to make public any details of the accident. Nothing about how it occurred, or about the gun or the snare."

The Superintendent and the Archdeacon had sat up late before the fire on the night before. Littlejohn seemed hardly to have settled in his feather-bed before he was out again. As he spoke to Knell, the Rev. Caesar Kinrade appeared at the head of the stairs in his nightshirt. Maggie Keggin, a dressing-gown over her nightdress, passed him with a sigh and glared at the telephone as she made her way to the kitchen to put on the coffee.

"More poor sermons to-morrow," she said as she ground at the coffee-mill.

"He won't be able to concentrate on what he's tellin' us. Whatever that Knell says, they're not leavin' this house without a proper breakfast."

She served them with Manx ham and eggs half an hour later and when Knell drew up at the door in a police car, she gave him the same without a cheerful word.

"Ye'll be the death of Master Kinrade before you've done," she told Knell as she saw them to the door.

"Then perhaps ye'll be satisfied."

She wound a muffler round the neck of the Venerable Archdeacon.

"Do ye want to die of the cold?"

The sun was clearing the mists from Barrule as they sped across Foxdale. The village was just awake and the smoke of cottage fires rose straight into the air and vanished in the blue. Now and then workmen passed on cycles and motorbikes. Littlejohn closed his eyes and breathed deeply the perfume of the wet leaves and grass and the faint sweetness of flowers he couldn't identify. Too nice a morning for another crime!

Casement had met his death from an expensive gun, the kind a poacher never handles in a lifetime. If the affair was a faked accident, someone had slipped up badly. And yet, the rest of the trick, the snare in which the foot had been entangled, the position of the body, the whole set-up had been carefully thought out. Why substitute a gun quite out of character for the likely cheap one a rough-and-tumble fellow like Casement would use?

Then a thought struck him.

"Call at Myrescogh Manor before we go to the scene of the accident, Knell."

"Very good, sir."

It sounded queer, but Knell was used to Littlejohn's hunches. He saw an arrest in the offing.

"Wuthering Heights," said Littlejohn to himself, as they turned in at the manor gates.

"I was thinking the same myself," said the Archdeacon, who had been quietly pondering over the case. As a scholar who had been first in his year in Logic and Method at Oxford years ago, he felt humbled to think that all his youthful days of training counted for nothing in a case like this. It concerned people, strange people, and, as his old nurse had often said seventy years ago, 'there's nowt queerer than folk.'

The drive to the manor was deserted. The trees met overhead and it was like travelling through a tunnel, with the blue sky showing here and there between the interlacing twigs above them. All around, the flat country was still and solemn, the sun shone on the hills, and, somewhere in the distance, a boy was whistling Knell's obsessive air, *Don't Knock the Rock.* The house looked deserted and dead. A thin trail of smoke arose from one chimney in the kitchen quarters.

Jinnie appeared at the door in answer to their knock.

She made a gesture of disgust until she saw the Archdeacon and then she gave him a look of apologetic reproach.

"It's no use ye comin' at this hour. She's asleep. Took her tablets last night and it won't be right to wake her yet. Come again, if ye must, about eleven."

"You can help us, Jinnie," said the parson.

"The Superintendent has a question to ask you."

"It wouldn't be right for me to talk without Lady Skollick knowing you were here."

"This is quite a minor matter, Jinnie," said Littlejohn.

"Do you have a gun-room in the house?"

"No, we don't, an' the less said about guns, the better for us all."

"Where did Sir Martin keep his gun?"

"He had six. He kept 'em up in his own room, which hasn't been turned out on her ladyship's orders and which I can't show you without she says so."

"Are they in cases?"

"You mean leather ones for carryin'? Two are. The rest are just standin' in the corner."

"May we see them please. This is important and concerns the matter of Sir Martin's death."

She folded her hands across her thin bosom and her lips grew tight.

"Not without Lady Skollick."

This looked like going on for hours. The Archdeacon intervened again.

"Take me up to the room then, Jinnie. I promise I'll stand by you if Lady Skollick objects."

"Very well, then. I don't mind you, Archdeacon, but I'll have no policemen in the private rooms without her permission. Come along and step quiet. She's asleep."

The pair of them vanished indoors, leaving Littlejohn and Knell to cool their heels. The parson was soon back carrying a gun-case.

"This, I think, will be the one you want."

An elegant leather affair containing one of a pair of splendid weapons. A label inside the lid. *Daintree and Hotcher, London, W.I.*

Littlejohn took out the gun and assembled it. He balanced it in his hand and raised it to his shoulder with admiration.

"I'll bet this pair cost Skollick a pretty penny." Jinnie, standing disapproving on the threshold, almost snarled.

"Pity he hadn't somethin' better to spend his money on."

"Where's the other gun, Jinnie? Is it in the corner?"

"It is not. Sir Martin always carried it about with him in the car. In case he saw any thin' about, he used to say. I have heard her ladyship grumblin' at him about it. A gun worth three hundred pounds. God save us! Left lyin' in a car for anybody to carry off."

Littlejohn replaced the gun and closed the case."

"Thank you, Jinnie. You've been a great help."

"I can't see that. Flatterin', that's what ye are."

She refused to let the Archdeacon take the case upstairs again.

"My bones is younger than yours, reverend."

Then, to the scene of the accident. There was nothing left to see. The body was in the morgue, the gun with the police, Moddey Beg, the little dog, cooling-off and refusing food and friendship in an outhouse at Killip's home.

"Where's the Great Dog?" everybody was asking. Since the death of Casement, Moddey Mooar hadn't been seen.

At the police-station in Ramsey Littlejohn inspected the Daintree and Hotcher gun. It was the twin of the one he had handled at

Myrescogh. It was plentifully sprinkled with the large fingerprints of Casement, and nobody else.

When Littlejohn made it known that Sir Martin had been in the habit of carrying the gun around with him in his car, the affair began to take reasonable shape. Casement might have stolen the gun from the unlocked car at some time or other. A vagabond with a grudge, who hated Sir Martin, he would easily think he was doing himself some good and obtaining an easy revenge on Skollick by filching his gun.

It all sounded so easy. Littlejohn, however, had formed a reasonable view of Casement from an impartial encounter. He might have revelled in poaching rabbits and game, but he had his own type of integrity and forthrightness. Not only would he have scruples about blatant robbery, but he had never struck Littlejohn as being a fool, and nobody but a fool would have thought of stealing a gun which could be identified among a thousand, one which would make its owner move heaven and earth to recover it, and could not be used or sold without arousing intense suspicion. Besides, Casement would be well aware that in the event of its disappearance, he would be thought of as a likely thief, along with the rest of the rascals of the neighbourhood.

They visited Casement's home in Ballaugh Glen. It stood almost at the end of the road, an old thatched cottage, which, when they entered, struck them as more like a factory for curing rabbit-skins than a dwelling-place. Skins everywhere, hanging from the bare beams, on nails driven in the walls, across the rooms on pieces of string. True, the man was out most of the day on the hills with his sheep and most of the night snaring and shooting on the mountains by torchlight. There was a squalid bed, a wash-place of sorts, primitive shaving table and a change of clothing. No signs of Casement's ability to read or write. Not a letter, not a bill. There was a Bible in Manx, an old herbal, a copy of *Pilgrim's Progress;* all of them seemed to have been inherited from Casement's family. *Pilgrim's Progress* was apparently the poacher's simple hiding-place. Among the leaves were sprinkled a number of pound notes, totalling about £25. It seemed to be all the wealth he possessed.

In one corner of the living-room stood an old hammer gun. It had lately been used and laid aside without cleaning. Littlejohn opened the breach and sniffed the barrels.

"This is the gun he used regularly."

It was in keeping with Casement and his poverty-stricken existence. An old Belgian model, cheap even when new. There were cartridges in a box on the mantelpiece over the wide old-fashioned fireplace. The same make as those found in the gun beside the body.

"There's nothing here to help us at all."

The Inspector from Ramsey who had accompanied them agreed.

"We turned the place upside down, but everything seems straight and above board. As though when he left, he intended to come back."

An interruption. A powerful-looking man in a tweed cap and countryman's go-to-town clothes put his head in at the door. A smiling, shy, pleasant sort of chap, with a ruddy clean face, and an air of well-being.

"Morning, Mr. Kneale."

The Inspector greeted him with respect, for Mr. Kneale was a J.P., and a local man of substance. Introductions all round.

"I saw you were here as I was passing on my way to Ramsey. Casement was shepherd for me. I'm sorry to lose him. A good man with the sheep. Honest enough, too, except for a bit of poaching-and shooting with lights on the hills.

Dependable, however, and honest in his way. Drank too much; otherwise, he should have had a nice bit put away."

Mr. Kneale seemed to think he had to speak well of the dead, give him a send-off from life with a good testimonial. "Was he at all strange in his behaviour of late, sir?"

"In what way, Superintendent?"

"Did he seem afraid, overjoyed, expectant? In other words, different from usual?"

"No. But then, he was a dour phlegmatic sort. The only queer thing lately was his asking me for a piece of paper, two envelopes, and a pencil. And why *two* envelopes? Perhaps in case he spoiled one. He was a rum fellow with some queer notions."

"When was that?"

"Friday, this week. I never knew he could write. He always came round to the farm and asked one of my boys to do any writing or figuring he had to do. This time, he seemed to want to do it himself. He'd never think of buying notepaper if he could cadge any. It was his way of looking at life, poaching and cadging."

"But not thieving?"

"Never. I always found him honest to the last penny."

"About the notepaper. Had he any relatives he might wish to write to? Any bills he'd have to render?"

"As far as I know, he'd one brother who died in the war. That was the last of his family. As for accounts to render, my boys used to make out the little bills he sent for his rabbit-skins if he'd more than he could deal with by mental arithmetic."

"You think he wanted to write someone a letter?"

"What-else could it be? Though what it was all about, I'm damned if I can even guess."

He drove away in his car assuring them of any help he could give and they locked the place and went away.

"Any sign of the Great Dog?" people asked along the way down Ballaugh Glen. But nobody had seen or heard of him since Casement's death.

"What's happened to Sullivan Lee?" asked Littlejohn as they drew into the village of Ballaugh.

"He's back at the vicarage, packing-up, sir. As soon as the police will allow him, he's leaving the Island and going to join the abbey he mentioned. He's going to become a monk."

"Let's make a brief call on him, then. There's some information he can give which may be useful."

It was like gleaning after harvest. A bit here, a bit there. Knell wondered where it was all leading, but was confident that it would all add up to a spectacular finish. He turned again into the curraghs.

Smoke was rising from the main chimney of Mylecharaine vicarage and inside they found the Rev. Sullivan Lee, as black as a chimney-sweep, burning papers in front of the grate. He seemed quite unperturbed about his appearance.

"I'm burning rubbish, Archdeacon, and as soon as I applied a light to the pile of papers in the grate, there was an appalling fall of soot. I haven't used the grate since I came here. Oil stove."

He pointed to an ancient, corroded tin affair which made them marvel that he hadn't blown himself out of the place with its assistance long ago. There was a mound of soot on the hearth. The cobwebs of the room were festooned with it and it lay thick on the furniture.

Mr. Lee had only been there since the evening before, but in his fervour to get away to his monastery, he'd already packed-up. The furniture was stacked awaiting the carrier's cart to the auction-rooms. An old tin trunk, a rush basket affair, a packing-case, and an oval tin hat-box were already waiting in the shabby hall, among a lot of books standing in piles.

"I thought those would do for the next jumble-sale," explained Mr. Lee, a propos of nothing at all. The Archdeacon, who stooped to read the titles, grunted. They were the sermons of ancient divines and about thirty volumes of treatises on faith, hope, charity, the Holy Land, and the communion of saints.

Only the little shrine to Mr. Lee's wife remained undisturbed and the light was burning in the small sanctuary lamp in front of it.

Littlejohn almost laughed as he addressed the vicar, for he looked to have just made himself up for a minstrel show. "I want to ask you to cast your mind back, sir, to the time when you stumbled across the dead body of Sir Martin Skollick."

Mr. Lee recoiled a pace and rolled his eyes.

"Please don't bring all the horror back, I beg you. I am trying to forget it, as well as my own foolish behaviour."

"But this is important, even vital, sir. I must ask you to pull yourself together and try."

Sullivan Lee braced himself and nodded.

"I admit I owe you a duty. Pray ask what you wish."

"Can you tell me how you found Skollick lying when you came upon his body?"

"Just face downward on the grass."

"Grass? He wasn't actually on the road?"

"No. On the grass verge. As I close my eyes, I can see the whole ghastly picture. He was at right-angles to the road."

Mr. Lee closed his eyes. His eyelids were white. "Where were his feet? On the grass verge or in the ditch?"

"No. Strangely enough, as I bring the scene before me, I recollect his strange position. There was a hedge, one of the familiar Manx hedges made of sods. He seemed to have been emerging from the top of the hedge, as though he had climbed over it and was just descending to the road. His body was sloping. I mean, his feet were higher than his head."

"In other words, if he'd been carrying a gun."

"But he wasn't."

"I know. But if he had been, it would have appeared that in climbing over the hedge, he'd tripped, fallen down, head first, and the gun had exploded in his face as he fell?"

Mr. Lee paused and rolled his eyes again.

"Exactly. You put it so plainly that you might be describing precisely what I see in my mind's-eye. You know, Superintendent, you have a great talent for description. The other day, during our conversation, you so vividly depicted what happened on the tragic night of Sir Martin's death, that I was completely carried away."

That was all. It remained to say good-bye to Mr. Lee and to wish him well. He had caused the police a lot of trouble, but at least he'd been responsible for bringing Littlejohn back to the Isle of Man. He got a good mark for that.

IT WAS good to be back at Grenaby. After the lush, damp flatness of the curraghs, the hidden village, with its tall trees, its circle of hills and its rattling little river, was a relief indeed.

Knell left them. He'd promised to take his wife to the pictures to see a crime film. It would be a bit of a rest and a change, he said. Littlejohn and the Archdeacon had the late afternoon and evening all to themselves. The parson assured the Superintendent that his sermons would be all right on the morrow. If, after sixty years in the church, he couldn't preach two sermons which would make a detective ask for more, he thought it was time to retire.

It gave Littlejohn time to breathe and think. Hitherto, he'd been rushing here and there gathering information, impressions, background. Now they must be put into shape and into proper perspective. On this operation, the Rev. Caesar Kinrade could hardly wait to make a start.

"Let's take a stroll up the hill to Ronague," he said, "and you can enlighten me about the state of affairs and we'll digest our late meal at the same time."

Nothing better.

They lit their pipes and climbed the old road which led into the deserted wilderness between Ronague and the Round Table. The setting sun cast long shafts of light across the moorland. The crests of the hills were massive and golden and the valleys lay in misty shadow. In the melancholy evening light, the deserted cottages, the *tholtans* of crofters who had tired of struggling to wring a poor living from arid soil and fishing, looked sad and forlorn. Nobody cared to remove the stones which might harbour the spirits of their departed or some hearth-fairy who refused to vacate. Some of the houses had stood the ravages of time well and were sturdily erect, roofless, their gardens wild and still blooming in memory of those who were gone. All that remained of others was a ground-plan of stones and rubble.

The Archdeacon and the Superintendent leaned over an old gate leading to a deserted croft and smoked in silence. It was as though neither wished to destroy the peace of the dying day by talking about murder.

"Funny thing, that as soon as Sullivan Lee is released and in circulation again, a second crime, similar to the first in many ways, is committed."

"I think it's purely fortuitous, parson. Both crimes were carefully planned by the look of things. Take the first, for example."

"Sir Martin."

"Yes. It seems likely he was murdered elsewhere and the body brought to the curragh. Although shooting after dark is illegal, it's a common practice in the hills, isn't it? The sportsman, if such he may be called, uses a powerful light from a torch to paralyse and pin-down the fascinated rabbits whilst he shoots them. This goes on in remote places all over the Island. A shot in the dead of night in those parts is a commonplace. A score of shots wouldn't waken anyone. But in the curraghs, it's too near habitation. The police could be there in a matter of minutes. A shot there at such an hour causes a commotion. In fact, the exact number of shots would be counted."

"Yes. There was one report on the night Skollick died.

That came from Lee's gun. But Lee's gun didn't kill Skollick, who died from a cartridge of smokeless powder. Therefore, Skollick was killed in some place where shooting after dark is a common event."

"We'll make a detective of you yet, sir."

"Judging from your questions to Lee and his replies, it would appear that the body of Skollick was brought to the curraghs and placed in a position where it would look as though he'd died from an accident, after he had climbed a bank with his gun."

"He might easily have been walking home after his car dried-up, and have taken his gun with him for safety. It was valuable and a means of defence in the dark. He was known to carry it in his car. It was therefore reasonable for him to have it with him. He was known to be 'out' for Casement, who was abroad in the curraghs at such unearthly hours."

"Climbed the hedge to investigate some sound or sight, fell down, and was killed by the accidental discharge of his own gun."

"Exactly, Archdeacon. The body was placed to substantiate such a theory."

"But the gun wasn't there when the body was found by Lee. In other words, someone passed by even at that hour in such a lonely place, took the gun, and callously ignored the dead body. Casement?"

"Yes. He was around, heard a car, which he said was without lights, held his peace until the coast was clear, went to investigate, and found the body and the gun. Or perhaps Lee in his confusion and terror overlooked the gun and left it behind when he carried away the body. Casement couldn't resist the gun. We know he was nearby, because Lee saw the dog. Probably Casement's queer conscience was clear about taking the gun. The owner was dead and he hated him. By removing it, he threw someone's cunning plan awry. And Lee almost put it to rights again by his tomfoolery. Had the gun from the jumble-sale been more modern and fired smokeless cartridges, he might have been in a tight spot."

They were now slowly climbing the old forsaken road to the Round Table, where the wheel-tracks of carts of crofters and fishermen, gone generations ago, were still visible among a knee-deep riot of bramble, bilberry and heather. A spectator from the heights they were approaching, might have mistaken them for father and son, engaged in argument, for the arm of the old man was linked with that of the massive younger one beside him, and they halted now and then to make a point, gesticulating or lighting a pipe forgotten in the discussion.

"Casement might have seen who brought the body to the curragh, then?"

"That is very likely. When first Casement and I met at Sulby he'd something on his mind. He was at pains to convince me, that whatever I heard about him and his hatred for Skollick, he himself hadn't killed Sir Martin. I can't bring myself to think of his blackmailing whoever he saw with the dead body that night. I quite took a fancy to Casement. He had a kind of fierce code of his own. I'd rather think that when we had him at Douglas police station and questioned him, the full significance of Lee's position struck him. The Reverend Sullivan Lee was perhaps going to be found guilty of a crime Casement knew he didn't commit. He decided he'd better talk over the matter with whoever he'd seen dump the body in the curragh. It was in keeping with his autocratic, independent ways. Instead of telling the police, he wrote a letter, arranging a rendezvous. He signed his own death-warrant when he wrote that letter, sir. And had it not been committed in the atmosphere of the first crime and tallied in many ways with it, Casement's death might easily have been put down to accident."

They turned round and retraced their steps towards Grenaby again. Night fell very gently. The last cries of roosting blackbirds ceased. The familiar noises of the day died away.

"Who committed these cunning crimes, Littlejohn? Have you any ideas?"

"No, sir. There's a handful of suspects, but nothing pointing particularly to anyone of them."

"All of them hating Skollick?"

"All with motives. Lady Skollick, who loved him and from whom it's said he wished to obtain a divorce. Dr. Pakeman, who loved Lady Skollick and hated Sir Martin for his cruelty and for taking her from him in the past. William Fayle, whose sister Skollick seduced. And Ellen herself, who told me Skollick had promised her marriage when he'd obtained a divorce, and yet, he didn't seem to have taken or intended to take steps to fulfil his promise. Mrs. Vacey, with whom Sir Martin had promised to break, according to Ellen, but who herself says Skollick never mentioned or intended such a thing."

"Some will have alibis."

"Most of them have. The Fayles were at their grandfather's deathbed that night. But deathbeds are emotional and stunning disasters and the comings and goings of an odd person are not always noticed. Ballagonny is only ten minutes from where Sir Martin was found. Pakeman was hurrying to the deathbed when the shots were heard, but at the actual time of the crime might have been anywhere. Lady Skollick says she was asleep in bed. Mrs. Vacey was at home."

"And Sullivan Lee was abroad in the night and has behaved like a madman ever since."

"Yes. That's the lot, so far. The investigation is only just starting, but on routine lines now."

"You'll be working tomorrow, too. Sunday?"

"Yes, parson. A policeman's job is usually for seven days a week. Crime takes no rest. I promise to hear you preach, however, at evensong."

They played chess all night until bedtime and the curraghs and their mysteries were forgotten until the morrow.

12
NINETY YEARS OLD

Littlejohn was wakened by the bell for early communion and lay for a minute or two, half asleep. Everything was still, and in the distance he could hear the bells of Malewand Arbory answering that of Grenaby like echoes. He felt ashamed to think that the Archdeacon must already be up and officiating in the church. He hurriedly got out of bed, bathed, and shaved, and was waiting for the vicar when he returned.

The Rev. Caesar Kinrade was excited. His blue eyes glistened and he gave Littlejohn a look and a greeting which had mystery in them.

"A letter, Littlejohn. The postman has just given it to me. I thought we'd open it together."

And he went on, as he slit the flap of the soiled envelope with his penknife, to explain that although there was no official postal delivery on Sundays, the Grenaby postman, who lived on the outskirts of the village and usually came to early service, would often bring with him letters which had arrived for the parson after the single delivery on Saturday and normally wouldn't arrive at the vicarage until Monday morning.

The envelope in the Archdeacon's hand was simply addressed in illiterate writing.

Rev. Kinred, Archdecn oj Mann Isle ot Mann.

It contained another envelope, sealed, and inscribed.

In case of mi deth, only to be oppened by Rev. Kinred, Archdecn, (sined) Finlo Casement.

The Archdeacon raised his eyebrows.
"The two envelopes of Mr. Kneale? Is it a confession, do you think?"

The second envelope held a single sheet of grubby paper, obviously mauled in Casement's efforts to write and make himself understood. A few lines of writing which must have taken much of Casement's time and cost him a lot of tiresome effort.

There was no date or address. The letter had been posted in Ballaugh, probably on the Friday night, for it bore Saturday's postmark.

Master Kinred.

Yew are the ony man I can trust proper. I have bisness to sea to. I mai not cum back. It not. there is' twenty five punds in Pilgrim Progress. Same to be used to by a stoan tor mi mother's grave in old Ballaugh, were I want to rest to.

Trusting yew and thanking yew tore favor.

Finlo Casement. (Sined)

Pleese look ajtur dogs. It not wanted by ennybody to be shot and bury with me.

The two men stood side by side reading the letter and when they had finished, they remained silent, deeply moved by the sad and kindly last wishes of the dead man.

"In spite of the illiterate writing and spelling, Littlejohn, it is a beautiful document. Not the kind written by a man off on the business of blackmail." said the Archdeacon at length. He must have posted it on his way to his death, and, instead of having the business, as he calls it, foremost in his mind, and telling us what it is, he thinks of his mother and his dogs. There was something very fine about Finlo Casement."

They were quiet over breakfast, as though they'd received bad news or were mourning a friend. Littlejohn was grim and anxious to be off on the case, Sunday or not. Skollick and his amours and the ghastly death they had brought him, were in a different class from Casement's. Sir Martin had courted misfortune for years. He was, as he had told Ellen Fayle, doomed. But Finlo Casement had been a harmless man who'd stumbled across some scene, some information in the dead of night, which had cost him his life.

"I'd better be off to the curragh again, parson. I'll be back for your evening sermon."

"Never mind the sermon; find who shot poor Casement in cold blood."

Knell was due there at ten with the car. It seemed hours before he arrived. He had to read the letter through twice, slowly, before the full implication dawned on him. His customary smile vanished.

"He wasn't going blackmailing, if this is the letter he wrote before he was murdered. I could kill whoever did it with my bare hands."

Littlejohn pocketed Casement's simple will, which the Archdeacon handed to him.

"Please, both of you, not a word to anyone about this letter, for the time being."

The early sun had been too bright and it began to drizzle as

Knell and Littlejohn reached the main road which runs from Castletown across Foxdale to Ramsey and the curraghs. The hillsides were misty and rain dripped from the overhanging trees.

"Where are we going, sir?"

The pair of them had merely hurried to the trail of murder without thinking much of anything except being on the spot which harboured the criminal.

"Pakeman's, Knell. And let's hope he isn't at home. I want a word with Mrs. Vondy alone, if possible."

The weather cleared at Kirk Michael, but low clouds still hung about the hills behind. Farther north, over the curraghs and the flat lands of the Ayre and Andreas, the sky was blue again and looked freshly shampooed. The rain of early morning had drenched the garden of Tantaloo and the scent of the wallflowers met them from the road. Pakeman was not at home.

"He's been away an hour, sir," Mrs. Vondy told them.

"He's gone with the gun and if it's urgent you'll get him at Mr. Baron's, Ballabreeve, Andreas."

"Might we come in and have a word with you, Mrs. Vondy?"

"If you don't mind the untidy house. I'm just giving it a clean-up while the doctor's out of the place. Come in. Maybe we'd better go in the study."

The same room again, fireless this time, and chilly. The dampness seemed to be ever about, ready to take possession as soon as the fire went out.

Mrs. Vondy entered behind them and stood for a moment wondering what they wanted.

"Sit down a minute."

The three of them sat down. Mrs. Vondy indicated by a shuffling gesture like that of a hen settling on a lot of eggs, and by a look of exaggerated repose, that she was ready to hear what Littlejohn had to say.

"We're enquiring from as many people as possible what

happened in this neighbourhood at the time of Sir Martin Skollick's death."

Mrs. Vondy's face assumed a stubborn expression.

"But I had nothin' whatever to do with it, sir. I was fast asleep in my bed when it was done."

"It's just a formality, Mrs. Vondy, and sometimes, some little thing remembered by people not connected with a case at all, may be of great use to us."

"You can ask your questions if you like, sir, although what use I'll be to you I can't think."

Littlejohn took out his envelope on which was scribbled the schedule of events on the fatal night.

"Early on the evening of Sir Martin's death, Dr. Pakeman tells me, he himself had gone to Ballabreeve, Andreas, to see the owner about some shooting."

"That's right, sir. Immediately after tea, he went."

"You were in all the evening, Mrs. Vondy?"

"Yes. My sister from Ramsey came and kept me company till nearly ten."

"At ten there was a telephone message?"

"Yes. From Ballagonny. Old Mr. William Fayle was bad again and they wanted the doctor. I took a message for when he got back."

"You write them on a pad near the telephone, I take it?"

"Yes."

"Is it there now?"

"No, sir. It's torn off every day and thrown away. Like as not, it's been burned. used to light the fire along with the other paper."

"Never mind, Mrs. Vondy."

She seemed bewildered and a bit afraid. She couldn't understand what it was all about. She was flushed with confusion.

"What time did you go to bed?"

"I didn't look at the clock, but I remember as soon as I'd wrote down the message from Ballagonny, I started to make my supper and get the doctor's tray ready with his meal, too. Then I went straight up to bed."

"Did you hear the doctor come in?"

"Yes. I'd been asleep, but I never settle proper till he's home. It half woke me."

"Any idea of the time, Mrs. Vondy?"

"Nearly midnight. I put the little lamp on I have at the side of my bed and looked at my mother's watch which I always keep there on the little table."

"And then you went to sleep again?"

"That's right."

"And slept till morning?"

"I heard the doctor go out to Ballagonny and turned over and fell asleep again."

"You heard him go out to Ballagonny! What time would that be?"

"Midnight, or just after."

"He'd come in, stayed about ten minutes."

"Just time to eat the supper I'd left him. He never took a hot drink with it. He mixed himself a glass of whisky. Then he was off out again."

"Did you hear the doctor return?"

"No. He always comes in quiet, leek, when he's been out late. So's he won't wake me. Very kind and considerate, always."

"Were there any other messages for him when he returned that night, Mrs. Vondy?"

"No, sir."

"Where's the telephone?"

"On the hall-stand, with an extension to the doctor's room."

"And there were no more calls that night?"

"No. I think the doctor rang-up Ballagonny just after he got in to let them know he was comin', and be like to ask how the poor old man was."

"You heard him speaking, then?"

"No. My room's too far from the telephone for that. I can just hear the bell when it rings."

"And you heard it that night just after the doctor got home."

"Yes. Or at least, I think I did."

"And why did you come to the conclusion it was an outgoing call and not one to the house?"

"It sounded too short for one comin' in. It sounded like, like the little tinkle you get when you put back the telephone on the stand. You know what I mean."

"Yes, I know what you mean, Mrs. Vondy. Or perhaps the doctor was near the telephone when it began to ring and snatched it so it wouldn't waken you. You say he's very considerate."

"It might have been that. Easily, it might. I must say, I'd never thought of it that way, though."

The sky had grown overcast again and through each successive breach in the clouds, the sun cast shafts of intermittent beams, like the limelight of a stage, which travelled swiftly across the landscape and vanished. Rain fell angrily against the windows and then ceased before the sun again. Melancholy daylight entered the room and the damp smell of the earth and trees mingled with that of the weather beaten flowers in the garden.

There was little more to ask. Mrs. Vondy still waited, her hands patiently laid in her lap, and in her nervousness, she had clasped the fingers together and was slowly rotating her thumbs one round the other.

"I think that will be all, thank you, Mrs. Vondy. I'm most grateful for your help."

"What is it all about, sir? How does whether I slept or not through the murder of Sir Martin matter?"

"It's just a formality. We're asking everybody questions, you see. Thank you again."

They left her still wondering, and quite sure to mention it to the doctor when he returned.

As they entered the car again, a large blue motor-coach which was travelling in the opposite direction, suddenly began to pull-up and the driver indicated by waving from his cab that he had something to say to the police. Littlejohn and Knell strolled in his direction.

The coach was half-full and Littlejohn was astonished by its contents. It reminded him of a tour on the Continent organized by a group of Americans. A dozen or fourteen souls all told, most of them wearing the modern hygienic looking bifocals of the U.S.A., clad in light suits and costumes, and many of the men carrying expensive-looking cameras.

The driver leaned from his cab. "The old man wants a word with you."

Littlejohn gently shrugged his shoulders. Another mystery. "You know who it is? It's old Juan Kilbeg. He's ninety years old to-day, and he's insisted on a run round the Island to celebrate. He's not really fit to travel, but we've had to humour him."

Littlejohn and Knell climbed aboard, helped by half a dozen welcoming American hands. The newcomers were passed along the bus to the front where sat Old Juan himself.

"I saw you. I saw you," said the ancient of days in a quavering brogue. "I knew this chap as soon as I put a sight on him."

Knell shook the frail hand, almost like a claw, lined with purple veins and withered and brown. He'd known Juan Kilbeg ever since he was a boy. He wished him many happy returns of his birthday and Old Juan replied he didn't want too many.

"And this is the other fellah. I seen his picture in the paper. Not so much about the police as I don't know."

He shook Littlejohn's hand, too, with a remarkably strong grip, and Littlejohn congratulated him, as well.

"They didn't want me to take me farewell trip rouri' the Islan'. But I won. Said I was too feeble. Except for me legs, I'm as good as a fellah of sixty. Now I've said good-bye to my lovely li'l Mannin-veen and I'm content."

He then insisted that his wife, who sat beside him, should introduce Littlejohn and Knell all round.

"My grandchildren from Americky. Here to wish me many happy returns. Come over with the homecomers."

A cascade of handshakes. Wash. or Washington, Stan. or Standish, and their wives. Then Wesley, Wilbur and Elmer, the last two twins and as alike as a pair of book-ends. Juan Hoover Kilbeg and his missus, and Brigham Young Kilbeg from Salt Lake City and descended from the Kilbeg who'd become a Mormon. A real decent lot and as proud as Punch of their aged ancestor.

Then Old Juan wanted another word with Littlejohn. His eyes sparkled. Littlejohn looked at the hollow of the thin mouth, the toothless jaws, and sharp nose almost like a billhook. The old man's vitality was amazing. He wished he knew more about this ancient who had led an adventurous life, no doubt, locked away in an obscure island village.

Hitherto, all that had been visible of Juan Kilbeg was his thin withered neck and his sharp, shrewd old face, with a head almost bald, covered in very thin down. The rest was swathed in rugs.

"Take these things off!"

On this day of days, Old Juan's word was law and his wife, a red-cheeked, smiling woman in her sixties and devoted to her husband, loosened the wrappings from his shoulders. Littlejohn received another shock.

The old man was wearing a policeman's tunic! It was made of better stuff than nowadays and of the cutaway variety of very long ago. The silver buttons were bright and bore the Three Legs of Man on each.

"I said I'd wear it again on me ninetieth birthday. Been in mothballs many a year. It's me warmest jacket, too. Used to be in the police-force, Superintendent. P.C. Juan Kilbeg of the Isle O' Man police, sir. Stationed in Ballaugh, an' there I stayed till I retired on me pension in nineteentwenty-eight."

He sat down and they tucked him in again.

"That's why we stopped. To ask the both of ye to my party to-night. I'd like a policeman or two about, specially the ones who's goin' to find out who killed Finlo Casement. My friend Finlo. Many's the rabbuts he's brought for me. I'm partial to rabbuts. Poor Finlo."

He wasn't sad for long. The old sly, shy smile returned as he rested from his talk and excitement.

"Don't get excited, dad," said his wife. "Who's gettin' excited? Not me."

He tugged Littlejohn's coat.

"Come to-night, won't you, the both of you? And bring the Venerable Archdeacon along to speak with me in the Manx."

Littlejohn was feeling a bit anxious. The old man was certainly excited, not only about his birthday, but about his new friends from the police. They could do no other than humour him.

"Very well, sir. We'll come. But I've a lot to do still, and to call and pick-up Mr. Kinrade. You'll excuse us, then, and we'll see you later in Ballaugh."

The old man's wife told them the day's programme.

"It's as well it's a Sunday. If it hadn't been, I don't know what he'd have had going-on. I can't control him. We've all to go to church this afternoon. There's to be a sermon in Manx."

Littlejohn smiled. None of the Americans presumably knew the language. He could imagine Old Kilbeg lapping it up and the rest sitting there like a lot of teetotallers escorting a wine taster.

"There's a tay at eight after church. It's in the schoolroom at The Cronk, so you'll find your way there."

Old Juan tugged at Littlejohn's coat again.

"You'll come along now, just for a minute, just to drink me health on me birthday. It's not far."

"We'll be very glad to, sir. We'll follow your coach in our car, but it'll have to be a very short drink. We've things to see to before coming to your party."

"A quiet party, it'll be. No dancin'. Glad of that. Used to do a bit of dancin' myself in my young days. When I see these moderns dancin'. 'Tain't dancin', but they call it that. When I see 'em, I thank the Lord I shan't be long before I die. Men aren't men any more. Dancin' was dancin' in my days."

Littlejohn and Knell left the rest to quieten Old Juan down and followed the party in the police-car. At his cottage outside the village of Ballaugh, his relatives hoisted him from the coach and carried him indoors, for he could not walk. There Littlejohn and Knell drank the old man's health among his many relatives. There were so many there that several of them overflowed into the road.

Old Juan was tired after his morning's efforts and was soon to go to bed to rest himself ready for his party. He sat in his chair by the fire and beckoned Littlejohn over. His voice had grown feeble.

"Sit by me a minute, leek." Littlejohn drew up a stool.

"Spoiled me birthday, it has, Finlo dyin' leek that. I've not told the rest. They been so kind to me an' comin' all that way over to wish an old useless bag of bones like me a happy ninetieth birthday. I didn't tell 'em, but it spoiled my fun. Finlo called to see me on his way to gettin' himself killed. He made me laugh tellin' me how he'd been telephonin' someborry from the call-box in the village. He didn' say who, but he imitated it. Very good at imitatin' was Finlo. He wasn' used to telephonin' and got himself in a bit of a mess to start with. 'Soon be your birthday, you ole rascal,' he sez to me and he gives me a fine rabbut. 'Blest if I ever reach that age,' he sez. 'In fac', I dunno I'll be around much longer,' an' he told me he'd just posted off his will to the Reverend Archdeacon. I been upset about it all the day."

"Have you told anyone that, sir?"

"No. Not a one. As I said, I can't bear to spoil it all for 'em."

"Please don't, then. But do you feel strong enough and able to assist the police, sir? I don't want to trouble you on your day o' days, but perhaps you could help without any effort.

"I'm still a policeman. As you know yourself, Superintendent, once a policeman, always a policeman. It 'ud do me good, be somethin' to remember in the few days I got left leek."

"Then, sir, I suppose quite a lot of people will be calling to congratulate you?"

"Oh, yes. The Governor himself, this afternoon. Chairman of the Ramsey Commissioners, Captains O' the Parishes of Ballaugh and Kirk Michael. A whole lot. Jest to wish me well. Very kind of 'em all."

"The doctor?"

"Aye. Dr. Pakeman, too. And Lady Skollick. Never 'ad much time for Sir Martin. But she's a lady. Comin' to see me in spite of her sorrow."

"The Fayles of Ballagonny?"

"Them above all. William Fayle, Ballagonny, was my oldest friend. Used to say to him, leek, which of us'll last longest. All my old friends have gone, now. William last month, and now Finlo."

"Could I ask you to tell the Fayles, the doctor, and Lady Skollick, when you see them, that Finlo Casement posted a letter late on Friday to the Archdeacon? Don't say it was his will. Just a letter. And before you tell them that, will you say that Finlo knew who killed Sir Martin Skollick and has written to the Archdeacon. Say Casement told you that, and that the letter should be at Grenaby vicarage first delivery on Monday morning."

The old man passed his thin hand across his sunken eyes.

"Am I asking you too much, sir? I'm sorry. I shouldn't have dared bother you, to-day of all days."

Juan Kilbeg made an irritable gesture.

"It's not that. I'm jest puttin' it carefully in my memory what you said. The doctor, Lady Skollick, the two Fayles. Did Finlo know who shot Skollick?"

"Yes, sir."

"Then why didn't he tell me, or the police?"

"He hated Skollick and didn't much care, until he got involved in our enquiry himself. After he found that the Reverend Lee didn't do it, he remembered somebody else he'd seen around that night. He had to think it over and make sure. He arranged to meet that somebody. It was his way of doing things. He lost his life through it."

The quavering lips met in a thin line.

"I got it. I'll tell 'em. But surely those four, those four wouldn't be killin' Finlo. They're nice people."

"Perhaps not, sir. But if you tell them about the letter, they may tell someone else and it might be like putting a ferret down a rabbit hole. It might make someone bolt into the daylight and help us catch them."

"I see what you mean. A ferret in a hole. I'll do it."

Mrs. Kilbeg interfered to tell them it was time for rest and the old man was taken to his adjoining bedroom.

"See you at my party. Ain't forgot what you said. Thank you for comin', Superintendent." He said as he left.

The many offspring of Juan Kilbeg piled in their motor coach and, after more handshakes and promises to meet Littlejohn and Knell again that evening, were taken off to their hotel in Douglas. All was quiet again, and the old gentleman slept.

"One more trip, Knell. To the manor again. Lady Skollick, if she's been to church, should be home by now."

He wondered if it would be yesterday's liver for lunch. The curragh folk had at last become fully aware of the Superintendent's frequent visits and his interest in them. Now, with the death of Casement, they manifested even greater curiosity in his comings and goings. His presence lulled many of them into a sense of greater security in the face of the killer at large in their midst.

As Knell slowly drove along the narrow roads which led to the manor and as they passed the clusters and the isolated dwellings in the fens, sentinels seemed to keep watch at every window and he was aware of curtains billowing as they passed, blinds trembling, doors moving ajar. An eye would be visible, sometimes accompanied by a flattened nose against a window-pane. News passed from house to house that he was about. Now and then, the watcher would appear entirely, but with a can or bucket in hand to make the gesture of feeding hens, watering a clump of flowers, or throwing clothes on the maiden in the corner.

There were other things Littlejohn did not know. Among the clumps of women who gathered in the hamlets every morning or in the schoolrooms to perform works of charity or help balance the chapel budgets, he was invested with great courage and skill. He was, according to all of them, biding his time, and then would pounce and denounce the criminal against whom they now double-barred their doors and the men cleaned and loaded their guns. And when finally someone more inquisitive than the rest found out about the Legion of Honour with which the Superintendent had been decorated for his work with the French underground during the war, their cup of gratitude and joy was full. The awe-stricken children who listened in silence to all this going-on were regularly given the same advice.

"Do your homework and be a good boy, and one day you'll be like him!"

Myrescogh Manor was as silent as ever as they approached it along the gloomy drive. Every time they visited the place, Littlejohn found and added another detail of it to his mental picture. Now, he noticed the gate on the north side which gave on to the open curragh and the derelict summerhouse, overgrown with brambles and with the roof falling in, in one corner of the garden. Ahead, the hills were tinged with bluish shadows alternating with patches of sunlight as the clouds floated across the sky. There had been rain in the curraghs earlier in the day. The forlorn garden of Myrescogh was drenched and the shrubs still wet from the showers. The daffodils and wallflowers, so bright and fresh when Littlejohn had first seen them, were beaten to the ground.

Jinnie appeared in answer to their knocking. She was still

resentful, her old dear-cut face expressing disgust and aggressive defiance.

"She's just eating her lunch."

"I'm sorry, Jinnie, but I'll have to disturb her. Please tell her I've called."

"Wait, then."

She returned quickly, looking all the more annoyed because she was to show him in. Knell remained in the car and the Superintendent entered the sitting-room on the ground floor where they had waited for Pakeman on their first visit there. Lady Skollick came to him at once.

This time she was sober, very sober, as presumably she'd been to church and had little time to brood or drink. She received him courteously and shook hands. Her trip out of doors had brought some colour and freshness to her cheeks. She looked now more like her picture taken with the horse at the show.

"You wished to see me?"

"Just to ask if you heard anything unusual on Friday night when Casement met his death?"

"No. I didn't even hear the shot which they said was fired."

"So, you can't help us on that score, Lady Skollick?"

"I'm sorry, no. Is that all you wish to know?"

"Yes. I'm glad to find you much better, and I thank you for seeing me again. You heard, of course, that Casement died from a shot from Sir Martin's gun?"

She nodded gravely, quite unmoved by the mention of it.

"He must have stolen it from the car. An impudent trick which did him no good at all."

"Are you interested in guns, Lady Skollick? The one in question was a very fine one."

"It was. I bought it for Sir Martin myself. A birthday present many years ago."

"You chose the pair yourself?"

"Yes. I grew interested in shooting after I married Sir Martin. I became quite a good shot myself. Why I tell you this, I really don't know. But you seem interested in guns, too."

"I am fond of shooting when I have the time. Dr. Pakeman does a fair amount, too. He's out at Andreas with the gun this morning."

"Is he?"

She said it in a bored tone, as though the doctor and his affairs were of little interest.

"You are old friends, he tells me."

"He has been our doctor since we came to live here, that's all."

"You weren't friends during your stage days, Lady Skollick?"

"No. Has someone told you we were?"

"I must be mistaken. He told me he was interested in opera and greatly admired your singing when he was in practice in London years ago."

"Did he? I never met him there. He's never mentioned his musical tastes whilst visiting us here. He and my husband were always very preoccupied with sport and particularly with fishing and shooting. I'm pleased to know I once gave him pleasure before I knew him personally."

She appeared to be quite natural about it all. Either she or Pakeman was a liar, and what it was all about Littlejohn could not think.

"He has some of your recordings. One of your singing Tosti's *Avril*."

"Has he, indeed! I'm flattered. Wait, though. How he got it, I can't say. It has been out of circulation a long time."

She went to the record cabinet in the corner and searched about in it.

"It's gone. I was playing it the night before my husband died. In fact, I left it on the turntable."

It struck Littlejohn that she might be the type who would listen appreciatively to her own recordings. And perhaps to those of nobody else.

She raised the lid of the radiogram.

"He must have taken it. Let's say borrowed it, when he called. A piece of impertinence."

There was nothing more to say. Lady Skollick mentioned that her lunch was growing cold. Littlejohn apologized and they said good-bye.

On the way back, a countryman lounging at his garden gate in his Sunday best raised a friendly hand and stopped them.

"I thought you'd like to know, master, that we think Casement's great dog, Moddey Mooar's about the curraghs. One or two heard howling in the night and as the little dog's tied up and friendly now at P.C. Killip's, it looks as if it's the other, leek. I wouldn' like to meet that fellah in the dark, 'specially since his boss was shot. If it's true what they say, that it's murder, then whoever done it had better look out."

13
THE HOUSE IN THE CURRAGH

Old Juan's ninetieth birthday party went very well. There were about fifty specially invited guests, including his family from America, but it had been widely advertised that anyone else who cared to call would be welcome.

The little school at The Cronk was filled to the doors.

Some were even compelled to eat and drink in the road, illuminated by the lights from the windows. Barricaded by a circle of old friends, Juan Kilbeg held court for about an hour and then he felt tired. The whole affair ended formally about half-past nine with the departure of the old man to bed. He expressed himself as not being very well pleased with the present generation, compared them unfavourably with the young men of his own youth, said he was glad he would soon die and join his long-gone friends in heaven, and insisted on the assembly singing his favourite hymn, *A Day's March Nearer Home*, before he left.

Littlejohn, Knell and the Venerable Archdeacon drove to The Cronk after evening service at Grenaby, enjoyed a hearty meal, and then Old Juan and the Rev. Caesar Kinrade talked Manx for half an hour, and Juan mentioned that he had passed on the news about Casement's letter to the Archdeacon. Meanwhile, Wash.

Kilbeg, a sporting member of the American line, entertained such as were interested on the finer points of baseball. Standish, a politician, explained the constitution of the United States to two travelling students who, passing by heavy-laden with rucksacks, had called in for a free meal. Elmer and Wilbur, the twins, meanwhile, had taken a few of the youthful element into a small adjoining room and were initiating them into the art of crap-shooting, a game which the thrifty Manxmen played for matches, greatly to the disgust of their instructors.

Old Juan decided it was time to go to bed just after J. Hoover Kilbeg and his wife, both of them eminent musicians and teachers in their home town, began to play a Beethoven sonata for horn and piano, which they had been practising in honour of the old man.

After Juan Kilbeg had left them, the guests gathered round for an hour's talk about old times and Manx news, including the Archdeacon who had been buttonholed by another Manx-speaking old gentleman who monopolized him for half an hour. Littlejohn slipped out into the open air, lit his pipe, and took a stroll for a breath of cool breeze from the sea. Knell, whom he left behind, had met a long lost second-cousin, who was in the process of talking him to death.

Littlejohn started off down the road which led to the curraghs. By this time, he thought he knew it well. He turned to the right and he found himself plunged at once into pitch darkness. The sudden change from the brightly lit schoolroom to the night around him made him pull up short. Above his head, a vault of branches and shadows obscured the stars; ahead blackness. There was a bitter tang of unknown plants on the air which mingled with the familiar smell of the marshes.

Then, suddenly, he was in the open again. The trees thinned out, he could see the stars overhead, and, in the distance, the lights of cottages dotted across the curraghs. He began to find his bearings and, as he paused to identify the places he had grown to know, an idea abruptly entered his mind to visit by night the scene of the crime and the strange events which followed it. The road he was following led straight past Mylecharaine school, the church, and then on, by a narrow path to the vicarage.

All the way to the church, about a mile away, Littlejohn met nobody. Old William Fayle's chapel was in darkness, the cottages scattered round the church at Mylecharaine were snugly closed and lights showed behind drawn curtains and blinds. Now and then, there were sounds of radio music or voices. The church was in darkness, too.

There were two lanes which led to the rectory. One through the churchyard, the 'parson's path', the other along the church wall and through the front gate. Littlejohn took the latter way and found himself unable to enter as the gate was overgrown with weeds and ivy. Furthermore, the hedge which enclosed the house had recently been re-enforced by wire-netting by a farmer whose cattle had only recently eaten half of it away. Through the clumps of neglected bushes which almost entirely hid the vicarage from where he was standing, Littlejohn could see a light burning in the front room.

He remained motionless, his eyes fixed on the illuminated window. As he did so, two figures materialized from within, stood for a minute in full view and then, engaged in earnest conversation, disappeared. They were the Rev. Sullivan Lee and Dr. Pakeman.

The Superintendent fumbled his way along the dilapidated hedge, seeking a way to the front door, and finally found the remnants of an old wall, topped by what felt to be ivy. He pulled himself up, threw his leg over, slipped down the other side, and was immediately above his ankles in mud. Risking making his presence obvious, he took out his torch and cast a pencil of light about his feet. He had just missed plunging into the black pool in an even darker corner of the garden and was now involved in part of its muddy bank.

The unkempt garden, overrun by bramble bushes and holly, had a haunted feel and a temperature several degrees below the surrounding countryside which chilled Littlejohn to the marrow. Dry twigs crackled underfoot as he leapt from the mud to drier land. The high tops of the surrounding trees must have held colonies of rooks, which he heard heavily flapping their wings, but not daring to take flight in the night or even to cry out. Ahead lay the sad house, which no amount of decoration, warmth, human habitation or change of season had ever succeeded in cheering. Amid its barren garden and the misty curraghs it reared itself like a doomed place.

The house was in full view and so unexpectedly near, that he had to draw back behind the bushes as he heard footsteps and voices in the hall behind the door. His foot caught a forgotten rake which lay in the wet grass and the handle rose and hit him on the chest. He cautiously thrust it beneath a stunted tree in case he encountered it again.

What a place! Littlejohn had no idea of the direction of The Cronk, where, less than an hour ago, he had been sitting, half-asleep, listening to the gentle drone of gossiping voices. Here, as soon as one took a step from the chartered paths, the twists, zig-zags and doubling back and forth of the hidden tracks led one into a complete labyrinth.

He took a few cautious steps and found himself close to the lighted window. The weather was fine, but water fell drop by drop from some spout or gutter overhead splattering his hat and coat. Although there appeared to be no wind to speak of, the trees overhead sighed gently.

Suddenly the knob of the front door was turned and in the dim light of the hall, Littlejohn could make out the forms of the two men again.

"Well, good-night, Mr. Lee. Let me know if anything turns up."

The doctor was buttoning his raincoat as he spoke.

"I will do that, doctor. I had him in the shed round the corner and when he vanished, I thought I'd better tell you. It may be dangerous."

"Quite right. You were lucky to come upon him the way you did. Well, good-night. My car's under the church wall by the main gate."

He made off in the dark across the parson's path and the vicar closed the door. Littlejohn watched him return to the lighted room, where he at once began sorting books which lay in piles on the worn linoleum of the floor. He still looked eager to get away and was merely waiting for police permission to catch the next boat to the mainland.

Gingerly Littlejohn felt his way round the house, now and then flashing a faint glimmer of his torch to guide him. There was a path, knee-deep in strong weeds, leading all the way and skirting this at the end of the front wall were two or three ramshackle wooden sheds, the rotten smell of which filled the air and told of their condition in spite of the pitch darkness. Rats scuttered about and, overhead, the rooks still flapped their nervous wings and seemed to follow every silent footstep beneath.

A large shed which might once have held a small car or a gig. The door was closed, but, when he shone his torch on the catch, he found that the hasp, which had held a locked chain, had been torn from its position in the rotten wood. Littlejohn opened the door and swept his light around. A rat scuttered through a hole in the timber and disappeared. There was a hole cut at the bottom of the door to admit a cat. A pity none was about at present to deal with the rats.

The place was full of dust, cobwebs, and other rubbish.

Old iron, decrepit garden tools, plant pots, battered boxes and tins. The floor however was interesting. An old enamel dish, half full of water; another of heavy earthenware which had probably held food and been licked clean by rats. Scattered here and there lumps of dog excrement.

The clues among the dust, the breaking open of the door by sheer bodily weight, the conversation between Lee and Pakeman could only mean one thing. Casement's Great Dog, Moddey Mooar, had probably been held prisoner there until he'd decided he'd had enough, and had forced his way out.

And then he noticed an astonishing thing. Half-way between the hole through which the rat had scrambled and the empty food dish lay another large rat. At first he thought it was dead, but a closer look revealed that it was unconscious. It lay there amazingly and peacefully asleep. Littlejohn frowned, and touched it. It was warm and he could feel its breathing and heartbeats.

Still frowning, he slowly left the shed, and closed the door and made for the front of the house again. The mud around his trousers-bottoms was growing hard and uncomfortable and the damp miasma surrounding the place was giving him a chill. He wondered why he'd ever set about this wild goose chase.

Littlejohn's knock on the front door of the vicarage sounded hollow through the silent, almost empty house. From where he was standing, with a good view through the adjacent lighted window, Littlejohn could see Lee almost leap in the air when his knock was heard. A pause. Lee peeped through the window into the dark night. Then he decided he'd better answer the door. His head peered out after he had rattled the bolts and chains which he had made secure when Pakeman left. He saw Littlejohn and, without even a word, stood aside to let him enter, as though finding it futile to resist. He stared timidly at the Superintendent as he entered the hall.

It was the same as when P.C. Killip had called on the eventful night of Skollick's death. A paraffin lamp smoked on a chair in the hall. Dark shadows hung like cloaks all-round the periphery of the room. Somewhere in the building a tap was running with an eerie wailing sound; otherwise, as the two men faced each other there was silence.

As Lee made no show of inviting him in, Littlejohn quietly

strolled into the lighted room. The illumination came from another paraffin lamp, this time made of brass and with a broken mantle, mounted on a brass stand. It looked like a candidate for another jumble-sale. Lee followed him hesitantly, like a boy about to be chastised and wasting time to defer the punishment.

"Why didn't you tell us that you'd been harbouring Casement's dog here, Mr. Lee?"

Lee's mouth opened, and yet he did not speak. He stood as though he expected Littlejohn to strike him any minute. "How did you capture it, in the first place?"

Lee approached with hesitant steps, his face tightening as he tried to assume a defiant air.

"He just came here and I fed him. He was wild and bewildered. He was in the garden drinking at the pool."

"You threw food in the shed and then locked him in?"

"Yes."

"Why didn't you inform the police?"

"I never thought of it. I have only just returned to the vicarage, as you know, and my mind is confused. I am preparing to leave as soon as the police give permission."

"Yet, you let Dr. Pakeman know?"

"He asked me to do so, if I saw the animal about."

"When did he ask you?"

"He called soon after I returned from prison, told me the dog was abroad and dangerous, and said if I saw it, I ought to let him know. He has told everyone on the curraghs, so I was not alone in the affair."

"What was he doing here to-night?"

"The dog came last night. I telephoned first thing this morning to the doctor's home, but he was out. He has just been to see me in answer to my message. Only to find that the dog had escaped."

Lee was nervously fumbling with a piece of knotted string which had lain on the floor. His fingers trembled so violently that he could not untie it. Littlejohn gently took it from him, untied the two knots, and then placed it on the table.

The candle guttered in front of the little shrine to Lee's wife. A long sliver of grease had formed down one side through the draught and stood like a minor support for the main column of wax. The room still stank of soot, although Lee had apparently cleaned away all traces of the fall down the chimney.

"Why are you giving up the parish and entering a monastery, sir?"

The question was so unexpected and irrelevant, that Lee paused before answering, as though wondering if it really had been asked.

"I don't know."

"Please, Mr. Lee, don't try to mislead me any more. You have been a very well-liked priest in this small community and you have done good work. Then, suddenly, you throw the whole business up and cannot pack quickly enough and get away. You wish to cut yourself off from the world."

"I have decided to enter the Roman church. I cannot, therefore, stay here."

"Is it not because of your spell in prison? Your parishioners think too much of you to hold that against you now you have been found innocent. They'll even think all the more of you for your quixotic effort to shield someone else."

Lee blinked and his face reddened.

"Mr. Lee, I beg of you, tell me the whole business, the truth about your own share in the death of Sir Martin. I don't suggest that you had anything to do with the murder; your innocence there has been proved. But you may get into very serious trouble as an accessory if you aren't careful. What are you doing meddling in this matter? This is probably your last chance to help the police. If, when the arrest is made, you are again implicated, the results may be very serious for you."

Lee's shoulders shivered and he turned an exhausted face with closed eyes to Littlejohn, as though not caring to give him a straight look because of some guilt which might be plainly seen.

"Please leave me alone. Let me go away. I swear I had nothing to do with the crime. That is all you wanted. Please leave me in peace."

"I'm going to talk to you as man to man, sir. I don't blame you for what you have done. Many another man has fallen in love with a woman whom he knows can only ruin his life."

He paused. The agonized eyes had opened and he was surprised to see them glistening with anger. Littlejohn feared the old stubborn streak was about to manifest itself again.

"I have no doubt, sir, that you have tried to be faithful to the memory of your late wife."

With a noise like a soft wail, Lee sat at the table among the dusty books and piles of sermons, and buried his head in his arms. Dry sobs shook him and he rolled from side to side as though seeking in movement some kind of relief.

"In another half-hour, sir, I shall be a policeman again.

Our ways will part then. But at present, I am trying simply to be your friend, to release you from the load of remorse you stubbornly persist in bearing. You wish to be faithful to your wife at all costs. But you have developed a passion for someone else. You are going to run away, therefore, and enter a monastery. Very well. But, through your emotions, you have got mixed in the machinery of the law."

Lee had fixed Littlejohn with an unwavering stare, full of hostility and distrust, as though the Superintendent were trying to trick him into another more fatal confession.

"Who has told you all this? It is not true."

"Nobody needed to tell me, sir. Forgive me if I draw painful conclusions, but it is, I trust, for your own good. When your wife died, you, like many others who have known happiness and great love with a woman, made yourself a little shrine to her memory. Can you tell me honestly that the one there is the same as when you first erected it? Dusty, fly-blown, an old candle askew. You didn't even remember to take it to prison with you; a place where it might be expected to comfort you most."

"Stop! Stop! I can bear no more of it! Will you please go and leave me to my packing. I must get away."

"Away from whom? Lady Skollick, who, until a few days ago, was another man's wife. Or, Gillian Vacey, notoriously loose in her ways, and mistress of Skollick and heaven knows whom else. Or, could it be Ellen Fayle, a girl almost forty years younger than yourself, who might cause tongues to wag here and elsewhere and make the pastoral work of a parson impossible? Which is it, sir?"

Lee's sins and troubles might have materialized into a swarm of bees, judging from his behaviour. He raised his hands and shielded his face and then started to flail around his head like someone beating off a cloud of insects.

"I wish that I, not Skollick, had met my death recently. I cannot face any more torture."

"I'm sorry, I can't prolong this interview. It is growing late and my friends don't know where I am and will be anxious. I tell you this, however. In a few days, we shall arrest the murderer of Skollick and Casement. You will then know who committed the crime. If it should happen to be this woman who has captivated you, sir, then she will disappear from your life. If not, her name will be cleared and you will have to decide what to do. Believe me, you are not alone in your trouble. Many a good man has faced it and solved it. When this sordid affair is over, you will be free, provided you have not involved yourself as an accessory. I ask you again, Mr. Lee, did you, on the night of the crime, see anyone in the vicinity of the body when you found it?"

"No."

"Why are you interested in capturing Casement's Great Dog?"

"I feared it would kill whoever shot its master."

"And you think you know who did?"

A chill breeze, smelling of damp leaves and earth, stole into the room through the open front door like a ghost from the marshes. In the distance, J. Hoover Kilbeg, drunk on rhubarb wine, was playing *Yankee Doodle* on his horn in the road at The Cronk and the notes floated across the curragh and into the vicarage like the trumpets of a different world.

"I cannot say who did it. I do not know who murdered Skollick. But I can think who might have done it, and no word of mine shall incriminate him."

"Why?"

The clenched jaws and the fluttering eyelids relaxed, and the will, strained beyond endurance, broke down. The Rev. Sullivan Lee's eyes burned and he raised his arms and thrashed the air again.

"Skollick was a scoundrel. An evil man. He ruined three women, at least. His wife, a drunkard now through his cruel indifference and unfaithfulness. Gillian Vacey, a decent woman until Skollick arrived and made her what she is. And Ellen Fayle, promised marriage after the divorce of Skollick, to try to expunge the sin she and Skollick committed together. Whoever killed Skollick wiped out a scourge, a menace, a plague, a hypocrite, a scoundrel."

The list of synonyms for a plain rotter ripped out from Lee's shouting mouth until he could utter no more, his throat gave out, he panted, and drank up the dregs of some cold tea which remained in a dirty cup on the table.

"What must I do?"

He calmed down suddenly and sprung his despairing question at the surprised Superintendent, as though Littlejohn himself were his father confessor.

"Tell me the truth. Who do you think killed Skollick?" Lee had suddenly grown calm. He had been stretched to breaking-point and past it, and now could resist no longer.

"It was Pakeman."

"And why, may I ask, did you not tell the police right away? What did you see on the night Skollick died?"

"As I already told you, I went to the school for my spectacles. What I did not tell you was that the lights of the room had been switched off at the main. I used my pocket torch. I recovered the glasses and was just about to leave, when I heard a car slowly drive past the school. It halted some distance along the road, and, as I stood behind the trees watching it, for its lights were extinguished, I saw someone inside light a cigarette. It was Dr. Pakeman."

"You saw the dog?"

"Yes; that was as I said. I had picked it out by the light of my torch at the school door. I did not fire at it. I stood watching the car. I had the gun in my hand in case I saw the dog again. By this, my eyes were used to the darkness. I saw Pakeman get out of the car and then hoist out what I assumed was a drunken person. I couldn't think who it might be or what it was all about. Then, suddenly, what appeared to be a scuffle ensued. I saw Pakeman take the other person in his arms, almost turn him upside down and then lay him head first, inclining down the bank of the hedge. Then he took out what looked like a gun from the car and seemed about to shoot the prostrate man. I hurried forward to prevent it, caught my foot against a root or some obstruction, fell, and fired the gun off. The rest you know. I collected myself, by which time the car had driven hurriedly away and I went and found the dead body of Skollick. I didn't know whether I or Pakeman had killed Skollick. As Pakeman did not fire the gun, I assumed, at first, that my shot had been the fatal one. I have given this much thought and until you told me you had scientific proof that I had not done the deed, I hesitated and refused to speak. I was sure that if Pakeman had killed Skollick before depositing him in the curragh, he would not have let me take the blame. I waited in prison for him to confess if he had committed the crime. I have known him a long time. I was sure he would speak. He did not. Therefore, I am justified in telling you this. You must take it as my own theory and must confirm it before acting upon it."

"Have you told Pakeman all this?"

"No. He must think I did not see him, or else that I refuse to speak of it. But I am sure Casement, who was there, too, must have told the doctor *he* was watching. Why else should he have killed Casement?"

"So, you've thought all that out, too, sir?"

"Over the past few days, I have had food for much thought. First, you told me that you had proof that my shots did not kill Skollick. Then, you said that probably the dog I saw was Casement's. He was presumably poaching in the vicinity and saw the crime committed or the body in the arms of Pakeman and perhaps blackmailed him. This would stimulate the murderer to wish to eliminate Casement. Had I told Pakeman that I was there, as well as Casement, I fear I would have suffered Casement's fate as well. I am afraid now for the first time. I fear that it may suddenly strike Pakeman that I know who killed Skollick. In fact, I wonder if that was the purpose of his call to-night. Your presence about the place saved me."

"But Pakeman had gone when I knocked at the door."

"He must have seen you in the garden. Did you make much noise or shine a torch?"

"I put on my torch for a brief second."

"That would be it. He said,

"There is someone in the garden. Have you been granted police protection, then?"

I said I had not, and he smiled and said, "They are on your trail. You are under observation still."

"You were released yesterday and slept here last night?"

"No. The Maddrells, in the village, kindly offered me a bed. This place had not been aired. So I accepted."

"I see. What do you propose to do to-night?"

"I don't quite know, Superintendent. If I bolt all the doors and fasten the windows?"

It was a great temptation to use Lee as bait and let him stay in the vicarage with the police hidden to spring the trap. Littlejohn resisted it. Lee was at the end of his tether, and, as likely as not would, at the approach of danger, go off the deep-end and spoil it all.

"You'd better come to the Maddrells' again with me, sir. Just for one more night."

"Very well. I'll be guided by you. They invited me, but I declined. One can't be cowering in fright for ever. I've got to pull myself together."

"One last question. May I ask you the name of the lady you mentioned? The one from whom you propose to flee."

Littlejohn said it half humorously, hoping to get under Lee's veneer of solemn sinfulness about his choice of a second love.

Lee's glance darkened.

"I ask it with friendliest of motives, sir."

"Very well, but I trust you not to mention it elsewhere. You have been most kind to me. It is Lady Skollick."

It was almost comic! The idea of persisting in running away from the lady of the manor! A little flattery, a little indulgence in operatic talk, a little patience, and the job would surely be done. Not only that, Lee would be good for her. His solemn and obstinate ways would probably result in her signing the pledge, encouraging the Band of Hope, enthusiastically persisting in increased good works in the curraghs, and generally making him a good partner.

"Haven't you a rival, sir?"

Lee reared and his eyebrows shot up. He even squared his shoulders, as though ready for the fray. It was like a dose of tonic.

"A rival! Whom, pray?"

"Dr. Pakeman, the man you say murdered her husband."

"But that is ridiculous! He has thoughts of only one woman. Mrs. Vacey."

It was Littlejohn's turn now to rear. "But who told you that, sir?"

"Not Pakeman, you may be sure. It was Sir Martin himself. During one of my pastoral visits to the manor, he returned somewhat the worse for drink. He chided me for calling during his absence and in drunken fashion hinted that I called to pay court to his wife. Then, impudently, for Lady Skollick was present, he said that we professional men were all the same. Pakeman took advantage of being Mrs. Vacey's doctor to importune her with declarations of love. She had told Sir Martin and they had been amused. Sir Martin talked of giving Pakeman and me the sack as medical and spiritual advisers. I am sure I would have known, in fact, she would have told me, for we are good friends, had Pakeman had the audacity to approach Lady Skollick in unseemly fashion."

"Let us go, then, sir. I'll see you safely to the Maddrells." They walked down the garden together, leaving behind them the candle still burning at the shrine. The damp air was mild and soothing after the musty house. Littlejohn turned aside for a minute to look in the shed again. The rat was still asleep and apparently coming to no harm.

"If I may say so, Mr. Lee, you ought to stay over here instead of running away. That's what you're doing. Running away. Lady Skollick, in her present state of health and mind, needs the guidance of a good man. Remember that. You might even make up to her for."

A car was approaching with headlights full on. It halted as the two men drew level and Knell thrust his head out of the window. The Archdeacon was sitting calmly with him.

"We thought you'd either got lost or kidnapped, sir."

He said in a voice so moved that Littlejohn hastened to apologize and excuse himself more profusely than was necessary.

They dropped Lee at the Maddrells', and then they drove home to Grenaby.

14
MONDAY MORNING

Monday, and a bright sunny morning. Sam Callister slid noisily between the quiet houses of Castletown in his little red van and steered out of the maze of silent streets to the road which led past Marown church to the cross-ways and thence to Grenaby. In spite of the weather, Sam wasn't feeling too cheerful.

"Mornin', Fred," he called out to the roadman who, although he'd enjoyed a good breakfast at home before leaving, was now eating another before starting to mow the grass verges.

"Mornin', Sam. Nice sunny mornin'."

Sam wished he were a roadmender. Anything rather than a postman. He passed the last houses of the little town, settled so securely under the walls of its great castle, and turned to look at it as if for the last time. Before he quite knew where he was, he was passing Malew churchyard. It gave him quite a turn. He eyed the granite memorials and the little white marble slabs and thought he might be there himself before long. He accelerated to the cross-roads and there, clad in a grey suit of Manx tweed, stood Inspector Knell. Callister resented the light suit. After all, they weren't going on a picnic!

Knell had arrived in a police-car in which Littlejohn and the Rev. Caesar Kinrade were now sitting. They were both smiling pleasantly and bade Sam a hearty good morning. Sam was a little chubby fellow, with red cheeks and jolly blue eyes, as a rule. This morning his eyes weren't so jolly and his cheeks were pale pink.

"Remember, Sam, just be natural. We'll see you come to no harm."

They'd briefed him earlier before he dealt with his mail.

When they'd told him that the post might be held-up that delivery, he hadn't quite realized what they meant. But after they'd gone and he'd had time to brood as he sorted his round, he hadn't liked it at all. True, they'd offered to dress a bobby in postman's uniform and let him do the round, but Sam had dismissed such a silly idea with great indignation. What would people say when he didn't turn-up as usual! Besides, the postmen were as good as the police any day. They'd proved that a time or two at the annual football matches between them. Sam had insisted on doing his own work whatever came along. He remembered the Wells-Fargo serials his kids read every week in their comics. Men pursuing a mail-coach firing bullets right and left. It wasn't comic to Sam.

"You're sure you've got it all. We'll look after you every inch of the way."

Knell was insisting on briefing Sam again and Callister resented it.

"Of course I'm sure. Get in."

Knell opened the back of the van and climbed inside. It contained one large mail bag, sagging with emptiness, because it wasn't a very busy morning. There were also an old tyre, a new one, Sam's lunch in a paper bag, the morning paper, and a large bunch of herbs which a colleague had given Sam as a specific for his wife's rheumatics.

Knell scrambled about among the contents, sat on Sam's lunch, which made strange noises as he squashed the hardboiled eggs, drew himself up just behind the driver's seat, and concealed himself behind the two tyres and the large bunch of comfrey. That was why Knell was wearing Manx tweeds. His gardening suit, which he could soil to his heart's content.

"Just be natural," he murmured to Sam, who was too disgusted to reply.

Somewhere between the cross-roads and Grenaby, they were sure somebody would try to waylay the postman and take Casement's letter addressed to the Archdeacon, which they thought was still on the way. The loneliest stretch of the round was approaching and in some quiet part of it the attempt would be made. It might be by force, or stealth, or a dodge, or even boldness. Sam was sure it would involve a man on horseback brandishing a six-shooter. After all, they hadn't told him a full tale for fear of upsetting him completely. He just knew there might be a plot to take his letters from him. He thought of teddy-boys, the I.R.A., Russians, rustlers, outlaws and bandits. He read his boys' comics as eagerly as they did themselves after they'd retired to bed. No reading in bed, he always told them, and made them leave their literature behind.

"Get moving, then, Sam." They were off.

It had all been planned beforehand. Every inch of the road was being watched. Policemen behind bushes, in barns, even among the branches of trees. And posted here and there were half-a-dozen marksmen with rifles who would shoot if Sam seemed in grave danger. Finally, here was Knell at his elbow, bent in the shape of a sack of flour.

"Have you got a revolver with you?"

"No, Sam. It'll hardly come to that," said Knell comfortably.

Oh, what's the use! thought Sam, and the sound of the whistle of the little train leaving Castletown for Douglas brought back so many happy memories, that the thought that he might never hear it again brought tears to Sam's eyes.

They called at several farms first. The countryside looked

clean and peaceful. Sam had never noticed before how patient and friendly it could be. The grass was very green, with dew still upon it, and all around there was a perfect riot of birdsong.

"Are you not too well, Sam?" asked Mrs. Robertson at Vollan Veg.

"Come in and I'll make you a cup of tea." Sam looked back at the van as though questioning Knell telepathically, and then decided he'd better get it over.

"No, thanks, Mrs. Robertson. I'll be all right. I'm late as it is."

A parcel for Ballahot, and then Sam would have to run the gauntlet. Ahead were the signpost and the turning to Grenaby, and the narrow country road running between hedges and wasteland, with hardly a farm or a living soul to be seen. As he turned and passed the fingerpost marked *Grenaby*, so well-known to Littlejohn, Sam cast his anguished eyes across at Fildraw, the place where he'd done his courting.

This was the dangerous stretch, with occasionally a bit of relief when Sam turned-in at the long "streets" which led to the isolated farms of Ballavell, Ballakewin, Ballabeg. There was only one letter between the three of them this morning. A free detergent coupon, but to Sam it seemed like a lifebuoy.

After Ballakewin, a long deserted span, with poor moorland soil on either side and ahead the massive wilderness of Moaney Mooar. Every bush, tree, tuft, ditch and hedge was a menace to Sam, harbouring hidden danger. And yet, there seemed to be nobody about! Looking at the road between the turning to Quayle's Orchard and the dip down to Grenaby itself, he couldn't see a soul in sight. Hardly a place to hide anybody, in fact. Sam's spirits began to rise. Perhaps it was a hoax, after all. Driving with one hand, he turned over with a forefinger of the other the spane Monday mail for Grenaby.

Ahead, the roadmen had parked an old steam-roller which had lain neglected there all last winter. This was the only remaining spot where anyone could hide, and, thought Sam, the police had surely taken care of that. The huge ungainly obstacle made single-line traffic absolutely essential where it poked its sprawling bulk into part of the roadway. Not that there was ever any need for regulating traffic in this god-forsaken bit of highway.

Suddenly something moved from behind the ancient contraption, and Sam Callister gasped and put on his brakes. Knell cautiously raised his head above his barricade of tyres and herbs. A huge dog was standing in the road ahead, sniffing the air. It was wild and unkempt as it slowly turned its head, divining the scent of what it was seeking. Then, before the red van reached it, it grew tense, turned its nose to the north, howled dismally, bounded off into the wasteland, and was lost in an instant.

Knell broke into a cold sweat. It was Casement's Great Dog, on the trail of his master's killer, and the killer was somewhere nearby!

"Looks like a giant sheep-dog gone wild," said Sam, accelerating for the last lap.

"Did you ever see the likes of that for size? Queer things always goin' on in the region of Grenaby."

He was feeling better. In fact, almost blithe, for the gauntlet was run and the danger was over. Only the tunnel of trees, the bridge over the stream, and there were the houses and the vicarage. The hold-up hadn't come-off.

Knell was puzzled, too. The murderer was obviously somewhere about. If not, what about Casement's dog? He was otherwise unlikely to be hanging around Grenaby, so far from his home ground. He wondered what all the scouts on the route were doing, and Littlejohn and the Archdeacon, parked and hidden in the last by-way in the loneliest part of the moor.

They were at the bridge and crossed it and the van pulled up at the house of Joe Henn, a recluse from Yorkshire who was gradually losing his wits in isolation. Joe was waiting at the gate for his mail. He wore a cap and a muffler, and his nightshirt was tucked down his trousers. Sam had a mere postcard for him from a nephew who was after his uncle's money. A view of Bermuda in vivid colours. "Having a lovely time. Wish you were here. Love from Walter and Lil." Joe merely looked at it, viciously tore it up, and threw the pieces in the river, for he had been expecting a dividend warrant. Then he went indoors for his breakfast.

Two letters and a parcel of books for the Rev. Caesar Kinrade. No use starting the van again for those. Sam picked the three from the remaining odds and ends, began to whistle, and walked to the parsonage with springing strides. He left Knell in the van, still wondering when things were going to get hot.

Sam opened the gate between the two thick fuchsia trees and halted. At the exact spot where the bushes concealed the path from the gate and the house, the two barrels of a gun were poking from the very body of a yew tree. Sam had just time to notice a pair of trousers and brown-brogued feet visible beneath, when a gruff voice spoke.

"Turn your back to me."

Sam obeyed mechanically, half wondering what it was that the heroes did in such circumstances in his boys' comics. They spun round and 'drew' as they spun. But then Sam had nothing to 'draw'. He wished he had as he turned his back square to the menacing barrels. A gloved hand took the letters from his own.

"Now, stay where you are until I say you may move." Sam stood there, frozen to the spot, waiting for the next order. None came. Instead, in the old neglected lane which ran under the vicarage wall and which had, long ago, been the drive to the parson's coach-house, there was the noise of a car starting-up, of an engine furiously driven, of the grinding of changing gears. Then a pause, shouts, squealing brakes, a resounding crash. A brief silence, a scream, and then two shattering reports from a sporting gun.

Sam thought it was time to turn round and found himself face to face with Maggie Keggin.

"Sam Callister! Whatever have you been up to?" Knell had, like

Sam, begun to think the whole business had become a farce. Just a lot of melodrama for nothing. And yet, Littlejohn had been so sure that the trap would attract the killer. He sat up in the van and thrust his hand in his pocket for his packet of cigarettes just as the postman opened the parsonage gate. As soon as Sam returned, he would climb down, stretch his legs, and call to see what Maggie Keggin had in the oven for breakfast. He could smell the ham and eggs already.

When the engine of the hidden car sprang into life among the vicarage trees, Knell didn't think of anything exciting. It might be the Superintendent and the Archdeacon who'd changed their plans and were now coming into the open after the whole affair had proved a frost.

The concealed car came out into the road. A small, fast sports model driven by a young man in a cap and with a scarf wound round his face showing merely his eyes.

"Hey!" It was the only strangled exclamation Knell could utter as he climbed into the driving-seat of the red van and pawed at the self-starter to go in pursuit. The word froze on his lips. He had a ringside seat for what followed.

Just beyond the lovely little stone bridge which crossed the river near Joe Herin's house, rose a grass bank leading to a plateau of cultivated land reached by a rough path with a gate at the top. As the sports car turned from the vicarage at a breakneck and still increasing speed, there appeared at the top of the bank a huge dog. It did not hesitate or halt in its tracks, but plunged downhill in time to stand in the very centre of the bridge, with hair bristling and fangs bared in a hideous snarl, as the car approached.

Instead of fleeing from it, the dog, without pausing, launched himself straight at the approaching vehicle, cleared the low bonnet, and crashed against the windscreen.

Knell briefly saw the masked face and the wild, staring eyes above the driver's scarf, and then the car swerved, hit the stone parapet a glancing blow, turned a complete somersault, and plunged into the stony river bed below.

Knell sprang from the van and scrambled down the bank of the river to the tangled wreckage. Joe Henn appeared, still masticating his breakfast, took in the scene, ran indoors again, returned with a gun into which he was driving a couple of cartridges as he ran, and shot the great dog which lay twitching in the road. So Moddey Mooar was buried with his master, as Casement had wished.

The usually silent little village suddenly became alive with police. Two cars drew up by the bridge and officers poured out. Littlejohn's was next and he and the vicar hastily emerged. Then policemen on bicycles. It might have been a policeman's picnic.

Knell stood waist-deep in the middle of the river. He bent over the wrecked car and, through the door which he had now forced open, he drew the body of the occupant, gently took it in his arms, waded to the bank, and carefully laid it on the damp grass. He shook his head.

"Dead." he said. "Broken neck and drowned before I could get the door open."

He had not examined the body carefully, but seemed instinctively sure.

Littlejohn hastily removed the cap and unwound the scarf. There was a concerted gasp from the surrounding police. A tangled wet mop of dark brown hair slid down and parted, revealing a calm pale face with tired closed eyes.

It was Gillian Vacey.

Knell's intuition had been right. The neck was broken, the woman quite dead. They gently carried her to the vicarage and someone telephoned to Castletown for an ambulance and a doctor, not that he would be much use.

"She doesn't look the sort who would kill anybody and come to a bad end," remarked a constable, just for something to say.

Invisible rooks in the vicarage trees cawed and answered his voice.

Littlejohn and the Archdeacon were left alone, guarding the body of Gillian Vacey. The Superintendent gently drew aside the sheet which Maggie Keggin had provided for a decent covering, and carefully thrust back the sleeves of the canary-coloured jumper one after another. The arms were both bruised cruelly and as he covered them again he made a clicking noise of pity through his teeth.

Then the shapely hands, with their long, carefully-manicured and red-varnished nails. Littlejohn held them in his own for a second and then crossed them over the breast.

The two men looked at each other silently and in the warm daylight their faces appeared leaden and drawn. They looked through the window over the empty mute garden and seemed to understand each other's thoughts even without words.

The old house appeared as peaceful and quiet as ever. The constables had gone. Only an Inspector and Knell remained and were in the kitchen, speaking in whispers, whilst Maggie Keggin, white-faced and erect, was putting on the kettle to make some tea.

"So this is the end of the case."

The Archdeacon's voice was full of sorrow. It may have been for the tragic ending or perhaps a little, too, that their work together was finished, and so lamentably.

Littlejohn seemed to wake from a trance of thought. He slowly covered the body again with the sheet and pulled himself up to his full height.

"No, sir. There's still a lot to be done. And I hope I haven't made a ghastly mistake. Excuse me."

He walked to the kitchen almost on tiptoe, as though anxious not to disturb the peace of death. Knell raised his troubled eyes.

"Knell. Where did Casement do his shooting by lamplight?"

The Inspector gave him a strange questioning look. He'd thought it was all over and done with, and the case neatly solved.

Now, Littlejohn didn't seem satisfied. He'd never seen him look so worried.

"As far as I know, sir, it's Narradale. That's a wild upland above Sulby, on the left of the road as you travel from Ramsey."

"Near the curragh where the body was found?"

"Right overlooking it, with the main road between. I'm sure it was Narradale, because I recollect Casement being caught there by Skollick and the local constable at the time Sir Martin was hounding him for poaching. He was prosecuted and fined."

"And suppose Casement wished to get, say, to the manor at Myrescogh in a hurry, which way would he go?"

"There's a good road right up to the hills. In fact, Skollick and the police went up there in Sir Martin's car the night they caught Casement. He was shooting not far from the road."

"But if Casement were in a hurry?"

"The road winds, because the gradient's so steep. A man like Casement would take the hill paths if he were in a hurry to get down to the main highway again. There's any number of old sheep tracks and Casement knew them like the back of his hand. Cross-country, he'd be down as quick a car going by the main Narradale road, because the curves and corners won't permit fast driving, unless you're a madman."

Littlejohn nodded his thanks and, taking Knell by the arm, led him into the hall.

"This is your case, Knell, and any further steps are your business. You realize, however, don't you, that it isn't ended by Mrs. Vacey's death?"

Knell nodded.

"There are one or two things I don't follow. I thought, maybe, when all this fuss is over and the body's been taken away, you'll just explain them to me."

Knell smiled modestly, as though he'd every trust in Littlejohn and that whatever he did was right.

"We'd better get off to Ramsey right away. Then, news of Mrs.

Vacey's death mustn't get around until we've finished the job. You warned the police from Castletown and the postman?"

"I did, sir. One or two of the village folk know, too, but they've no telephones, so any news they pass on will have to be on foot."

They waited for the ambulance to take away the body of Mrs. Vacey and then the Archdeacon joined Littlejohn and Knell.

"We've one more job to do, parson. Some questions to put to Dr. Pakeman, and then all should be tidy."

Dead silence fell over the old grey house again. The three stern-faced men set out for Ramsey just as there was a shrill and eerie whistling in the kitchen to give the signal that Maggie Keggin's kettle was boiling.

15

THE HORROR AT NARRADALE

Littlejohn's bulky figure seemed to fill the whole of the car as he sat slumped beside Knell on the familiar road to Ramsey again. Nobody spoke. The Archdeacon, comfortably settled in the back, was smoking his pipe and lost in thought. Knell was paying full attention to his driving. Littlejohn had asked him to get there as fast as he could.

"And I'd like to call on old Mr. Kilbeg, too, on the way."

Knell had never seen Littlejohn so pale and drawn. His face was grey, as though the strain of a long and trying case had drained all his energy away. His cold pipe dangled from his mouth and his hands were thrust deep in the pockets of his raincoat.

"Can't we go a little faster, Knell?"

They had done sixty along the straight moorland road over the Barrule plantation to Foxdale and the passage through the village was a bit tricky. All the same, Knell accelerated again and with his horn blowing, shot past the groups of housewives gossiping at their doors. The village bobby appeared, looking ready to pursue them on his bike, until he saw the sign *Police* on the car. Then, he gave it up as a bad job.

Littlejohn didn't wake from his thoughts until they drew up at

Old Juan Kilbeg's cottage. His wife was at the door shaking the mats and sweeping out the debris of the previous day's celebrations.

"Don't stop the engine, Knell. I won't be a minute." Mrs. Kilbeg stared hard at Littlejohn.

"You don't look so well, Superintendent. I'll make you a cup of tea if you'll wait a minute."

"Please don't trouble, Mrs. Kilbeg. I've already had one. Is Mr. Kilbeg all right after his party?"

"He certainly is. He was awake at seven asking for his breakfast and wanting to get up and go through all his birthday presents again. He'll be terrible cross if he knows you've been and not put a sight on him."

"Just for a minute, then. We're going to Ramsey and I thought I'd enquire about him."

"Come in. What about the Archdeacon and Mr. Knell?" So, they all had to call and greet the old man. He was sitting up in bed, wrapped in a quilted purple bed-jacket, the gift of Mr. and Mrs. Jefferson J. Kilbeg, of Honolulu, sent by post because Jeff J. was too far away to bring it in person.

"Ain't it fine and dandy?" said the old man before he even bade them good morning. He also showed them an alarm clock which would brew a pot of tea, pour it out, and then switch itself off, after playing *Happy Birthday to You* on a musical-box. This from Robert E. Lee-Kilbeg, another absentee, travelling for hardware in Alaska.

"And there's a good, warm Manx rug from Lady Skollick and a pound of my favourite baccy from Dr. Pakeman"

"Did Mrs. Vacey call?"

The old man's face blackened. "Nope!"

He'd learned the negative from Wash. Kilbeg and was proud that he said it like a real American, or so they told him.

The old clock in the hall struck eleven. Then it decided to have a repeat performance and struck eighteen.

"Don't take any notice of that clock. It's old and ticklish on its feet and gets upset now and then when shook up, like me. Somebody must have kicked it in the shindy yesterday."

All the same, it gave the visitors a chance to talk about leaving and, after promising Old Juan to return before long, they went on their way.

The walled garden of Tantaloo looked sweet and fresh in the morning sunshine and the air was full of the scent of flowers. Mrs. Vondy's face appeared at an upper window as they walked down the path and she opened the door before they had time to knock.

"Is the doctor in, Mrs. Vondy?"

"Yes. He's just finishing his breakfast. I know it's late, but he's been called out twice in the night, which doesn't happen often these days."

"By telephone?"

"Yes, both by telephone."

It was the doctor's voice which gave the answer and he appeared from the shadows of the hall and stood on the doorstep before them. He, too, looked drawn and grey. Littlejohn was surprised at the change in him. Even his moustache seemed to droop with fatigue.

"You'd better all come inside. Would you care for some coffee?"

The newcomers excused themselves. Mrs. Vondy looked anxiously at the knot of grim men as they filed into the front room.

"Will there be anything?"

"No, Mrs. Vondy. You can clear my breakfast dishes and then get on with what you were doing."

The doctor was nervous and impatient as he waited for his housekeeper to gather up the dirty dishes. Finally, he helped her himself to load the tray and carried it out for her.

At last they were alone, the four of them, and the doctor spoke first.

"To what do I owe the pleasure of this early visit?" He said it wearily and sat down as though eager to feel the comfort and support of his armchair.

"Mrs. Vacey died this morning."

Pakeman made no impulsive or astonished gesture. In fact, he hardly moved. He gave a faint sound like that of a brave man who suffers pain and stifles his cries, and turned his head so that his cheek rested against the leather back of his chair. Then he pulled himself together, and more drawn than ever, looked full at Littlejohn.

"How did it happen?" It was said in a whisper.

"She skidded into the bridge at Grenaby, her car overturned, she fell in the river-bed, and her neck was broken."

Knell turned and looked hard at Littlejohn, wondering at the careful recital of so many details, but there was no anger in the Superintendent's face.

Pakeman turned his cheek to the chair-back again as though finding comfort in the cool leather and this time put his hand across his eyes and squeezed his temples until the knuckles grew white.

"Where were you last night, doctor?"

"Am I supposed to provide an alibi even when someone is killed by accident?"

"Yes."

"Well, if you must know, I had two patients to see. I was called out at one o'clock to a heart case. I got back at two, went to bed, and was out again at five at a difficult confinement until eight."

"Did you call on Mrs. Vacey on your way to either of these patients?"

The shock of the question seemed to electrify the other three. Knell's mouth fell open and Pakeman grew red and raised his head angrily.

"Certainly not! Why should I? Both calls were urgent and, if you don't believe me, you can check them in every detail. I'll give you the addresses. I'd no time to be making social calls, even had I wanted to."

The atmosphere had suddenly changed. Pakeman had become an angry, affronted man.

"I don't know why you've all called. After a night of work, I'm not in much shape for answering a lot of silly questions. I appreciate your coming to tell me the sad news, but if you don't mind, I'll try to get an odd hour's rest before I make my morning calls. I'm all-in, sorry to seem rude, but I'm sure you'll understand."

Knell and the Archdeacon rose ready to go, but Littlejohn remained seated.

In a quiet, monotonous voice, as though he himself were tired-out, Littlejohn spoke.

"Have you nothing you wish to tell me, doctor? Nothing you want to get off your mind?"

Pakeman looked flabbergasted, as though Littlejohn had taken leave of his senses.

"What do you *want* me to say? That I followed Mrs. Vacey to Grenaby? That I murdered her? I thought you said there'd been an accident."

In the kitchen behind, Mrs. Vondy had switched on the radio. A suave voice was trotting out recipes and other domestic advice. Pakeman's nerves were on edge. He went to the door and called out to his housekeeper.

"For God's sake turn off that noise, Mrs. Vondy!"

The broadcast ceased suddenly and a shocked silence reigned in the rooms behind.

"If I tell you, doctor, that the accident was caused by Casement's big dog, Moddey Mooar, will that give you a clue as to what I want you to talk about?"

Every face was strained and Knell's and the parson's registered puzzled surprise.

"No. Why should it? What's come over you, Littlejohn? I've never known you like this."

"I have never been like this before. Will you please sit down, doctor, and you and Knell, too, if you please, Archdeacon?"

It was said quietly, but might have been an order. All three men slowly subsided.

"Was Skollick dead when you found him injured at Mrs. Vacey's on the night he died?"

"I don't know what you're talking about."

"Listen to me! If you won't explain what happened, I will. First of all, Casement's letter to the Archdeacon, which was expected through the post this morning, did not arrive."

Slowly and in an effort to hide his feelings, Pakeman drew a deep breath and trembled.

"It was delivered by hand yesterday by the postman on his way to church."

Pakeman changed colour; this time the blood drained from his face until he almost looked jaundiced. He tried to speak casually, but was too hasty about it.

"Old Kilbeg mentioned it yesterday when I called to greet him on his birthday, but I thought it was a bit of gossip. I wasn't interested."

"Yet you told Mrs. Vacey that it was on the way. Please don't deny it. She was out to intercept the letter when she met her death. She held-up the postman, took all the Archdeacon's mail, and would have got away with it, had not the dog leapt on the fast-moving car and made her swerve."

Pakeman waved his hands, dismissing the subject.

"That has nothing to do with me. Why go into details all over again?"

Littlejohn didn't answer at first and the silence only heightened the tension.

"If you won't tell me, I must tell you then, doctor."

Ellen Fayle had a child by Sir Martin Skollick. Becoming a father was an experience quite new to Skollick. He was fond of children. He made up his mind to become a family man, turn over a new leaf, and marry Ellen. He had to finish with his mistress and then get a divorce from his wife. He tackled Mrs. Vacey first. There were words, a quarrel, and then a scuffle. She struck him down and apparently with some justification. He mauled her badly and bruised her arms from top to bottom, trying to hold her. She must have lost her temper and control and hit him with some heavy object. He ended either dead or unconscious. Which was it, Pakeman?"

Everybody was deadly calm now. They were all thunderstruck and their strained faces made them look as if they hadn't slept for a week.

"Are you trying to make out that I had something to do with Skollick's death?"

"Yes. You either killed an unconscious man or butchered the dead body. Mrs. Vacey had very long nails. Like claws, in fact. In the course of the struggle, I presume she scratched Skollick's face badly. Had the police found the body at once, their thoughts would have turned to the mistress with the long, vicious nails. The marks on Skollick's face had to be eliminated. In fact, the face had to be removed!"

Pakeman sat taut and scowling, but did not speak. He seemed to be searching in his mind for something to say.

"You gave me an account of your movements on the night Skollick died, doctor. It was correct only until the time you arrived home from Andreas. After your meal, you didn't fall asleep in your chair. You were called-out at midnight by telephone. Mrs. Vacey had the unconscious or dead body of Sir Martin on her hands and wanted your help. You answered the call at once."

Pakeman leapt to his feet. He was obviously under a great strain, but had not lost his self-possession.

"This is ridiculous. I've no more time to listen to it. You must have gone mad."

"It was very foolish of you, Pakeman, to try to draw the limelight from Mrs. Vacey to Lady Skollick, by pretending that you loved Lady Skollick. To bear this out, wasn't it a bit childish to steal records from Myrescogh and have them lying about here to call my attention to your devotion and then when I asked if you loved Lady Skollick, to be so eager to bare your private sentiments."

"I don't understand you, at all, Littlejohn. I thought we were friends. At least, I've always thought well of you. Why try to pin these crimes on me, when it's so obvious that Mrs. Vacey killed Sir Martin in self-defence?"

"What about Casement's death, though?"

"I know nothing of that. It might have been an accident. There's no proof that he was murdered."

"There never will be any proof of how he died, now that Mrs. Vacey is gone. But this we know. Casement was going to meet someone, someone he thought might do him violence. He made his will before he went to the rendezvous and that, not a statement about who killed Skollick, was what he sent to the Archdeacon before he was killed."

Pakeman turned grey.

"So, Mrs. Vacey died for nothing. I was right. I've always been right. Skollick was doomed, and anybody who had anything intimately to do with him was doomed as well."

"Including yourself, doctor?"

"What do you mean by that?"

"Gillian Vacey called you out on the night Skollick died."

I grant that you might have found him dead."

"I did. I may as well tell you what happened. She rang me. I am her doctor. I found Skollick dead. He had, in a scuffle, stumbled backwards over the hearthrug, fallen, and struck his head against the marble kerb. Mrs. Vacey was in a fearful state. He had bruised and battered her in his efforts to free himself from the mad attack she had made on him when he told her he was finishing with her. Skollick in turn, had his face torn from eye to chin by Gillian's nails. It was a shocking affair."

"Why didn't you report it to the police? They'd have believed the story of self-defence, surely."

"Gillian was hysterical and half drunk. She said that the past relations she'd had with Skollick were well known and it would come out that he had broken with her. Her account of the struggles and Skollick's death might not be believed. She asked me to get rid of the body."

"And you, willing to do anything for her, infatuated by her, obeyed."

"In the heat and excitement of the minute, her point of view seemed reasonable."

"So, you took the body by car to a deserted spot. Narradale, in fact. It was a lonely place, where the shots of poachers by night are a commonplace. And with Skollick's own gun, which he carried in his car, you shot him in the head badly enough to eliminate all traces of the claw-marks of Mrs. Vacey."

"I resent your sarcasm, Littlejohn. She's dead now, and although she and I quarrelled and parted in anger before she died, I still respect her and object to your contempt for her."

"You set-out from Ramsey with the body in Skollick's car, intent on clearing Mrs. Vacey completely by making the death look like an accident. You drove the car, and Mrs. Vacey followed in her own to bring you safely back after you'd planted the body and concocted the mock misadventure. You must have had a shock when the car ran out of petrol. You forgot that Skollick was in the habit of filling up on his way home and had almost let his tank run dry."

"I had to transfer the body to Mrs. Vacey's car and leave Skollick's on the road. It didn't alter the plan very much. It was far enough away from Ramsey and it looked as though Skollick had walked home. The trouble was with Gillian. She was hysterical. I had to slap her to keep her quiet and then I put the body in the boot."

"Then off to Narradale. Casement was there poaching and saw and heard what went on. When you had finished with the body and loaded it back in the car, he was curious about it all. He went off cross-country like a hare and caught up with you as you were planting the corpse near Mylecharaine and staging things to look like an accident."

"I suppose I shall be regarded as an accessory to the whole affair. I ought to have reported it right away. I admit it was my duty. But you've only to put yourself in my place."

"Loving Gillian Vacey, under her spell, and hating Skollick for what he'd done to her in the past and present, you'd no objection at all to blowing a dead man's head off, had you, Pakeman?"

"I admit, I was foolish."

"You were indeed. But the pair of you might have got away with it if Casement hadn't been abroad, or, what is more fantastic, Sullivan Lee prowling in the schoolroom after his reading glasses. He saw you halt your car and light a cigarette."

"It was Gillian who lit the cigarette. She said she *must* smoke. She had Skollick's lighter with her and as she flicked it alight, I dashed it out and it fell from her hand and was lost. We'd no time to wait and hunt for it."

"Lee made out your face in the brief glimmer of the lighter. He saw you, a shadow in the darkness, get out and hoist Skollick from the car. He thought Skollick was drunk and there ensued what Lee thought was a scuffle between you. He saw you arranging the body, to be exact, and when you took out the gun, he rushed to prevent your using it, for he thought the pair of you were fighting. He fell, and the gun he was carrying to protect himself against Casement's dog, which was prowling about and which he thought was some spectral hound or other, went off. By the time Lee had gathered himself together, you had made off."

"I heard the shots."

"Lee thought he'd killed Skollick and went berserk. You know how he behaved. He wouldn't make a statement about his movements at the time he found the body. He went to gaol instead. He was sure that if you had killed Skollick, you would come and clear him. He trusted you that much. Instead, you left him in prison and he was only released because we proved he could not have killed Skollick with the gun he fired."

"I wouldn't have allowed him to."

"You ought never to have allowed him to go to gaol at all. He is a simple, decent man, whose mind was deranged by the horror of events. You let him fight it out alone."

"Well, he's cleared now."

"You won't forget, though, that Casement was on the spot, too. He arrived hot-foot from Narradale and added to the confounding of your plot by carrying away Skollick's gun which you'd placed with the body and which Lee, when he took the corpse to the church, left behind. So all your scheming went awry and instead, Lee was left to take the blame."

"I admit I was wrong. I've said so before. I'm prepared to take my punishment for my share in the whole sorry affair."

"For Casement's death, as well?"

Pakeman stiffened and he seemed to hold his breath like someone hiding and trying to prevent discovery.

"I'm afraid you can't pin that on me, Littlejohn. It was apparently an accident. He was out poaching, tripped over one of his own snares, and the gun went off."

Littlejohn's turn to stiffen now. There was another dead silence. Cars hummed past outside, the birds sang in the garden, and a bee entered the room and droned its way here and there trying to get out again, just as Pakeman was doing in the turmoil in which he was involved.

"Who told you Casement tripped over one of his snares?"

"I don't really know. Mrs. Vondy, I think, got the full tale and passed it on to me."

Littlejohn strode to the door and called to the kitchen. "Are you there, Mrs. Vondy? Can you spare us a minute?"

Mrs. Vondy arrived slowly. She had been weeping. Pakeman's anger with her about the radio was something new and she couldn't understand or bear it. She stood at the door, avoiding the doctor's eye.

"Mrs. Vondy. You heard of the death of Casement? How did he die?"

She looked stupefied, her mouth opened, and she shook her head.

"I hope I didn't do anything wrong. The news came with the postman. I told the doctor, who didn't know. He can tell you what I said."

"Of course I can. You can go, Mrs. Vondy. The Superintendent has no right to bully you."

Pakeman was standing beside Littlejohn now, waving his hand at Mrs. Vondy in dismissal.

"Kindly go and sit down, doctor. This is my business.

Knell, please take the doctor to a chair."

In the diversion caused by Knell's confused attempt to deal with Pakeman, Littlejohn asked his simple question. "Did you tell the doctor that Casement tripped and was killed by his own gun?"

"No. I said he'd accidentally shot himself in the dark. Nobody knew how. I never said he tripped because I didn't know."

"Did you know he put snares down in the fields?"

"Yes. We thought he might have been out seeing if there was anything in them. The postman said he might have bent down to put in a snare and his gun went off."

"Thank you, Mrs. Vondy. That will be all."

She went away quickly to the refuge of her kitchen, closed the door, and was quiet again.

"Well, Pakeman? Nobody knew about the snare, but the police and whoever committed the crime. I suggest that Casement telephoned you and either charged you with being involved in the killing of Skollick, or else asked you some other awkward questions. And you dealt with him after the pattern of Skollick and faked another accident."

"You've no proof of that! As we said, with Mrs. Vacey dead, nobody will even know the truth. I didn't kill Casement. I say it again. *I didn't.* And now, if you don't mind, I'm busy."

Littlejohn ignored him.

"I agree Mrs. Vacey won't now be able to deny responsibility for Casement's death or even produce an alibi. Her death has made you very sure of yourself."

"I've said I'm busy."

"You know what caused Mrs. Vacey's death, Pakeman. It was Casement's Great Dog, as I said before."

The Archdeacon, who had been sitting there without a word, raised his eyes to those of Littlejohn, as though sensing a climax.

"Moddey Mooar was, in this case, just as much a lethal weapon as a gun or a knife."

"Except that the weapon was not wielded. It was alive and acted on instinct. And don't you think this has gone far enough, Littlejohn?"

"Not quite. Let me just finish it. You evidently know exactly how Casement was killed. And yet, you did not kill him."

"I told you I didn't. Why persist?"

"Mrs. Vacey shot Casement. He didn't see either of you on the night she killed Sir Martin. It was only the chance flare of the petrol-lighter that showed your face to Sullivan Lee. It was Mrs. Vacey's car that Casement recognized and, after he'd thought matters out, he made up his mind to have it out with her. He rang her on the telephone. What he said to her, I don't know, but it sealed his fate. She arranged to meet him, shot him, took the body to the curragh, and we know the rest."

Pakeman nodded and sighed.

"I'm glad you aren't making the mistake of accusing me. Why don't you? You're working on theory. Why *not* accuse me? It would be as sensible as the rest of your fantastic deductions."

"I'm not accusing you, because Casement's dog showed no interest in you whatever. Moddey Mooar was present when his master was killed. He knew who did it. He also recognized the car when he saw it in Grenaby. *Because it smelled of his master and his master's blood!*"

Pakeman recoiled, wide eyed, his hands before him as though fending off some evil.

"What did Mrs. Vacey tell you when she rang you up, afterwards, Pakeman?"

"She told me."

"Go on. You may as well. She's dead now and is past human judgment or retribution."

"She rang me up from the telephone-box near Sulby."

"She was in a terrible state and said she'd collapsed. I went out and found her nearby, sitting in her car, with the lights out. Casement had rung her up. He'd said he wanted to see her at once about what happened to Sir Martin. She'd tried to get me on the telephone to help her, but I was out on a confinement. She arranged to meet him in Sulby Claddagh, which is lonely and safe from interference after dark. We both knew that Casement was around when we took Skollick's body to the curragh. We saw the dog, too, but were sure that, in the dark, he'd not recognize us. We were reassured when he didn't come forward after the arrest of Lee."

"Yes?"

"She said she'd shot Casement as soon as they met. He'd his gun across his arm and she was certain he meant to kill her. She was as hard as nails. Both dogs were there. The little one ran off into the darkness when she threatened him, but the big one attacked her. She struck him down with the barrels of the gun and left him, she thought, dead. She loaded Casement's body in the boot of the car, took it to the curragh, and, seeing a wire snare half out of his pocket, she used it in arranging the scene to make it look like an accident."

"What did you do, then?"

"I was horror-struck. This was cold-blooded murder and as I saw her face, frozen with fear and horror, yet unrelenting in her purpose, I realized that she was mad, and I hated her. She poured abuse on me for being out when she rang up. I gave her some brandy from my flask. She said I must help her home, that I was in it, too, and unless I supported her, she'd see that I suffered exactly the same as she did. I'd been her accomplice in the Skollick affair; this 'accident' of Casement's was just the same-a double job. Nobody would believe I wasn't involved. It seemed to me that she was right. I calmed her by pretending I understood and sympathized, and I told her to get in her car and drive slowly behind me. I took her home. Then, she said the boot was stained with blood. We had to shut ourselves with her car in the garage and dean it. Stained with blood was an understatement. It was swimming in it. I shall never forget."

Pakeman paled, sat in his chair again and tugged at his collar. All the blood had again drained from his face as though he were living the horror over again. Knell half-filled a glass with whisky and passed it to Pakeman, who gulped it eagerly down.

"I tied Skollick's head in a plastic bag when we handled him. Gillian had taken no such precautions."

He was breathing hard and struggled to speak. And as he struggled he seemed somehow to enjoy it, like a martyr blessing the irons and flames. The Archdeacon rose and unfastened Pakeman's collar and tie.

"It's all right, sir. It's just the thought of it all. I feel better again now."

But he didn't look it.

"So that's how it happened. I shall have to take my punishment, although I didn't commit either crime. I simply got involved in something beyond me and before I knew where I was, I was in it, up to the neck."

"Yes, Pakeman, and you thought you'd found an excellent way out. If Mrs. Vacey died, especially through the dog, she would bear all the blame and you might get away with it! The dog wasn't dead. He recovered, turned wild, and in his faithful way, set out after his master's killer. He prowled the curraghs with one instinct. He'd no time for anyone except Mrs. Vacey, who had about her still, in her car, the scent of his master's blood. That was how Sullivan Lee came to find him, half-starved, foraging for scraps of food round the vicarage and when he telephoned you to say he'd got Moddey Mooar locked up in the shed there, an idea came to you. Old Juan Kilbeg had told you that Casement had written to the Archdeacon before he died. You thought the letter contained a denunciation of Mrs. Vacey. You had no intention of allowing her to obtain and destroy it. For her to be caught, or better still, found dead with it in her possession would solve everything and incriminate her fully. Or, what is perhaps more likely, you wished her to die, either to be rid of her whom now you hated, or else to be avenged on her for her treatment of you. You telephoned and told her about the letter."

"No, no. It's a lie. I didn't."

"You told her it would be delivered on the first round on Monday. You followed her to Grenaby."

"You were there. I appeal to you, Knell. Archdeacon. I was nowhere about. He's trying to incriminate me for his own ends."

"You called on Lee after his message about the dog. You slipped a dish of drugged food into the shed. Before he had eaten it all, the dog was asleep. You smuggled him away in your car. The rats finished the rest. One of them ate too much. He, too, collapsed under the drug. He's probably lying there dead by now. When you followed Mrs. Vacey, you had Moddey Mooar, now fully conscious, in the boot of your car. You watched her and then you released the now savage hound either to kill her or impede her until she was captured. Unfortunately for her, perhaps, he took some time finding the scent. Had he come upon her hiding in the Archdeacon's garden waiting for the postman, she would probably have had to shoot him with the gun she held. Instead, he caught the scent of the car as she drove along the road to the bridge. He sprang."

Pakeman was on his feet, unsteadily groping for the bell by the side of the fireplace. He pressed the button. Mrs. Vondy entered and looked at him in horror.

"Oh, sir. You're ill again. Your heart."

"Be quiet! Open the front door. Open it, I say." Slowly, her eyes wide with terror, she went into the hall and obeyed.

In two swift strides, Pakeman had reached the corner and turned to face Littlejohn, his gun in his hand.

"Now, get out. All of you, get out or I'll blow you out." The Rev. Caesar Kinrade was the first to act. Before the others could move, he rose, fixed Pakeman with his calm blue eyes, and walked sternly to him.

"Give me that gun. You'll do some damage. Give it to me, I say."

Pakeman, like someone bemused, slowly and calmly surrendered the weapon to the old man.

And then, he sprang to the door. Before the other three had quite realized it, he was running up the garden path, out of the gate, and along the footway which borders the Lezayre Road. The rest of them followed, Knell and Littlejohn at the trot, the Archdeacon at his usual calm pace. His face was set and grim and then he calmly gestured with his hand to the other two.

"Let him go. He won't get far. Don't you see."

He was right. Pakeman, running in the distance, steadily, looking neither to right nor left, unheeding the flabbergasted stares of passers-by, threw up his hands, flung himself forward, and lay sprawling and still, on the roadside.

When they reached him, the doctor was gasping for breath, his face blue, his eyes staring, and they gently carried him home.

Mrs. Vondy met them at the door. She was almost hysterical and they had to shake her to calm her and get her to help them with the sick man.

"His heart was terrible bad," she said as they followed her upstairs and laid Pakeman on his bed. "He used to take tablets that kept him well. Lately, he's not been taking them, in spite of the way I reminded him. I got to countin' them in the box and I wondered why. I thought he was feelin' quite better again. He shouldn't have left them off."

Pakeman opened his eyes and smiled wanly.

"It was all as you said, Littlejohn. I loved her till I found out what a fiend she was. She only loved her first husband. The rest, she used for her own ends. She was poor and she told me later that Skollick gave her all she wanted.

There's nothing you can do for *me* now. I'm better dead.

I've lost everything. My faith, my love, my reputation."

He clutched his chest and was seized by a horrible spasm of pain.

"My heart has been bad. Took tablets which kept me well and going. It only needed a little overexertion, and then. More ways of killing oneself than by poison. I always had this way out if I needed it. See that whoever takes-over my patients gets my notebook in the middle desk drawer."

With a final convulsion, Pakeman died. The old springer spaniel, sunning himself in the garden beneath the bedroom window, suddenly opened his alarmed eyes, whined, and then raising his muzzle in the air, he howled dismally.

ABOUT THE AUTHOR

George Bellairs is the pseudonym under which Harold Blundell (1902–1982) wrote police procedural thrillers in rural British settings. He was born in Lancashire, England, and worked as a bank manager in Manchester. After retiring, Bellairs moved to the Isle of Man, where several of his novels are set, to be with friends and family.

In 1941 Bellairs wrote his first mystery, *Littlejohn on Leave*, during spare moments at his air raid warden's post. The title introduced Thomas Littlejohn, the detective who appears in fifty-seven of his novels. Bellairs was also a regular contributor to the *Manchester Guardian* and worked as a freelance writer for newspapers both local and national.

THE INSPECTOR LITTLEJOHN MYSTERIES

FROM OPEN ROAD MEDIA

OPEN ROAD
INTEGRATED MEDIA

Find a full list of our authors and titles at www.openroadmedia.com

FOLLOW US
@OpenRoadMedia

EARLY BIRD BOOKS
FRESH DEALS, DELIVERED DAILY

Love to read? Love great sales?

Get fantastic deals on bestselling ebooks delivered to your inbox every day!

Sign up today at
earlybirdbooks.com/book

Printed in Dunstable, United Kingdom